BONDAGE

OTHER BOOKS AND AUDIO BOOKS
BY H.B. MOORE

Out of Jerusalem: Of Goodly Parents

Out of Jerusalem: A Light in the Wilderness

Out of Jerusalem: Towards the Promised Land

Out of Jerusalem: Land of Inheritance

Abinadi

Alma

Alma the Younger

Ammon

Daughters of Jared

Esther the Queen

OTHER BOOKS BY
HEATHER B. MOORE

Women of the Book of Mormon: Insights & Inspirations

Christ's Gifts to Women

Divinity of Women: Inspiration and Insights from Women of the Scriptures

Athena

Ruby's Secret

Tying the Knot

THE
MOSES
CHRONICLES

Volume I
BONDAGE

a novel

H.B. MOORE

Covenant Communications, Inc.

Cover Credits

Reference Photography: Figure photography by McKenzie Deakins; *Pyramids of Giza, Egypt* ©
DavidCallan courtesy of istockphoto.com ; *Baby in the Bullrushes* © hidesy courtesy of istockphoto.com;
Blue Sky Background in Grunge Style © elenavolkova courtesy of istockphoto.com.

Painting by David Malan. For more information visit davemalan.com.

Cover design copyright © 2015 by Covenant Communications, Inc.

Published by Covenant Communications, Inc.
American Fork, Utah

Printed in the United States of America
First Printing: May 2015

21 20 19 18 17 16 15   10 9 8 7 6 5 4 3 2 1

ISBN: 978-1-68047-166-3

To Lu Ann Staheli
Mentor & Friend

For I brought thee up out of the land of Egypt,
and redeemed thee out of the house of servants; and I sent
before thee Moses, Aaron, and Miriam.

(Micah 6:4)

CHARACTER NAMES

Denotes Historical Figures

*Moses
*Miriam, Moses's sister
*Aaron, Moses's brother
Salome, Aaron's wife
*Jochebed, Moses's mother
*Amram, father of Moses
*Ramses II, crown prince of Egypt, son of Seti I
*Nefertari, betrothed to Ramses
*Seti I, pharaoh of Egypt
*Bithiah, Moses's adoptive mother, daughter of Seti I
*Mered, palace scribe, of the tribe of Judah
*Caleb, son of Jephunneh, of the tribe of Judah
Pentu, cousin to Ramses II
Reuven, Hebrew slave
Deborah, widow in Hebrew village
Cena, daughter of Vizier Amon
Katu, desert dweller

CHAPTER ONE

MIRIAM

1281 BC

MIRIAM SETTLED IN HER USUAL spot, about two paces from the river's edge. The River Nile was lazy today, ebbing around the reeds as the deep green water shimmered in the afternoon sun, glinting gold with each ripple. The air felt heavy, wet, and silent. If Miriam hadn't been waiting to catch sight of her brother, she might have fallen asleep.

A male voice sounded down the river, not far from her hiding spot, and every part of Miriam went on alert. It took a great deal of strength to stay in her concealed position behind a thick group of rushes. Soon she'd see her brother, a strong, young man who lived in the pharaoh's palace in Mennefer. A young man who lived with all the privileges of royalty. A young man who didn't know Miriam existed and didn't know his older sister and brother were slaves. Who didn't know his parents, Amram and Jochebed, mourned his loss every day.

Miriam leaned forward, pushing her face through the reeds, trying to secure a good view.

Moses laughed.

She would know the sound of his laughter anywhere. She could close her eyes and pick out his voice in a crowd. And they had been in the same crowd together once—the year before during the Flame Festival, when Moses had passed by in the royal procession with his princess-mother, the woman who'd adopted Moses after she'd fetched him out of the river as an infant so many years ago.

Miriam could never tell anyone her secret, that she'd been the one to follow the basket containing her infant brother along the River Nile, had nudged it a time or two with a large stick to keep it moving. She couldn't tell anyone she'd watched the pharaoh's daughter, Bithiah, find the basket as she was wading with her handmaidens at the river's bank. And she couldn't tell anyone how her mother had disobeyed pharaoh's royal order to exterminate all firstborn Hebrew males.

She could definitely never tell anyone that each moon she crept to that same river's bank, praying to catch sight of her brother. She'd kept her secrets hidden for more than eighteen years now. If the reeds along the River Nile could speak, they'd have a lot to say.

"Let's race, then." Moses's voice carried through the gentle breeze, sending a jolt through Miriam.

Moments later he came into view, walking with two other young men, both of whom Miriam recognized as members of the court who seemed to be close friends with her brother. They wore fine linen kilts the color of alabaster, and gold armbands set off their dark skin. Moses was the fairest-skinned among the friends, but his tan was a close enough match. Their heads were shaved after the tradition of the royals.

Her brother was a member of the pharaoh's family. It was hard to believe sometimes, especially when she and her family spent their days in hard labor and their nights struggling to sleep with so little food in their stomachs.

As the men grew closer, Miriam stifled a gasp. One of them was Prince Ramses, heir to the throne of Egypt.

Moses laughed again and pushed the shoulder of the other young man in front of him. They were daring each other in a race . . . across the river. It might be safe in the heat of the day when the crocodiles and hippopotamuses stayed well below the surface, but the sun was setting, and the river was starting to come alive. As Moses and his friends splashed into the water only a dozen paces from her, Miriam scrambled backward, trying not to make a sound or any movement that might draw their attention.

She had just about reached the line of palms when she ran into someone. "Oh!" Miriam covered her mouth to keep quiet, turning around. She was expecting the worst—an Egyptian taskmaster or a member of the court.

Instead, it was Caleb.

The knot of dread loosened, but her anger quickly replaced it. "What are you doing?" she hissed at Caleb, pushing past him and hurrying toward the palms. Once she was safely away from the river, she turned to face Caleb.

His intense gaze jarred her senses; Miriam told herself it was because he'd startled her. He was yet unmarried—one of the taller men in the village, with broad shoulders and dark curls that nearly reached his shoulders. Miriam focused on his light-brown eyes. "You followed me."

"I did." His eyes searched hers as if he could decipher what she'd been up to by studying her face. "Why are you here? You know you'll get in trouble if you're caught this far from our village, especially before work is finished for the day."

It was a risk; it was always a risk. Miriam had witnessed firsthand the beatings the Hebrews were given when they disobeyed curfew or left their worksites before sundown. But she had her reasons. "You shouldn't have followed me." She narrowed her eyes, realizing she didn't know Caleb all that well. He was a friend of her older brother Aaron, but he'd only lived in their village a few months. At the moment, she couldn't remember where he'd lived before. All she knew was that he was from the tribe of Judah.

"You shouldn't be here," Caleb persisted. "And you shouldn't be alone."

He was right, but Miriam tried to ignore the foreboding that crept in with Caleb's words. It was foolish to travel about on her own, a defenseless female slave. Hebrew women had disappeared from her village more than once. But it was late afternoon, and everyone should have been working and not paying attention to her. "I was just about to return to the village."

She walked around him and set off toward the path that wound through the palms, giving her sporadic glimpses of the slow-moving river.

"Miri, wait," he said, easily catching up to her.

Keeping her gaze forward, she said, "My name's *Miriam*." She didn't know where he got the courage to shorten her name, but something about it made her more aware of him, and she needed to put a stop to it.

He fell into step beside her. "Right. Whether or not you want to tell me why you come to this part of the river and spy on the Egyptians every week, I'm going to continue to follow you. To keep you safe."

She stopped dead. "*Continue?* You've followed me more than once?"

He looked away, but not before Miriam saw the admission in his eyes. "Did Aaron put you up to this?"

"He didn't have to."

That didn't exactly answer her question, but it did tell her that the two men were in agreement. "Maybe I'll start coming at night, then." She turned away, intent on putting distance between them.

She knew Caleb followed because she could hear his footsteps, hear his occasional sigh, and when the hot wind shifted, she could smell the spice on his skin. But he stayed a few paces behind her. She refused to turn around again and instead kept her thoughts focused on the scolding she'd give Aaron when she returned to the village.

CHAPTER TWO

MOSES

THE MURKY WATER SURROUNDED MOSES, blocking out all sounds and sights, making him feel like he was in another world. Perhaps this was what the afterlife felt like: body suspended, weightless, protected from the eyes and voices of the living. He dove deeper, wondering how far it was to the bottom of the river. The water cooled and darkened even more, and his heart thumped as he thought of what creatures might be able to see him now.

A foot kicked his shoulder, and Moses shot up to the surface.

"There you are," Ramses said, a grin on his wet face. "Thought you were eaten by a croc."

Moses wiped the water from his face. "They don't come to these parts."

"That's right. They're too full from eating the Hebrews." Ramses laughed at himself, and his cousin Pentu joined in.

Moses pushed through the water, leaving the laughter behind as he moved toward the bank of reeds until he stood knee-deep in the river. The race along the river had been exhilarating, but when Ramses and Pentu started in on mocking the Hebrew slaves, a knot had formed in Moses's stomach.

"Where are you going, Moses?" Ramses called after him.

"I'm starving," Moses said, causing more laughter. It was always a good way to put some space between him and his cousins. Technically, Ram, his full name Ramses II, and heir to the throne of Egypt, was Moses's uncle, but they referred to each other as cousins. At eighteen, Moses was the eldest of the group; Ramses was only fourteen, while Pentu was nearly eighteen as well. Ramses was already betrothed. It had been an important event the year before, and all the dignitaries in the land would attend his upcoming marriage.

Outside the court, Ramses seemed like a regular young man—a royal young man, perhaps, but it was still hard to imagine him on the throne. Of course, there was no guarantee that Ramses would become the next pharaoh. There was plenty of palace intrigue, secrets whispered in corners, sudden illnesses, and, as always, impending threats to the throne from distant cousins.

Yet Ramses was smart and proud. Both attributes combined to make him a favorite of the people. Even if a distant cousin tried to conquer the throne, the people of Egypt would be on Ramses II's side.

Moses headed toward the palace, and Ramses and Pentu teased each other as they followed him. They were constantly comparing their fighting skills, but they both knew Moses would win in any competition, so they usually left him out of their betting. Moses might not be the most eloquent orator in their law and history lessons—when it came to oration, he'd rather pluck out his toenails—but he was naturally skilled in sword fighting and wrestling.

He glanced over his shoulder and tuned back in to Ramses and Pentu's conversation, which was more of an argument.

"They're not ready to race," Ramses was saying.

Pentu shoved Ramses in the shoulder. "That's what you said about your other horses."

Moses slowed and waited for the two to catch up. "You're still using that excuse, Ram?"

"What? You think your horses can beat mine?" the prince asked.

Moses looked over at Pentu, who grinned at him. "Yes." Moses had been training a couple of two-year-old fillies, but they were as strong and fast as the other seasoned chariot racers.

"Let's do it, then. Tonight after the banquet," Ramses said.

"In the dark?" Pentu asked.

"In the moonlight," Moses said, excitement building in him. It would be dangerous, but he could test out his horses without a crowd of spectators. It would be perfect.

"What does the winner get?" Pentu asked. "Gold armbands?"

"Something better," Ramses said, looking over at Pentu. "If I win, you have to show us where the Hebrew girls bathe."

Pentu's eyes widened. "I promised Ptah I wouldn't tell anyone. We'll get caught if too many of us go to watch."

Moses knew about Ptah and his stories. He didn't believe half of what the man said, but if there was truth in this, he didn't want anything to do with it.

"So?" Ramses asked with a laugh. "What would happen if we were caught? Nothing."

"I don't want any of the harem women to find out," Pentu said, his voice sullen. "They won't think I'm Egyptian enough for them. You know how gossip travels. My future wife might hate me before we're even married."

"We'll never tell," Ramses said, slapping Moses's shoulder. "Right, Moses?"

Ramses and Pentu had already initiated visits to the harem. They'd teased Moses more than once about his reluctance to join them. So far he'd come up with hardy excuses not to go on the evenings they escaped. It wasn't that he wasn't interested in women, but the thought of entering into a temporary dalliance with a girl that might result in her becoming with child made him hesitate. His mother had no husband; he had no father, and he'd felt the shame his entire life.

"That's no prize," Moses said, hoping he sounded lighthearted enough to not reflect the disappointment he felt. "The winner should get the losing horses."

"You only say that because you'll probably win," Pentu said to Moses.

He shrugged and grinned. "Might as well be a fine prize, then."

"It's a deal," Ramses pronounced. He always seemed to have the last word.

Pentu's face pulled into a scowl. "You have more horses than a woman has necklaces. If I lose my horses, it could be months before I get any more."

"Then you'll have more to fight for," Moses said, and Ramses laughed. Pentu was the son of one of the pharaoh's consorts. He wasn't as skilled as Moses, so he never won competitions that might bring him more wealth or status.

"Tonight, then. Midnight," Pentu said, his face red.

CHAPTER THREE

MIRIAM

"I WON'T MARRY," MIRIAM SAID as she sat behind the small hut she shared with her parents, threading the wool strands through her loom and refusing to look at her brother Aaron. After Miriam shared a silent meal with her mother and father, Aaron had conveniently showed up—obviously to reason with his stubborn sister. Two burning lamps provided just enough light for her weaving but still concealed her face, which was probably red from embarrassment and frustration. She focused on threading the next color of wool through the loom and pulled the thread tight. When she didn't want to talk about something, she stayed busy, so busy that she couldn't be bothered to carry on a discussion.

She wouldn't give in. Not to Aaron, not to anyone. Her parents were aging, and they needed someone to care for them. It wasn't fair to Aaron and his wife, Salome, who was with child, to always be looking after them.

When Aaron didn't respond, it made her even more irritated. He was like that, staying quiet until she'd more than spoken her mind, until all of her words were spent, until she was ready to listen. At this rate, she'd be finished with the rug tonight. "And making your friends spy on me isn't going to change my mind," she added.

"Caleb's not *spying* on you," Aaron said, then coughed into his hand.

"You can't even lie about it." Miriam peeked up at him.

His lips twitched, but he kept a straight face. "He's just watching out for you," Aaron said. "And since you keep leaving the village, that requires a bit of following around."

"That's called *spying*, Aaron." Now she looked at him fully, pausing in her work. He looked so much like Moses, although Aaron had a full head of hair and was thin with hard labor. "I know what you are doing. You're trying to get Caleb interested in your poor, unmarried sister—one who's too plain to attract the men she grew up around."

Aaron's expression was stoic as he watched her throw words in his face. Nothing she said ever seemed to upset him. His calmness was eerie sometimes and annoying all of the time.

"I mean it, Aaron." She wove in another wool thread, a bit too quickly, missing the weft pattern. She pulled it out and started over. "Don't force Caleb, or any other man, to follow me around. The last thing I want is to be in an arranged marriage."

"No one has ever asked that of you," Aaron said above her.

She hated his composed voice. And the truth it spoke. "Not in words, but it's expected now that no one has spoken for me. I've heard Mother tell Father she wished she would have used a matchmaker years ago. Now that I'm too old and stubborn, it's too late."

Aaron barked out a laugh, startling Miriam. "You're only in your twenty-fifth year, sister," he said. "Hardly old. But I can't disagree with the *stubborn* assessment."

"Which is why you need to stop trying to change my mind," she said, suddenly feeling tired. She'd done her weaving work quickly today and then walked all the way to the palace to spy on Moses. Then she'd had that encounter with Caleb, and now this argument with Aaron while she madly worked at the loom. It was exhausting. Why didn't her brother take his condemnation somewhere else?

"Don't you have something to do?" she asked, looking up at him coyly. "Like meet with the elders or something?"

One side of his mouth lifted again. If she could get him to laugh, he'd forget his purpose in talking to her. She could go inside the hut in peace, and after fixing her parents some tea, she'd go straight to sleep. Mornings always came too early.

"I do have someplace to be, but you're more important than that place." Aaron folded his arms.

She hated it when he talked like that, about how important she was, about how he did care about her thoughts, and how concerned he was for her. There was far too much concern going around in her family. Couldn't they just keep to themselves for one single day? She took her time choosing the next color of thread, as if it were a very important decision too. Never mind that her weaving was known throughout the Hebrew villages as being among the most colorful and lively. Most of her rugs went to the Egyptian aristocracy, but what little she could hold back was highly prized by those who knew her work.

She always tried to do something different in her patterns. Instead of alternating two or three colors, she'd throw in a fourth or even a fifth color sometimes. She created her own dyes, using plants she collected along the riverbank near the palace.

"Miriam."

She let out a sigh and looked up at her brother.

"I know why you go to the riverbank, and it's not only to collect plants." His voice was quiet. "I know who you are watching."

Her chest tightened, and her eyes burned. She couldn't look at Aaron's steady gaze anymore. "Is it so wrong?"

Aaron crouched down beside her so he was at eye level. "He doesn't even know us," he said in a soft voice. "He doesn't know he has a sister. If he saw you, Miriam, what do you think he'd do?"

All sorts of horrible answers floated through her mind as she thought of the fate of Hebrew girls who were caught in the wrong places. "He's not like that."

Aaron dropped his head. "He was raised by Egyptians," he finally said. "He has been educated like them. If there's one thing they all have in common, it's that they despise our race. He will not see you as a sister, Miriam. He will see you only as another Hebrew slave."

"No," Miriam whispered. Then she was on her feet. "Moses is not like them. He is one of *us*."

Aaron shot to his feet and covered her mouth. "Don't ever say his name aloud." His eyes bore into hers, more serious than she'd ever seen them. "If someone overheard . . . if someone knew what our family has done . . . we could all be killed. Even *him*."

Miriam stepped back, her eyes stinging. It was true. Her family had disobeyed pharaoh Seti I. They'd hidden their younger brother for three moons while the other male infants were being killed in their village. After pharaoh's daughter had rescued Moses from the river, Miriam talked her into bringing in a Hebrew slave to suckle the abandoned infant.

Then Miriam had fetched her own mother and brought her to the pharaoh's daughter. For nearly three years, her mother had breast-fed Moses, and then she'd been sent away. But they'd had those three years. Miriam had been with her mother each time. She'd played with the young boy, never being able to tell him she was his true sister.

Moses might be an Egyptian and a member of the royal family now, but he was her brother. He was still the little child whose life she'd helped save. He was *not* like them. But now fear had settled in her stomach, planted there by Aaron.

"If you insist on traveling to the riverbank, Caleb will follow you," Aaron said, his voice calm again. "Know that it's not only your life you are putting in danger. You are risking Caleb's life and our parents' lives. What do you think Mother would do if something happened to you?"

Miriam sank onto her stool, fighting the tears.

"She's already lost one child," Aaron said in a quiet voice.

Miriam brushed at the wetness on her face. She might give in to Aaron now and might even make a promise, but tomorrow or next week, she'd be making her way to the center of Mennefer once again.

"And, Miriam?" Aaron said. He waited until she looked up at him. Instead of seeing anger on his face, she saw that his expression was tender. "I never sent Caleb. He came to me and told me of his concerns. I gave him permission to watch over you." Before Miriam could comprehend what he'd said, Aaron leaned down and kissed her cheek. "Despite what you say, I don't think you'll remain unmarried for long, even if your heart stays stubborn."

CHAPTER FOUR

Bithiah

Bithiah adjusted the Nubian wig on her head, then let her hands fall as her lady servant began to apply kohl to her eyes. Tonight was a feast celebrating the sudden announcement of the official coronation of Ramses II as crown prince and coregent. He was only fourteen. Bithiah supposed she should be grateful she'd been invited to the celebration, since she wasn't among the favored daughters of the pharaoh.

"Mother," a male voice spoke from the doorway.

She turned to face her handsome son, and a smile spread across her face. "Moses. Come in." And just like that, the bitterness fled.

Her son strode toward her, then grasped her hand and leaned over to kiss her cheek. Bithiah took pride in his strong physique and intelligence and kind nature. Despite the uproar she'd caused in the palace and among her family when she'd insisted on keeping the abandoned child, the price was worth it.

She had given up any prospects of a royal husband since the gossips had convinced the court that she'd secretly given birth to Moses. Her parents knew the truth, and Bithiah had to be content with that, although neither of them had been pleased. They had tried to talk her out of keeping the child, adding threats of exile, but she had remained firm. From the moment she had picked up the infant out of the basket in the river and he had clung to her with a cry, she'd known she could not abandon him. And she certainly could never reveal that her adopted son was a Hebrew.

Despite her father's edict to kill all of the Hebrew male infants, it must have been Hapi's will that she find the child and Hapi's will that she raise him. After all, Hapi, god of the River Nile, had delivered this child to her.

And now this young man before her filled her heart in a way she doubted an arranged marriage to a vizier and bearing him a brood of children could ever do. She may not have given birth to Moses, but her soul was bonded to his. He knew no different and believed she was his physical mother. And even if he did one day discover the truth, their love would never be broken.

"You are ready early," Bithiah said. "Have you come to escort me to the ceremony?"

"I have," Moses said, a smile playing on his face. "And I'm not early. As usual, you are late."

"Oh." Bithiah laughed. "I was waiting for my escort."

Moses held out his hand, his eyes amused. "Of course you were."

Bithiah rose to her feet and glanced in the long copper square that showed her image. She needed to make a good impression on the court so her father would be pleased. She was surprised he was holding this ceremony with Ramses II so young and her father in good health. But it was a sign that life was moving forward quickly, and gratefully, events like finding an abandoned child in a basket floating down the river were events of the past.

Once outside her chamber, they walked along the wide corridor, passing granite pillars and statues of various gods and creatures. Others were arriving—family members, court officials, and a few selected from the upper tier of society.

As they neared the throne room, a woman escorted by several guards came into view from the main entrance.

"Nefertari is here?" Bithiah said.

Moses glanced over at the entourage. "It is an important day for her future husband."

"Yes," she said, wondering why she felt surprised. Typically the betrothed couple was kept quite separate in the months leading up to the wedding. Her mind started to spin as she considered what this might mean. It seemed the pharaoh wanted the people to witness Nefertari's close association with the royal family.

Bithiah's breathing increased as she entered the throne room. Was the pharaoh ill? Did he feel his days were short? She tried to remain calm as Moses led her to the group of women she normally sat with. He released her arm and kissed her cheek.

"Thank you," she said, then turned to greet her cousins. They'd already settled among the cushions and had started to pour the wine. The women's black Nubian wigs glistened in the torchlight, and their oiled arms and hennaed chests gleamed. There was no shortage of jewels and gold adorning their bodies. Tonight was an honorable banquet for those in attendance.

Bithiah planned to watch the pharaoh closely. If something happened to him, she hoped Ramses II would be a kinder ruler toward Moses. While the pharaoh had allowed Moses to become educated with the other royal children, he hadn't given him an occupation yet. Even Ramses's cousin, Pentu, had been elected as the next overseer of the taskmasters. Pentu would organize and dictate the taskmasters' duties as they managed the Hebrew slaves. Bithiah shuddered at the thought. Pentu was a boisterous young man, often in a pout since he lost almost every competition to Moses or Ramses. Bithiah couldn't ignore his quick temper and penchant for luxurious living. He certainly indulged in everything a young royal could indulge in.

She knew Moses would like a position in the military or perhaps with training the royal horses. His athletic abilities were natural, and he had a way with animals. As all of these thoughts went through her head, she kept a placid smile on her face, nodding from time to time when someone spoke to her.

A murmur ran through the assembly, and everyone rose to their feet as the pharaoh and Queen Tuya entered. Bithiah prostrated herself along with the others. The procession was impressive, including Ramses II and his two sisters, Tia and Henutmire. The young man's face was sober, but Bithiah recognized the sense of pride behind his forward-focused gaze. From the time Ramses was a young boy, he had acted the part of a crown prince, and today would only make it official in the eyes of Egypt.

It wasn't until the pharaoh and Ramses were on the dais that Bithiah dared look for Mered, the Hebrew scribe who attended all the official ceremonies as well as judgment days. He was unlike any man Bithiah knew—was it because he was Hebrew? Mered was intelligent yet humble. His dark eyes had a depth and sincerity to them that Bithiah rarely saw in the men who sought her company during royal banquets.

Every time she'd heard him speak, she'd been impressed with his patience when confronted with the many delays that occurred in working with Pharaoh. Mered seemed to have an incredible memory—he almost always had the answers to Pharaoh's questions about a law or a piece of history.

Bithiah's heart leapt when she saw him, and she immediately berated herself. They couldn't come from more opposite backgrounds. He was

Hebrew, and she was Egyptian royalty. He would never break any rules of propriety and look at her during a ceremony. Their gazes had only caught a few times in passing, yet Bithiah frequently imagined that they were friends, that they weren't forbidden to talk or interact, that she could ask him questions about his life and she could tell him about hers.

Mered wasn't a typical Hebrew slave, since he was compensated for his work by living in a home the pharaoh provided. And certainly Mered never went hungry, as was evidenced by his solid and strong build. In fact, Bithiah had witnessed him competing with the Egyptians a few times in their never-ending games. Mered could hold his own against them, but he always kept an unobtrusive attitude and was hardly noticed.

Bithiah thought that a time or two, he'd probably allowed one of the Egyptian studs to win. And now he was here, preparing to record the historical event of Ramses II declared as the crown prince and heir to Pharaoh Seti's throne.

She dragged her eyes from the Hebrew man to focus on the ceremony that was beginning. The high priest had taken his place on the dais, and he began by saying, "In the name of Amun, and through the will of Osiris, you are appointed crown prince to the pharaoh of Egypt, Seti I."

Ramses lowered his head, and the high priest poured oil on top of Ramses's head. The oil slid along his skin, down his neck, and onto his shoulders.

"And now you will wash in the sacred pool, representing the acceptance of this sacred position as crown prince of Egypt." The high priest led Ramses to the pool of clear water behind the dais, where Ramses washed off.

He then stepped into a curtained area, and when he emerged, he was wearing the traditional *shendyt* kilt. Once Ramses stepped onto the dais again, the high priest placed a striped *Khat* head cloth and the gold *uraeus* on Ramses's head. The prince would wear it only during the ceremony since the crowned pharaoh was still living.

The high priest presented Ramses with the crook and flail of Egypt and said, "Ramses II is now crown prince of Egypt. May he be blessed with prosperity and long life and the love of his people."

Bithiah joined the audience in bowing to the floor and prostrating herself to the new crown prince. When she rose, the audience began to disperse, talking among themselves. Those who had brought gifts formed a line in order to present them to Ramses.

Bithiah watched Mered walk among the priests and other scribes who were leaving the ceremony. Just as he moved in front of her, he glanced over. He looked away before it turned into an outright stare, but Bithiah had seen into the depths of his eyes. And she knew he had seen *her*. Her breath came short, and she averted her gaze, hoping no one would notice the flush on her face. She could no longer watch Mered and hope for a life that would never happen. If anyone knew of her feelings toward a Hebrew man, she would lose everything.

CHAPTER FIVE

MIRIAM

MIRIAM EDGED CLOSER TO THE front of the gathering. At least a couple dozen Hebrews met every few days to hear the reports of the palace from Mered, a palace scribe. Many envied the Judahite's elevated position, his privileges and luxuries, but he was under intense scrutiny, and one misstep could bring an execution sentence.

Tonight he was to relay the details of the most recent ceremony to establish Ramses as the crown prince of Egypt. Miriam hoped to hear any mention of the princes, and more specifically Moses. On the other side of the crowd, she caught her brother's eye. He was frowning at her, obviously having guessed her motive to pay close attention tonight. She wanted more than anything to be able to question Mered in private. But how would she ask what she really wanted to know without revealing her dangerous secret?

Another man caught her eye, and Miriam turned her gaze away before she could be noticed. Caleb hadn't spoken to her after that day she'd caught him following her to the river, but she'd seen him watching her often. Normally she would have been annoyed at the obvious interest, especially after Aaron had implied that Caleb was watching over her of his own accord, but Miriam found that she wasn't annoyed; she was more . . . flattered, or maybe flustered. She didn't want the attention. She didn't want to be followed. And she'd never asked to be protected.

So why was he doing it? Again her brother's suggestion came to mind, making her feel too warm. She hadn't entirely ruled out the possibility of marriage, but she had never welcomed the thought either. There had simply been no reason for her to marry. Bearing children only to have them become another generation of slaves to the Egyptians was far from appealing. And who would care for her parents in their old age? Besides, giving up her brother had left a large hole in her heart, one she doubted a child of her own could ever fill.

Mered started to speak, and Miriam focused on his account of the ceremony. He talked about the foreign dignitaries who had attended and the ritual the high priest had performed. Several in the group hissed their disapproval. The Egyptians worshipped myriad gods, none of them the true God. But Miriam didn't want to listen to any criticisms. Mered was a good storyteller and remembered interesting details, such as the fine kilt Ramses had worn and how the women had been adorned with necklaces and armbands of gold.

Some in the crowd asked questions, and finally Miriam couldn't wait anymore to ask her own. She lifted her hand, and when Mered called on her, she said, "Has the princess Bithiah taken a husband yet?"

If Mered could tell her about Moses's adopted mother, Miriam might learn something more about Moses. To her surprise, Mered's face flushed, and his eyes widened. Miriam watched him with curiosity while he seemed to stumble for an answer. He had never been one to be at a loss for words.

"She has not married," Mered finally said. He seemed ready to add something else when a petite woman standing a few paces behind Miriam interrupted.

"She'll not marry, either, on account of her illegitimate child," the woman said. "Even the royals have their own rules within their ranks."

Miriam's face heated. She didn't turn to see who was speaking because she believed her expression would give away too much. Moses was *not* illegitimate, and Bithiah was nothing but compassionate. The princess had saved Miriam's brother's life.

Someone else asked a question, but Miriam was too consumed with her thoughts to pay attention any longer. She turned to leave, surprised to see Aaron moving through the crowd toward her.

When he reached her, he grasped her arm and spoke in a low voice. "Let's go home." His tone was calm, but Miriam shivered at his underlying firmness.

The walk home with Aaron was painful, literally. He kept hold of her arm too tightly, and even though he didn't speak a word, she knew he was furious. When he deposited her on their parents' doorstep, he only said, "You are becoming reckless."

He disappeared into the dark, and she could only imagine what he might tell her parents when he next spoke to them. Miriam was grateful they were asleep, as evidenced by the dark home.

She stayed in front of her home for several minutes, not ready to go inside the slumbering hut yet. She was feeling too reckless, which Aaron had just accused her of, but instead of making her want to change her ways, it only increased her stubbornness. Why shouldn't she find a way to learn more about their brother?

With the emotions pulsing through her, she knew it would be awhile before she could fall asleep, and she knew she'd regret staying up when the morning came. It always came early. She decided to sit in the courtyard and study the maps in the sky. The night sky always seemed to bring calm. But as she left the front of the hut and walked into the courtyard, she saw the outline of a man walking along the road, approaching the hut. Miriam sat on the bench, knowing she'd be mostly concealed by the waist-high wall. She wasn't particularly afraid, but she was curious.

Soon she recognized Mered, who, instead of heading in the direction of the village, was walking away, toward the palace. It made sense because he lived close to it, but something made Miriam stand up and greet him.

"You should be inside your hut. It's very late." Mered's first words seemed to echo those of everyone else Miriam knew.

"I was thinking about what you said at the gathering." She knew she had to be careful, but she couldn't resist. When else would she have a chance to talk to this man without anyone else around? "I hope my question wasn't out of line."

Mered shifted on his feet so the moonlight caught his facial features. He definitely looked disapproving. "It does us no good to speculate about the royalty," he said. "Especially on things we don't know much about."

"Do you see Moses often?" Miriam said, then shut her mouth quickly. She'd gone too far.

Mered's eyes shifted and seemed to darken. He was silent for a moment. "You are very curious."

"I apologize." Miriam took a step back and turned toward the hut.

Mered's voice stopped her. "I usually know of events he's involved in, but I've never personally spoken to him. He is chariot-racing Ramses and Pentu tonight."

Miriam turned back to Mered and gave a quick nod, then a quiet "Thank you."

When she reached the door of her hut, she looked back. Mered had already started down the road again. She watched him until he disappeared from sight.

She felt caught between the desire to follow and watch the chariot racing and the rare side of her that cautioned her to stay home. She crept to her silent home, seeing that her mother had already laid out the fire for the next morning's cooking. Miriam could picture her mother's wrinkled fingers doing the work after her father was in bed. It seemed her mother never stopped working, which was why she slept so deeply.

Miriam could leave and return, and neither of her parents would know. Her heart hammered as she paused, thinking of what might happen if she was caught by either her brother or her parents or, even worse, by an Egyptian along the road.

She took a deep breath, then reached for the cloak hanging by the door. Slipping it on, she left the hut without making a sound.

CHAPTER SIX

Moses

Moses brushed through the manes of the horses in his private stable. They were restless tonight. One was an older stallion; the other two were fillies. He would be hard-pressed to lose with the two fillies, and he wouldn't mind adding Pentu's new horses to his stable.

As he led the two younger horses out of the stable and into the arena, he was surprised at the size of the assembled audience. There were several dozen gathered, and torches had been placed around the arena to light the track. Moses chuckled to himself as he spotted Pentu, who was already arguing with Ramses over something.

Ramses looked calm, as usual, a wry smile on his face, while Pentu's hands were flying everywhere, emphasizing the perspiration on his shaved head.

"What's the problem?" Moses said, walking over to them after securing his horses to a side post.

Pentu turned sharply. "Ram is pulling out. We need more than two contenders."

Moses looked over at Ramses with surprise. "Why are you pulling out?"

"Nefertari's cousin is marrying tonight, and she wants me to accompany her," Ramses said.

"Nefertari commands you now?" Pentu cut in, his voice thick with disdain.

Moses glanced over the crowd, and not seeing Ramses's betrothed, he said, "Pentu's right. Doesn't Nefertari know you're the crown prince?"

Ramses snapped his gaze back to Moses and narrowed his eyes, probably suspecting where Moses was going to take this.

"You'll be pharaoh of Egypt one day, ruler over us all, and that includes your wife," Pentu said, jumping in before Moses could speak.

Ramses drew his brows together and shrugged. "I don't want to race either, so it happens to be my wish as well."

Moses laughed, and Pentu joined in. Every muscle in Ramses's body was geared for competition. Even now his stance told Moses that Ramses was ready to race. After he caught his breath, Moses said, "When has Ramses II ever not wanted to compete?"

"You're going soft like a kitten, Ram," Pentu chided. He lowered his voice and leaned toward Ramses. "And I'm not the only one who thinks so."

Ramses shook his head, looking toward the crowd. Then he straightened his shoulders and looked over at Pentu and Moses. His jaw tight, he spat out the words, "I'll race."

Moses grinned and clapped him on the back. "Wise choice, my friend. All of Egypt will thank you later."

"For what?" Ramses said.

"For never backing down from a challenge," Moses said, looking over at Pentu, who was also grinning and trying to hold back another laugh.

Pentu's smile only faltered when Moses hooked up his horses to his chariot. Pentu's horses from the north were fine specimens, but they didn't have the height and mass that Moses's fillies had.

As they prepared the chariots and horses, the audience started to call out the names of their favorites until that became a competition too. Moses worked quickly so he could be the first to the start line. The longer his horses stared down the track, the more tightly wound up they would be.

By the time Pentu and Ramses joined him, Moses's horses were straining against their harnesses. The three chariots were lined up side by side, and the crowd started to cheer. Moses kept the tension on the reins steady. A young woman dressed in a flowing tunic, and who was likely from the harem, stepped forward and raised her arms to prepare for the starting signal. When she lowered them, Moses let his horses take over. He shot out in front of both Ramses and Pentu, barreling down the track.

Moses rode hard but held the horses back just enough that they would have plenty of strength on the final paces. On the first turn, Pentu caught up, with Ramses close behind. It was hard to see the track in the dark, and it gave Moses the sensation that he was flying through the air with no ground beneath him. He focused on the general shape of the arena he was so familiar with and guided his horses accordingly.

Moses pulled ahead again, with Ramses keeping pace. They rode close together, their chariots almost touching, dust billowing between them. From Moses's peripheral vision, he could see Pentu gaining, but there wasn't much room for him to take over. Moses refocused on the track ahead, feeling the chariot's rocking movements beneath him and concentrating on how much more he could push his horses.

As the finish line loomed, Ramses suddenly fell away, and Pentu was beside Moses. The moment had come, and Moses yelled a command to his horses and gave them more lead to sprint. Pentu was in a strong position, but the strategy he'd used with Ramses wasn't enough, and Moses was able to stay ahead. He crossed the finish line first, elation soaring through him.

He slowed his horses, letting them gradually ease to a stop. Then he twisted to see how far behind Ramses had fallen. His stomach lurched when he saw the overturned chariot and Ramses lying next to it.

Moses jumped off his chariot and ran to the accident. He called upon every god and goddess he knew to spare the prince's life. When he reached Ramses, Moses knelt in the dirt. "Ramses!"

The prince moaned, and relief shot through Moses.

He leaned close to the prince and said loudly, "Are you all right? Can you move?"

Ramses's eyes opened. "Stop shouting," he hissed. "My head hurts." He rose up on his elbows and spit out a mouthful of dirt.

Others had gathered around them, but Moses was only focused on Ramses. "Can you move your legs?"

With another moan, Ramses moved to a full sitting position. He looked down at his legs, then bent one of his knees. "I can." His eyes searched the gathered crowd. "Where did Pentu go?"

"Pentu's probably sulking somewhere," Moses said. He stood and held out his hand to help Ramses stand. "Come on. I'll help you up."

Ramses put his hand into Moses's, and Moses hauled him to his feet. He'd never been so relieved in his life to know the prince was alive and safe.

"He ran toward the hills!" someone in the crowd shouted. "He was trying to kill you!"

Ramses whipped around and faced the man who'd accused Pentu. "What do you know?"

The man kept his head raised, his gaze bold. "Why would Pentu run unless he was guilty?"

Ramses turned back to Moses. "Is it possible? Did Pentu cut me off on purpose?" Ramses asked, his voice bitter.

A gasp went through the crowd, and Moses stared at Ramses. It seemed impossible, yet . . . there was no teasing in Ramses's expression or voice. Moses scanned the crowd for Pentu, but he wasn't anywhere to be seen.

Surely it was an accident, one made in the heat of a race. Moses couldn't let himself consider that Pentu had purposely put the crown prince of Egypt in mortal danger.

"Find him!" Ramses ordered those closest to him as he brushed dirt from his kilt.

Moses had hesitated with his answer too long. But he didn't need to be told to find Pentu; he was already pushing through the crowd, looking for his reckless cousin. The people dispersed, many calling out for the runaway. It took only moments for the frenzy to grow and for the young men to call for revenge in the name of Prince Ramses. If Pentu was found, his life could be over before he was brought to court.

Moses hurried toward the stands. They were mostly empty, and there was no sign of Pentu. He thought fast, trying to decide where his cousin might flee to. The sooner he was found and absolved, the better. If he disappeared overnight, a manhunt would be ordered, and his fate would be decided.

Outside the arena, the land was swathed in the darkness of night. Moses looked toward the palace, wondering if Pentu would dare return there—maybe to fetch some valuables. Moses scanned the collection of pools and the elegant trees surrounding them. They'd create enough cover to hide Pentu.

Moses set out for them at a quick run as shouts came from the arena, where the crowd was still focusing its search inside. This gave Moses the chance to slip away without being noticed. He needed to talk to Pentu without everyone accusing him too.

Once he reached the pools, Moses instinctively knew Pentu wasn't around. The water was too smooth and quiet, and the trees were as still as statues. Behind him, people exited the arena, carrying torchlights. They were on the move. Moses looked toward the hills that contained an old temple site now in ruins. Could Pentu have made it that far?

Moses calculated the time from the end of the race until now. If Pentu had run, he could be most of the way to the old site. Besides, the cover of night would have concealed him. Mind made up, Moses set out, moving as fast as he dared over the uneven ground, with only the moonlight to guide him.

"Pentu," he called out as he reached the ruins. He didn't think Pentu could have made it much farther, and beyond the ruins was the western desert. "Pentu! It's Moses. I'm here to help you!"

He stopped and listened over his labored breathing. No sound or movement reached him, but his thumping heart told him Pentu was close by.

He moved past the crumbled walls and toppled statues. When he reached a partially buried worship building, he remembered the interior reached deep into the hillside.

He bent and stepped into the low opening. "Pentu! Everyone is looking for you. Let me help you!"

No response. No sound at all.

Moses backed out of the opening, and then he heard it—a skitter of rocks.

"Pentu, it's better this way," Moses called out. "If you hide, they'll not stop hunting you. They'll think you're guilty because you won't come back. And when they do find you, you'll be executed without a trial of any sort." He paused, listening over the thundering of his apprehension.

"Ram will never forgive me." It was Pentu's voice, hollow yet close.

Moses took a few tentative steps inside. "Pentu? You've known Ramses your entire life. You're his cousin and friend. He'll pardon you. I know it."

Pentu's laugh was bitter. "How can you know anything? I've always been second best even though you're the bastard child."

A hard knot formed in Moses's throat, but he swallowed against it and ignored the anger Pentu incited. "Come out," Moses said, "and we can discuss this. I'll help you in any way I can." Relief shot through him when he heard more rocks skitter, then heard the sound of shuffling. Moses backed out, waiting. Moments later, Pentu came out of the opening.

The man looked like a skittish desert fox. He wouldn't even meet Moses's gaze, staying close to the cave's entrance.

"What happened in the arena?" Moses asked.

Pentu's eyes flashed black beneath the moon, and he folded his arms. "I was tired of losing."

Moses felt as if he'd been punched. Pentu had deliberately put the prince in danger. "You planned the accident?" he said, barely keeping his voice controlled.

Pentu scuffed his sandals against the rocky ground. "Not exactly. I was planning to cut *you* off, but you were ahead just enough that I couldn't reach you." He hesitated. The first sign of remorse. "It was foolish."

Moses wanted to wrap his hands around Pentu's neck and squeeze sense into him. "It was more than foolish. They are calling for your execution down there. You know Pharaoh will listen to the crowd, especially if it has to do with defending the safety and honor of his heir."

Pentu was silent for so long Moses wondered if the man was right in the head. Maybe he'd been fooling everyone for a long time.

Finally, Pentu stepped away from Moses. "I'll hide until Ram's no longer angry or until you can secure mercy for me."

"No," Moses said as Pentu moved farther away from him toward a tumbled wall. "You'll face Ramses now. The sooner, the better. If you hide, you'll never be welcomed back. Even I can see that."

Someone shouted far away by the pools, and Moses looked behind him. A group of men with torches was searching through the trees. It wouldn't be long now until they thought to come into the hills.

"You don't understand," Pentu said in a fierce whisper. "My family will suffer disgrace and be banished if I'm found guilty."

"Then tell Ram the truth. Let the tempers cool, and he'll know it was an accident." Moses exhaled. He needed to work on cooling his own temper. "Your family will be worse off if you hide than if you face your actions. At least there will be honor in that. Admitting your mistake and asking for mercy will not bring disgrace upon your family."

Voices floated up the hillside. The men were coming toward the temple site. "Pentu—"

But Pentu was shaking his head and moving farther away. "I can't take the risk." He turned and started up the hill, stumbling in his haste.

Moses didn't have time to carefully consider his actions. He lunged after Pentu and caught him around the waist. The two tumbled to the ground, and Moses quickly pinned Pentu beneath him. Pentu struggled and thrashed beneath Moses's weight, but Moses was able to hold him down.

The others had spotted them, and the shouting started.

"I hate you," Pentu said, spitting in Moses's face.

Moses didn't flinch as the spittle struck just below his eye, then dripped off his cheek. He kept Pentu locked to the ground as he stared into the defiant eyes.

As the voices grew closer, Pentu started to struggle again, then it seemed he knew he couldn't escape Moses's grip. He stilled and closed his eyes.

CHAPTER SEVEN

MIRIAM

MIRIAM THOUGHT HER HEART MIGHT stop in terror. The men with the torches were coming closer to the trees where she hid. She'd fled the arena as soon as the uproar had started and made her way toward the royal pools concealed by trees.

No one had paid attention to her, her cloak covering her hair and face. She'd even seen Mered sitting high up in the arena, but he hadn't noticed her. Now she could be discovered. She shrank against a tree trunk, trying to make herself as small as possible.

The voices moved in and out of the trees as they searched for a man named Pentu, whom Moses had raced against. Miriam assumed Pentu was a member of the court or even a royal. Whatever his station, he was now being called a traitor. She shuddered at the angry tone in the searchers' voices. And then the tones changed.

"He may have gone to the hills! Moses may have captured him."

Miriam held herself as still as possible as the men headed the other way. When the voices faded, she straightened. Sure enough, the men were heading for the slope, and others were coming from the arena to join them, men and women alike.

Miriam moved through the trees and joined the group that followed the lead men. No one seemed to be aware of her presence—she was just one of the crowd. When the people ahead of her stepped to the side and prostrated themselves, she realized Prince Ramses was coming up the hill as well. She turned to see the prince striding toward her.

She dropped into a prostrate, making sure the hood of the cloak kept her well concealed on this already dark night, and he walked by without any word or acknowledgment that there was a Hebrew woman in their midst. After he passed, Miriam rose, her throat tight. She had just bowed to the next pharaoh of Egypt. As much as she hated all that his father had done to her people, she wasn't about to be sentenced to execution tonight. Or even worse, become a plaything in the harem.

Maybe it was a bad idea to come to the chariot races, but she couldn't very well walk in the opposite direction now. She climbed the hill with the others, remaining on the outskirts of the crowd. Ramses walked right up to where Moses stood with the other chariot racer. Miriam noticed Moses's grip was tight on the man who looked like he wanted to be anywhere but facing the crown prince.

"You!" Ramses shouted, and the crowd immediately fell dead silent.

Miriam brought a hand to her throat as Ramses drove his fist into the other man's face. The victim would have collapsed, but Moses held him upright.

It seemed the Hebrews weren't the only ones who were beaten.

"You're a fool, Pentu. You've always been a fool," the prince hissed.

Even in the light of the moon, Miriam saw the bulging veins in the prince's neck. Tension rippled through the gathering, and the people started to edge away from the three men.

"Let him speak before you condemn him," Moses said, his voice clear in the silence.

Miriam found herself holding her breath as those around her gasped. If Moses had courage to say such things to Prince Ramses, they must be as close as brothers, Miriam decided, which only made her wonder more about his life.

"I've heard enough from him over the years," Prince Ramses ground out.

The man named Pentu hung his head, silent sobs moving his shoulders.

Miriam had seen the dangerous movements Pentu had made in the arena, yet she felt compassion for the fearful man.

"Ram," Moses said in a calm, firm voice, "he was foolish, I agree. But he meant you no real harm. He—"

"I can speak for myself," Pentu said, raising his head. His voice was thick with emotion, but he looked Ramses in the eye. "Moses is right. I was a fool. I *am* a fool. But I will spend the rest of my days working for your forgiveness. I should never have raced. I was childish and let the greed of competition control me." Pentu sank to his knees, Moses still keeping a grip on his arm to prevent him from fleeing. "Forgive me, Your Highness. I will be your most faithful servant for the rest of my life."

By the set of Prince Ramses's shoulders, it was plain he was listening to his competitor. Miriam let out a breath. Would the prince forgive this man? Was it so impossible to believe an Egyptian harbored any sort of compassion? She expected it of Moses, but of a royal?

Pentu continued to plead with Prince Ramses, and the longer the crown prince stayed silent, the more assured Miriam was that Pentu would not meet a horrible fate. And it seemed to be thanks to Moses, who was now asking for mercy on Pentu's behalf.

Finally Prince Ramses said the words. "You are pardoned, Pentu. But I don't want to see you for a few days, until I can stop my hands from squeezing the life out of you." He stared at Pentu for several seconds, then he made his way down the hillside. The crowd followed at a slower pace than the prince, possibly too afraid to get too close to him.

Miriam remained rooted to her place, watching all that unfolded and marveling that Prince Ramses was a kinder man than she'd thought.

Only a few people remained now, surrounding Moses and Pentu. Miriam moved off to the side, hoping no one would take particular notice of her. Perhaps tonight she'd be able to hear more from Moses and learn more about him. But before she could make any sort of plan, a hand wrapped around her upper arm.

"Come with me," a voice said close to her ear.

She turned her head. "Mered?"

His grasp tightened into a bruising grip, and he tugged her with him down the hillside, across the uneven landscape, past the pools and trees, then past the arena.

"You can let go of me now," Miriam whispered to him.

"Can I?" Mered asked, stopping, his grip not in the least loosened.

"I can walk on my own; I'm not a child," Miriam insisted. She regretted coming tonight and only wished to return to her home without further incident.

Mered's usually gentle face wrinkled into a scoff. "Miriam, daughter of Amram and Jochebed, you are a thorn in your parents' side."

She tried to pull away, but he was much stronger than she.

"I will spare them this night of news that will only bring sorrow to their old bones," he said, leaning closer and speaking in a fierce tone. "But you will face your brother."

At first Miriam thought he meant Moses, but then she realized he meant Aaron. She tried to pull away again.

Mered didn't even seem bothered that she was struggling against him. "You're not leaving my side until you are safely in your brother's home."

The walk back to the village was painful—both because Mered was true to his promise and didn't release her and because her heart was twisting at the thought of facing her brother. Aaron was already making it difficult for her to check on Moses; what would happen when he discovered where she'd been tonight?

Aaron's hut was pitch-black when Mered marched Miriam into the courtyard, but that didn't stop the man's determination. He rapped on the door, keeping his grip firm on her arm. She expected a whole series of bruises to appear by morning.

When Aaron answered the door, his sleepy expression immediately turned sharp as he took in the sight of Miriam. He slipped out of the door and pulled it shut behind him. Crossing his arms, he said, "What has she done now?"

"I'll let her explain," Mered said. "Then I'll leave her in your care."

In a shaky voice, Miriam told Aaron what she'd done, and when she finished, Mered finally, blessedly, removed his hand.

Aaron hadn't said a word through the entire explanation. And when he did talk, instead of speaking to Miriam, he thanked Mered. Miriam dropped her gaze and kept her eyes on her sandaled feet as she heard Mered's footsteps move away. The man might be gone, but she still felt his grip. Tears burned in her eyes. She'd confessed her deeds without a single tear, but now that it was just Aaron and her, she couldn't stop the tears from falling.

Aaron didn't move, didn't speak. He didn't have to. His thoughts sounded in Miriam's mind. She knew what he was about to say and what he was about to threaten. No, the time for threats had passed. They would become actions now.

* * *

Miriam hadn't slept the night before, and she'd spent all day weaving until her fingers ached. She ignored the pain, though, and continued to work through the midday break and then through the evening meal.

At one point, her mother came into the courtyard. She wore her frequently repaired tunic that was too big for her thin shoulders. Jochebed might be aging, with three adult children raised, but her hair was still thick and abundant. Its dark loveliness framed her round face and large dark eyes. "Come eat, Miriam. You must be hungry."

Miriam shook her head once, and eventually her mother left. Tonight there was to be a council between her parents and Aaron, in which they would decide her fate.

The thought alone made Miriam feel ill, and she knew if she had anything in her stomach, it wouldn't stay. As the sun settled against the horizon, her mother came into the courtyard again, saying nothing this time, and lit a torch. The orange glow provided enough light for Miriam to continue weaving, but truthfully, she could have done it with her eyes closed.

When a heavier step shuffled into the courtyard some time later, Miriam finally looked up. It was her father. Amram looked like an older version of Moses and Aaron—though he kept his hair grown to his shoulders. His long face and dark brows gave little doubt about whose father he was. While Miriam took after her mother, round faced with thick hair, her brothers were the younger version of their father.

"Come inside, daughter," her father said.

His tone was soft, but Miriam heard the tremor of disapproval. She followed him inside, where Aaron and her mother sat on the cushions in the central room. Miriam was exhausted both in body and mind, and she was ready to concede to her parents' wishes. The hurt in their faces had been enough for her to beg their forgiveness. And now she'd just have to listen to their pronouncement.

She settled next to her mother and clasped her hands in her lap.

Her father's raspy voice began first. "You have been living in the past for too long, Miriam. You must think of your future."

Miriam's throat grew tighter with each word her father spoke.

"Yoseph spoke with me this week, and he asked after you," her father continued.

She stared at her father. Had he made a promise to Yoseph?

Her father's gaze didn't waver. "He's a good man, and he has a young daughter who needs a mother."

Her mother reached over and patted Miriam's hand, then held it, her eyes steady on Miriam. "You are past the age to be acting on impulses. It's time you do your duty as a Hebrew woman. Marry and be a good wife and mother. It's the Adonai's calling for you."

Miriam exhaled slowly. Did the Lord Adonai want her to marry a widower just to be a mother to his child? Yoseph's daughter was a sweet little thing, but was that cause to marry Yoseph? Miriam let her eyes slide shut, and when she opened them again, Aaron spoke.

"You do not like widower Yoseph?" Aaron asked.

Had her brother read her thoughts? At least he always seemed to know she was going to get into trouble before she did.

"I have never spoken to him," she admitted. She'd seen him during market days, of course.

"We will invite him over tomorrow night and begin the courting process," her father said.

"Wait," Miriam said. "Is . . . is he the only man who has asked about me?" She looked to Aaron. Surely he would not condone her marrying someone she didn't at least care for. "I-I mean, surely . . . I know the available men are few in our village, and because of my age, I will have to likely settle for a widower, but I know so little about Yoseph that I wonder if he was the only man to express interest."

Both of her parents seemed surprised. She had never spoken so much about a possible suitor.

Aaron looked upward as if he was beseeching heaven itself for patience.

"Aaron, what is it?" her father asked. "*Have* other men inquired after your sister?"

"Miriam knows it is so," Aaron said, keeping his eyes trained on some imaginary Deity.

"Then why has no one spoken to me?" her father continued.

Aaron finally lowered his eyes and directed his gaze at Miriam. "She finds a way to frighten them off."

Her mother gasped and turned to Miriam. "*Why?* You could have been married by now, and I wouldn't have had to suffer the humiliation of Mered dragging my daughter back from an Egyptian chariot race!" Her mother's voice broke.

Miriam felt awful.

"David has asked after her," Aaron said.

She glowered at Aaron; he'd only made what had already been bad worse. Despite her commitment to obey her parents from here on out, she couldn't stop from speaking her mind. "Is it so wrong to want a husband with *two* legs? Not to mention he puts his crutch to good use against the small animals wandering the marketplace."

"David is good with his hands—a master carpenter," Aaron countered. "You'd always have good furniture."

"And most women would prefer a husband whose temper is not short and who doesn't spit on her when he speaks," Miriam continued, her neck growing warm.

"Would it be so hard to stand back a pace or two? And perhaps marriage will soften him," Aaron cut in. "What about Reuven? He has fine, strong features, and your children would be the most handsome in the village."

"And should I be expected to cover my nose each time my husband enters our home? And make excuses as to why he doesn't observe Sabbath?" Miriam said. Reuven was handsome, but he was also rude and abrasive. And it bothered her how he made no secret of breaking the Sabbath.

"As a dutiful wife, it would be within your influence to encourage Reuven to bathe regularly. And I'm sure you can convince him to observe Sabbath with your sweet talking." Aaron leaned forward, his voice turning into a growl. "Avner is kindhearted and doesn't smell."

"That's because he wears women's scented oil and has the habit of paying more attention to his male friends than seeking a wife."

Aaron narrowed his eyes. "He inquired after *you*."

"Only because he felt sorry for me with that big kind heart of his."

Their parents looked back and forth between the siblings. "All of these men—" her mother began.

"Yes, Mother," Aaron interrupted. "They all questioned me about Miriam and whether or not she was betrothed. When I passed on the message to Miriam, you would have thought she'd been stung by an entire horde of hornets at the thought of a man's interest."

Her mother snapped her head to stare at Miriam. "You do want to marry, do you not?"

"I do," Miriam said, frustration in her words. "But why is it so hard to find a man with both legs, who doesn't spit when he talks, who can be in the same room as another without the other passing out from the stink, and who would care for me more than he cares for his gaggle of friends?"

Her mother's eyes narrowed. "Then you cannot be opposed to Yoseph. He will be a good match, and your father and I will give you our blessing."

CHAPTER EIGHT

MOSES

MOSES OPENED HIS EYES TO the sunlight streaming into his bedchamber. Something wasn't right, and as soon as he turned his head to look toward the late-morning light, he remembered. The disastrous chariot race two days before between Pentu and Ramses . . . Moses had been the peacemaker between them that night . . . But in the two intervening days, there had been palpable contention between Ramses and Pentu, until the pharaoh himself had intervened.

Moses groaned as he thought about the pharaoh's proclamation to the three men the night before: "Tomorrow you will meet your brides. You're men now, and you have too much time on your hands. It's time you marry, and it's time you participated in all court events instead of running free and stirring up trouble."

Moses and Pentu had both stared at the pharaoh. Ramses was already betrothed, so the men knew Pharaoh wasn't referring to him. Pharaoh was ordering them to marry and join the court.

Pentu had immediately started arguing with Pharaoh, and Moses couldn't recall the words between the two men because he had gone absolutely still, his thoughts tumbling against each other.

His mother had been no help.

"Moses!" his mother's voice said as if he'd just conjured her up by thinking about her.

She came into his room, already dressed for the day, wearing her elegant tunic and fine jewels.

"You're not even out of bed. You need to prepare yourself quickly, son," she said, her tone far from chastising. She sounded merry.

He couldn't believe she was so happy about the sudden turn of events. He groaned again as his mother placed a firm hand on his shoulder.

"What's this? You're not about to disobey Pharaoh's orders, are you?" she said in a teasing voice. She knew he'd never do that. Not being the son of an unmarried princess.

"If I didn't know better, I'd think you gave Pharaoh the idea." Moses sat up in bed and stretched his arms. When his mother didn't laugh, he looked over at her.

She'd moved to the windows overlooking the courtyard and had stopped to look out the window openings. She wrapped her arms about her torso, tilting her head.

"What is it, Mother?" Moses said, climbing out of bed and rubbing his hand over his shaved head, still trying to wake up.

She shook her head slightly. "It's just that . . . I didn't expect this day to arrive so quickly."

Moses crossed to stand by her. She wasn't crying, so that was good, but her tone was now somber. "I am no longer a child, Mother," Moses said. "But I hoped I could avoid marriage for a few more years."

His mother turned. "You are still my little boy," she said in a soft voice. "I pray you will be given the kindest and most beautiful wife in all of Egypt."

Moses smiled and pulled his mother into his arms. "You see, that's impossible, because no one is as kind and as beautiful as you."

She tightened her hold about him, and for a moment, Moses believed he'd fooled her into thinking he was going to the betrothal meeting willingly. But in truth, he felt ill at the thought of it. He didn't want to worry his mother though; he could see that it brought her comfort to think the pharaoh had singled him out to arrange a special marriage for him.

He could see she thought he was rising in the pharaoh's favor and an important commission would naturally follow. But Moses wasn't convinced that was the case. The royal court was for nothing more than moving pawns from one place to another, and the pharaoh only did something if it pleased or benefited himself personally or increased his position in the kingdom.

Moses saw his and Pentu's sudden betrothals as an opportunity for Pharaoh to help himself or the kingdom in some way. If he was right, he'd be betrothed to a wealthy merchant's daughter or to a rich vizier's daughter—daughters of men the pharaoh wanted to elevate so he could have claim to their connections and wealth.

All this Moses suspected, and all this he kept from his mother. He believed she would never marry, especially if she had gone this long without a husband. Grandchildren would bring her joy.

"Your betrothal will last a year," his mother was saying as she withdrew herself from his embrace. "That will give you plenty of time to get to know her and her family." She placed her hands on each side of his face. "You'll make a wonderful husband."

Moses laughed. "You are overlooking many things to say that, Mother."

"I know who you are," she said, patting him on the chest. "You have a pure heart and will be kind to your wife." She lowered her hands and walked past him toward his small chamber of clothing.

But she didn't move fast enough; Moses saw the shadow in her eyes. Had she been in love with his father? Had he already been married? Had he been cruel? Moses exhaled. Every time he brought up marriage in reference to his mother, she always said she had enough love in her life—in the form of him—and she didn't want to give up her freedoms.

Yet, as she pulled out the kilt she wanted him to wear, he wondered if this day and his eventual marriage would be hard on her, and if marriage was something she still wished for herself.

"This will be a fine one to wear," his mother said, holding up an indigo-dyed kilt with gold edging. "I'll send the servant in to dress you."

Moses took the kilt from her, and before he could ask her any questions, she opened the door and called to the servant.

It didn't take long for the servant to prepare him, and soon he was walking along the corridor to the king's private banquet room. It would be a small banquet with the families of the two women the pharaoh had found for them.

When Moses reached the outer doors of the banquet room, his mother was standing there waiting, a smile on her face. In the time it had taken him to get ready, she had chased the shadows from her eyes. She grasped his arm and kissed his cheek. "I saw the families arrive," she said in a whisper to avoid being overheard by the guards. "Both women are beautiful, but I hope you get the taller one."

Moses bit back a laugh. He was taller than Pentu, but that wouldn't be a deciding factor. It would be purely political. He entered the room with his mother, and the people inside stood and bowed before Moses.

Pentu was already there with his father, and Moses could see that Pentu was clearly amused and enjoying himself. It wouldn't matter to Pentu whether he was married or not; he'd still enjoy his pursuits in the harem despite his marital status.

Pharaoh wouldn't be in attendance, since he had more important matters to attend to, so Vizier Horus was orchestrating the meeting.

Pentu winked at Moses, and Moses wanted to shake his head. Instead, he smiled politely as Vizier Horus, a short stocky, man, began the introductions.

"This is Commander Thoth, his wife, and their daughter Beset," Vizier Horus said.

Moses recognized Commander Thoth's name and knew he was over the Akhetaton division in Upper Egypt. The recognition was plain on Pentu's face as well. The daughter, Beset, was a petite woman with a narrow face and piercing eyes. The henna on her chest and the kohl on her eyes made her appear as striking as the royal women at court. She openly studied Moses and then Pentu.

When Vizier Horus said, "Beset has been chosen for Pentu," Moses was not in the least surprised. Pentu had already been given a commander position and was likely acquainted with Thoth. With the two commanders tied by marriage, Pharaoh had orchestrated unity within his military ranks.

It was with great interest that Moses then turned his attention to the second family. The daughter of this family would be *his* betrothed. He looked over at the woman who stood nearly behind her father. Her eyes were modestly lowered, and she had her hands clasped in front of her. She was tall and willowy, and while she wasn't walking or moving, her gracefulness was plain. She raised her head, and their eyes locked.

It was the depths of her eyes that stopped Moses. She wasn't a simple woman with simple desires. In only a moment of looking at her, he knew she was calculating and hard and had just made her own assessment of Moses. Something turned in Moses's stomach. But it wasn't the twist of interest or excitement that he was about to be betrothed to a beautiful woman—and there was no doubt she was beautiful.

He looked quickly away, doubting his impression, wondering how he could sense that about a woman he'd only just looked upon for the first time.

Vizier Horus introduced the second family. "This is Vizier Amon and his daughter, Cena. His wife passed away last year."

Moses's gaze was drawn again to Cena; instead of seeing the proper expression of sorrow he expected on her face at the mention of her deceased mother, he saw only indifference.

A shudder traveled through him, and he tried to suppress it, knowing his own mother was at his side and would certainly recognize his distress. He glanced at her, and she was all smiles. The introductions continued, but Moses knew he'd remember very little. He hardly remembered the meal, except for the times a question was repeated to him and he had to focus in order to answer. He'd spent the entire meal staring into the amber eyes of a temptress who had plans of her own.

The parents told stories of their daughters and their many talents and gifts. It was as if they were trying to convince Pentu and Moses their daughters were lovely and virtuous. But the longer Moses sat on his cushion and picked at the food on the platter in front of him, the more he thought of ways to break the betrothal. Only her father could agree to end it.

As the meal came to an end, Vizier Horus stood. "And now the couples will have a chance to walk in the garden and discuss their futures."

Moses shot a look at Pentu to see what he might do. Pentu leapt to his feet and eagerly held out his hand to Beset. The woman smiled and rose, placing her hand in his, and before Moses realized it, Pentu and Beset were walking out the rear doors into the pharaoh's private courtyard.

Moses swallowed against the tightness in his throat. He must follow suit. With a glance at his mother, and receiving an encouraging smile and nod in return, he stood and held out his hand to Cena.

She rose gracefully, her fingers barely touching his as she stood.

Everyone was smiling at them as if their stroll through the gardens would be the most wonderful thing in the world.

Moses led Cena to the courtyard, only to find that Pentu and Beset had already walked far enough that they were nearly out of sight.

"You don't look like your mother," Cena said, her voice soft.

Moses looked over at her with surprise. "It's because—" He stopped himself before he could go further. Wouldn't Cena know about his scandalous birth? How his mother had become pregnant out of wedlock and had almost been banished?

"You must look like your father, then," Cena said. "Where is he? Has he died?"

Moses felt like she'd stabbed him in his heart. "I never knew my father," he said.

Cena stopped and withdrew her arm from his. Her narrow eyebrows lifted. "You don't know your father? So he has died. Was he a prince?"

Moses's face heated. In truth, his mother had never told him anything about his father. He knew she'd been shamed, and he didn't want to add to her burden or remind her of her past. "He was not a prince." Although he might have been, it was better to dispel Cena's calculating expression.

She continued to study him, and soon Moses felt as if he was a piece of cloth being examined in the marketplace. She shook her head, looking thoughtful. "When my father told me I was to be betrothed to a princess's son," she said in a low tone, "I expected more."

Moses's anger burned hot. He'd never been more insulted in his life. He set his jaw, trying to prevent himself from saying something he'd regret. There wasn't any doubt in his mind that this woman would be too happy to proclaim his faults to anyone who might listen.

"Tell me about your father," Moses finally said, keeping his voice even, although he had the urge to leave the courtyard and keep walking until he plunged into the River Nile.

"He's wealthy, and it's because he's brilliant," Cena said with a bright smile, but her eyes bore into Moses. "My father wasn't pampered, and he had to work for everything. He's created a trading enterprise with the Hittites." She leaned close and lowered her voice. "And I believe the Hittites respect him more than they do Pharaoh." She straightened, a triumphant smile on her face.

Moses couldn't help but inhale her mysterious scent of flower and spice. If he had seen her across the courtyard at a festival, he would have thought she was beautiful, both on the inside and out. But her eyes and her words made her seem as dangerous as a coiled snake ready to strike.

"Your father must be a great man," Moses said, feeling it was his duty to say so.

"He is." Her eyes were back on Moses, scanning him from head to foot.

Moses wanted to turn away, go back to his chamber, and pretend that this day hadn't happened, but because it was happening, there would be many more like it. And what would marriage bring? A dull pain throbbed at his temples.

"At least you are handsome," Cena said, stunning Moses. She lifted her hands and placed them on each side of his face, much like his mother had just that morning, but this was entirely different. Cena lifted up on her feet and moved very close to Moses, close enough that her breath filled the space between them. "You are handsome, and you are strong. You will do, Moses." She released him and took a few steps back. "But you have a lot of work ahead of you to keep a woman like me pleased." With a lift of her brows, she added, "I intend to have everything Egypt can offer me."

CHAPTER NINE

MIRIAM

As was Hebrew custom, Miriam prepared the meal for their guest a week after it was decided that Yoseph would be invited to their home. Miriam had spent the previous evening washing grape leaves and grinding wheat into coarse flour. She wanted the grape leaves to soak a full day before she added the spiced barley and bits of lamb she'd boiled, then cut into small bits.

"How is it coming?" her mother said, entering the cooking area on the side of the house. Unlike Miriam, her mother wore a clean tunic and her face was free from perspiration.

"I'm nearly finished," Miriam said as she rolled the grape leaves. "But I'm not ready yet."

"Let me finish with the grape leaves," her mother said. "You get ready so you can impress Yoseph."

Is he that selective? Miriam wanted to retort, but she stayed silent. She hurried to her tiny bedchamber and changed into her nicest tunic. It was the color of the morning sky, and whenever she wore it, she received compliments. As she brushed out her hair, then replaited it, she thought of what she might say to Yoseph. She'd paid particular attention to him on the last market day, knowing she'd be, in effect, allowing him to court her. Yet she hadn't ever actually spoken to him.

The only thing she knew was that he wasn't going to be bringing his daughter tonight. Miriam almost wished he would; at least that would divert any awkward conversation. When Miriam finished with her hair, she breathed in with determination. Despite her disobedience, her family was the most important thing to her. Without them, she was no one. She didn't relish the changes a marriage would bring upon her, but it was her parents' greatest wish for her. So here she was, about to accept an official request to be courted.

Voices arose from outside, coming through the high window opening in her bedchamber: Aaron's and his wife, Salome's, and her father's and . . . another man's, Yoseph.

Miriam checked her reflection in the small square of brass hanging on her wall. She was way past the bloom of youth, but she supposed she was acceptable to take over the family of another woman who had died too early. If nothing else, Miriam was resourceful and a hard worker. That should please any widower.

"Miriam." Her mother's whisper cut through her thoughts.

Miriam turned to see her mother in the doorway to her room.

"Our guests are here."

Miriam gave a stiff nod, and after smoothing her tunic, she followed her mother into the modest central room where extra cushions had been placed around the newly brushed rug. Aaron and Salome, who was petite and appeared to be delicate but who loved fiercely, greeted her warmly with embraces and kisses on the cheek. Miriam returned the warmth enthusiastically, if for no other reason than to demonstrate to Yoseph that they were a cheerful and happy family.

Then her father introduced her to Yoseph. Of course she'd seen him a few times, so his appearance came as no surprise. She was surprised, however, that he was shorter than she thought. Apparently a glance across the marketplace at a man with a young daughter rendered him taller than he actually was. In fact, Miriam was taller by a half-hand's width.

He smiled, and Miriam smiled back. At least his manner seemed pleasant, and his smile made his rather round face appear friendly. His dark eyes gave her a quick appraisal, and Miriam didn't notice any hesitation in them, which was both good and bad—good because it meant he was pleased with Miriam and her extra height didn't bother him; bad because if they were already committed to each other, he wouldn't have to win her.

Miriam gave a silent sigh of disappointment. There was no other man stepping forward to give Yoseph any competition, so why shouldn't he be sure of his place? His confident stature was well placed. The men seated themselves, and Miriam, her mother, and her sister-in-law proceeded to the cooking area to gather the platters of food and serve the men.

"You've outdone yourself," Salome said, picking up a platter of flatbread and small bowls of spiced oil. She flashed Miriam a smile. Miriam marveled at Salome's constant cheerfulness, even though she was with child and had suffered much illness due to the baby she was carrying.

Miriam returned the smile although a knot had formed in her stomach. It was one thing to prepare this meal but another to have a guest actually eat it. She hoped it would be delicious, not because she thought the fate of a betrothal would be determined by her cooking skills but because she wanted to please her parents.

She didn't regret the concern she caused her brother, but she was very sorry for the duress she'd put her parents through, and this would be a small token of her gratitude for them being in her life.

Yoseph exclaimed enthusiastically as each dish was brought in. As she retreated to the cooking area, she heard his compliments on the food. It was no wonder, Miriam thought, keeping a smile hidden. He did appear to enjoy food immensely. Compared to that of Miriam's father and brother, Yoseph's girth was generous. She wouldn't put him in the category of indulgent—that was nearly impossible in their slave position—but he didn't seem to be affected by any previously poor rations. She and her mother and sister-in-law ate together in the cooking area, keeping relatively silent so they could hear the men's conversation.

"Tell me, Miriam," Yoseph said, when Miriam had stepped into the gathering room to serve a dish of relish. She was surprised at the direct question. "How did you like the Egyptian chariot race?"

Miriam's face heated. Did everyone in the village know about that? If so, did everyone know she was cooking for Yoseph tonight too? She quickly served the relish, wanting to leave as soon as possible, but her brother and father were looking at her, waiting for her reply. Aaron had a bit of a mischievous glint in his eye. He was going to get a talking-to later.

"It was too dark to see much," Miriam said at last. "I'll have to return in the day sometime."

Yoseph laughed, but Miriam's father and brother both frowned. The last thing they wanted was for Miriam's suitor to encourage her in her antics.

"It's no wonder your parents invited me over tonight," Yoseph said, his voice still containing laughter but his eyes narrowing slightly.

Miriam edged toward the cooking area, wishing her face wasn't so easily flushed with embarrassment.

"At the young age of six, my daughter already knows what's expected of her." His dark eyes flickered to Miriam, then over to her father. "She knows her greatest calling will be to marry and bear children."

The silence around the low table was such that it seemed the men were holding their breath. When Yoseph gave a nod, Miriam took it as a dismissal and disappeared into the cooking area again. She didn't disagree that her greatest calling was marrying and bearing children, *if* she married, but the way Yoseph had said it made her feel . . . less than a person. She was already a slave, already a woman, and now . . . It seemed she was even less in the eyes of a widower desperate for a mother to raise his daughter.

When Miriam stepped into the cooking area where her mother was waiting, her mother's eyes were wide. She'd heard everything Yoseph had said. Her mother handed over a platter of honeyed cakes. "Take this in there and tell him to share them with his daughter." Her eyes narrowed in warning. "Talk sweetly."

Miriam took the platter and moved back into the gathering room where the men sat. She did as her mother said and noticed her father seemed to exhale with relief. His previously cheerful expression had slipped a little, but his eyes were as stoic as ever.

Miriam was grateful for the opportunity to leave again and collect her muddled thoughts. She hadn't expected to fall in love with Yoseph, but she had hoped for some kindness and respect on his part. Her mother gave her a nod of approval, then she and Salome started to clean up the dishes. While Miriam arranged cups for the after-meal wine on a platter, she went over Yoseph's words in her head. Nothing was exactly anger inducing, but it had bothered her nonetheless. Perhaps her parents had given her too much freedom. Or perhaps she'd been rebelling too long to become part of a marriage union.

Stubbornness rose in her chest, and she tamped it down by thinking of what was best for her family, her parents. They wanted her married. They wanted her happy. But she wasn't sure if those were the same thing.

As she walked into the gathering room to serve the wine, she knew Yoseph would not make her happy. She'd have to find that within herself somehow.

Yoseph praised the sweet cakes and took the cup of wine from Miriam with a smile. He rose ceremoniously to his feet and gave a little bow to Miriam. "I would like to invite you and your family to my home for a meal. It will be very humble."

Everyone in her family watched her as she accepted before she could think about it. Yoseph was all smiles again. But as he left, Miriam felt she had made a mistake. Yet how could she have rejected him in front of everyone? Her parents would have been heartbroken once again.

While Aaron and Salome prepared to leave, Miriam stepped into the courtyard, relishing the cooling air. There might be a limited number of evenings like this after she married. She'd work all day weaving for the Egyptians and then spend the evening caring for a child another woman had borne.

Aaron and Salome exited, and Miriam bid them farewell, taking note of Aaron's firm jawline. He was the closest person to her, and he had likely seen her dislike of Yoseph. His gaze told her it was time to take responsibility for her future. It was time to stop thinking of herself.

Miriam sank onto the bench in the courtyard, wishing she could have looked upon Yoseph with more favor. Did it have to be so hard? Couldn't she just see the good in him? With an exasperated sigh, she closed her eyes and forced herself to do just that. He had good teeth, a nice smile. He enjoyed her cooking. He already had a daughter, and she was a sweet girl, so there was no need to train him to be a father. He had invited her to his home, so he must find her acceptable.

She opened her eyes. Surely all of that was enough. Marriage was a part of life, it was work, and she would just have to accept that. A movement near the road caught her eye. It wasn't all that late in the night, but not many people traveled alone after the sun set—with the exception of her, but she could not be that person anymore.

At that moment, the person saw that she was watching him, and he turned and walked the other way. Miriam rose to her feet. How strange. It was like he didn't want her to see him. Without thinking twice, she strode across the courtyard and stepped onto the road. The man was walking quickly, and just as she reached the middle of the road, he stumbled.

He was trying to get away from her, which meant she had nothing to be afraid of. She hurried toward him, recognizing him as she grew closer. "Caleb? What are you doing?"

"I-I was—"

Miriam folded her arms across her chest. "Aaron sent you, didn't he? My brother still doesn't trust me—even after I cooked for Yoseph."

"You cooked for Yoseph?" Caleb asked.

"I did. But it seems no matter what I do, Aaron still has no faith in me." Anger pulsed through her. "I even accepted an invitation to share a meal at the widower's home!"

Caleb was completely silent, which made Miriam even more upset. And embarrassed. She couldn't believe her brother's lack of faith in her to do the right thing and couldn't believe Caleb had to be involved. She wasn't a small child who couldn't even be trusted to sit in her courtyard after a long day of weaving and cooking.

She kept her arms folded. "What are you going to do, Caleb? Spy on me when I'm a married woman too? Follow me around the market as I walk with Yoseph's daughter? Peer through the window when I'm having supper with him?"

He took a step forward, his eyes dark and unreadable in the night. "If your brother asks me to, I will."

"Oh!" She gave an empty laugh. "You're just a fool with no thoughts for yourself. You do what Aaron asks with no questions."

"I have thoughts for myself—" Caleb started.

"What influence does Aaron have over you?" Miriam cut in. "Why do you follow him around?"

His brows lifted. "Who said Aaron has anything over me?"

"Why else would you waste all of this time following me around?" she asked. "Did he save your life and now you owe him a debt? Did he wrestle a leopard so you might run free?"

Caleb laughed, and the sound startled Miriam. She wasn't sure if she'd ever heard him laugh before.

"No, nothing like that," Caleb said, still smiling.

Then something occurred to her, and she didn't like the direction her thoughts were taking her. Not at all. Caleb couldn't be interested in her, could he? If so, he would have spoken to her father. She would have definitely heard from her parents if he had. Caleb had no family that she knew of, yet he was still an upstanding part of their community.

Several thoughts ran through her mind unbidden, thoughts comparing him to Yoseph. Caleb was much taller, much leaner, his shoulders broad. His hair was thicker and longer than Yoseph's, and it was too dark to see his eyes right now, but she knew for a fact they were light brown, whereas Yoseph's were a nondescript murky gray.

Also, Caleb wasn't a widower, and he didn't have a child from another woman. He observed the Sabbath, and he wasn't known to have a temper.

Miriam took a step back, putting a little distance between her and Caleb. She wasn't happy with her thoughts, and she was starting to become suspicious of both Aaron and Caleb. What if Caleb did like her? Was Aaron trying to play a trick on her? Putting them together over and over so she'd start to like him?

She bit her lower lip as she considered her brother's possible deviousness. Caleb was still watching her, his expression amused as he stayed quiet, which reminded her of her brother's habit—how Aaron would wait until she'd spilled all of her words and secrets before mustering a reply.

Miriam wouldn't give Caleb the benefit. "Whatever you owe my brother, whether or not you are willing to confess it, you can consider it repaid. I'm a proper daughter and sister now. No more escapades."

He was still smiling, and it annoyed Miriam more than ever.

"Are you sure about that?" he said, his voice low, nearly a whisper. "You mean your brother and I will never have to worry about you spying on the Egyptian royalty again?"

It was mostly the truth, Miriam decided, so she nodded.

"Is that a promise?" Caleb asked.

She wondered why he cared so much in the first place. She opened her mouth to reply, but she couldn't get the words out.

"It is just as I thought," Caleb said, moving closer to her. Too close for Miriam to think as clearly as she needed to. "You haven't completely transformed. Not even agreeing to prepare a meal for Yoseph could change who you truly are."

"It can," Miriam shot out. The last thing she wanted was for Caleb to report back to Aaron about her hesitation. "And it will. Yoseph has a deep sense of duty to family, and I plan to emulate that in every way possible. He has . . . He has helped me understand my duty."

The amusement left Caleb's eyes. "You would marry someone who wants to change you?"

Miriam lifted her chin. "He's right in his criticisms."

"Yoseph *criticized* you?" Caleb's eyes bore into hers, and she had to look away.

"You're not my brother nor my father," Miriam said, unsettled at how quick he was to defend her when he himself had been charged with keeping her out of trouble. "And my choices are of no concern to you." She felt awful the moment she spoke the words, but she couldn't retract them now.

"I am definitely not your brother or your father," Caleb said in a soft voice, "but I'm just as concerned for your well-being as they are."

This surprised Miriam despite the fact that Caleb had said similar things before. But his tone was different. It wasn't lighthearted or that of a man scolding a child. It carried a new somberness.

"Miri," he said, ignoring the fact that she'd told him before not to call her that. He grasped her arm, and she froze at his touch. It wasn't entirely unwelcome, but it was something new. "Surely you know I care for you."

His statement silenced her. What was he saying? She knew what he was saying, but how could he mean it? His hand was still on her arm, and the warmth of his palm on her skin seemed to spread up her arm and heat her neck.

"My name is Miriam," she stumbled out. He had just declared his feelings for her—if that was what she understood—and she was correcting him on her name.

"Miriam." His voice was soft, almost a caress, and a shudder went through her. Not the type of shudder that had gone through her as she'd thought about becoming Yoseph's wife, but the type of shudder she wouldn't mind experiencing again. "I'd like to speak to your father."

Her breath nearly stopped. So Caleb was in earnest. Her mind was spinning too fast to form a reply. She should have been ready with an answer, but he had done the unexpected. She couldn't come up with an excuse. Not aloud or even in her mind. He wasn't a short widower, he had both legs, he didn't smell like the animals, he didn't spit when he talked, and he certainly wasn't too old to marry. Her face flushed, and she was grateful for the near darkness.

He was watching her, but she could only look down at her twisting hands. Long moments of silence passed, and finally he released a sigh and dropped his hand. She missed his touch as soon as it left her. That thought frightened her more than spying on Moses. How could she let herself consider Caleb as a husband? He was obnoxious, he never did as she asked him to, and he owed some strange favor to her brother.

On the other hand, he was only a few years older than she was, he had all of his teeth, he was strong, and he was passably handsome if a woman liked deep golden skin, dark curls, and warm brown eyes. She swallowed over the lump in her throat.

Her heart had begun a slow crescendo. "Do you think you could stand my cooking?" she asked.

He blinked as if he didn't understand what she was saying. Then a slow smile moved his lips upward. "What did Yoseph think?"

"He was very complimentary and ate with relish." She felt her own lips tug upward against her will.

Caleb raised his eyebrows, his smile growing. "Then I shall eat twice as much."

* * *

Preparing the evening meal had been a disaster so far. Even the honey cakes were on the border of being too crispy and burnt. Miriam spent the time before Caleb's arrival scraping off the edges. The main dish of lamb and cooked barley wasn't much better. She'd added extra spice to the barley, but it still didn't taste right, and the pigeons were dry and nearly burnt. One bite of the overcooked food, and Caleb would spit it out. Or he'd swallow and turn pale, possibly choke. She didn't know which would be worse.

Yoseph had stopped by twice since the meal at his home the week before. Perhaps he had heard of Caleb's invitation and that had increased the widower's interest level. It was just as well, Miriam decided. Caleb wouldn't be back after tonight. Perhaps she could weave a rug for him. A man always needed a rug, right?

"The burnt smell isn't so strong," her mother said, coming into the cooking area. "I don't think he'll even notice."

Miriam had grown used to the acrid scent, but she was sure her mother was just trying to soothe her. "I've been all thumbs today," Miriam said. "I had to undo half of my weaving."

Her mother smiled and rested her hand on Miriam's shoulder. "That's wonderful."

"*Wonderful?* It's awful. I should go to bed and hope that tomorrow is better. But it will be too late"—she waved her hand toward the singed cakes—"for this to be fixed."

Her mother's smile didn't change as she slipped her arm around Miriam's shoulders and whispered, "I think it's wonderful that you *care* so much."

Miriam stilled. *Did* she care? She surveyed the cooking area and saw only disarray. She had wanted the meal to be delicious and praiseworthy, and it would be far from that. She wrinkled her nose, and then she straightened her shoulders. Somehow she'd prepared the perfect meal for Yoseph, but he'd still found faults in her character. Now she'd have a barely passable meal to present to Caleb. What he thought of her character had yet to be determined. Tonight would be a true test. Voices sounded from the courtyard: Aaron's and the deeper voice of Caleb. Their guests had arrived. Salome remained home tonight, as she wasn't feeling well again.

As Miriam heard her father greet them, she realized her hair was damp with perspiration and her tunic was stained from cooking. There was no chance of her making it past Caleb without being seen. If she excused herself to her bedchamber, it would be quite obvious how much of an effort she was making. And she didn't want to demonstrate anything like that in front of her brother.

He would be too pleased.

"Are you all right?" her mother asked in a quiet voice.

Miriam exhaled, trying to feel and act calm when inside she was anything but. "I will be. Let's begin."

Carrying the platter of barley and pigeon, Miriam entered the gathering room. She glanced at Caleb, then started serving. She felt his gaze on her, but she knew if she looked up, her face would flush. It was difficult enough to know that he'd be eating her cooking in just a few moments.

She served the food, then went back to the cooking area, pausing to listen for any words Caleb spoke. She tasted the remaining food on the platter while she waited. Her mother took the platter from her and started to dish up their own portions.

Miriam chewed and found the food was a bit spicier than she'd intended. She'd added the extra spice to cover the slight burnt taste. Her eyes started to sting, and her nose tingled. She hurried to the far side of the cooking area and reached for the goatskin of water, hoping the stinging was because she'd swallowed wrong.

"What's wrong?" her mother asked.

"Too spicy," Miriam whispered, panic rushing through her. She moved toward the gathering room and peeked in.

Caleb didn't look like he was faring much better. His eyes were watering, and he looked like he was trying not to cough.

Miriam backed out, swallowing quickly as the spice burned deeper in her throat. "This is terrible," she hissed at her mother. She took another drink from the goatskin, but the burning continued. She grabbed a piece of flatbread and took a bite, hoping to calm the taste of fire in her mouth, but the flatbread was hard and dry, making it difficult to swallow.

"Are the men reacting too?" her mother whispered.

"Yes, we must take them the wine. The water isn't enough." Miriam poured some wine into a cup for herself and took a few swallows. It soothed the burn.

Her mother grabbed the wine jug, and Miriam followed after her to serve the men. By the time they entered the gathering room, her father was coughing. She quickly poured the wine into cups for the men.

"Very sorry," she murmured, feeling her eyes burn for a different reason. She couldn't look at anyone; she didn't want to see their pity.

She cleared the platters and went back into the cooking area, where she stared at the vegetables cooked in goat's milk that she was to bring out next. But she couldn't bring herself to pick up the platter. She didn't know how long she stood there before her mother touched her shoulder. "Miriam, it will be fine."

At her mother's words, tears formed in Miriam's eyes. She blinked them away and turned to face her mother. "I can't go out there again."

Her mother pursed her lips, her eyes filled with compassion. "It wasn't that awful."

"It was."

"All right, the food could have been better, but I think Caleb is staying." She took a step forward. "I've ruined many meals, and your father is still around."

Miriam cracked a small smile. "I know I'm being foolish. I just wanted everything to go well." There wasn't anything more that had to be said. Miriam could see what her mother was hoping for Miriam.

"Finish serving the men," her mother said, picking up the platter of vegetables. "Someday you'll look back, and you'll be glad you did."

That someday couldn't come fast enough.

Miriam added some more flatbread to a basket and carried it out. No one acted like anything was wrong. Caleb and Aaron were talking about the aqueduct the pharaoh had ordered to be built, and her father seemed content to listen to them.

After serving the flatbread, Miriam returned to the cooking room and ate the vegetables with her mother. Once she finished, she arranged the honey cakes on a platter. She hoped the too-spicy main dish was now a distant memory. Laughter spilled into the cooking area from the men, and she took a deep breath. Perhaps the evening would be a success after all. But how might she define that success—an eventual proposal from Caleb? She could hardly believe she was thinking about it.

Marriage.

When she'd first agreed to host Yoseph, she'd been doing so out of duty and obedience. But Caleb was . . . He was someone she could fall in love with. She stood utterly still as the sounds from the other room faded. Her thoughts jumped forward by a week, a month, a year. Where would she be, and what would she be doing? Could she envision herself married to Caleb? Caring for him? Bringing forth a child?

Her pulse quickened as she realized she could, that it was possible.

Head held high and cheeks hot, Miriam entered the gathering room and served the honey cakes. She didn't comment on the scraped edges. She was sure nothing could be worse than the spicy barley dish, not even burnt honey cakes.

Again Caleb's eyes were on her, and again Miriam didn't meet his gaze. Her recent admission to herself had left her unsteady, and she was afraid that if she looked at Caleb or any of her family members, they'd be able to interpret her thoughts.

Before she left the room, the first bites of the honey cakes had been taken. There was no coughing or watering eyes. That meant they weren't horrible. When she met her mother again in the cooking area, her mother said, "I'll clear the rest when they finish. You may see to our guests."

Miriam's heart thumped. That meant she was to walk Caleb to the gate, and if Aaron lagged behind, there would be a private conversation. She'd never had trouble conversing with Caleb before, though their conversations had mostly consisted of arguing, but this was different. The expectation hung thick in the air around her. But Aaron was the first one out the door, making an excuse to hurry home to see to Salome. Her father grasped Caleb's hand for a moment, then he too left, moving toward the back of the hut.

Miriam pushed through the front door and crossed the courtyard. She'd barely realized she'd left Caleb behind until she heard him walk up to where she stood by the gate.

"Are you always that quiet around your family?" he asked.

She looked up at him. Twilight had fully descended so the usual gold of his skin was more of a burnished bronze. She looked away from his thick shoulders and inquisitive eyes. "Maybe I've changed."

His laughter rang out. She allowed herself to smile but only a little.

"I must apologize for the spices," she said. "I overcooked the barley and—"

"Shh," Caleb said, taking her hand in his.

His touch was unexpected, and she drew her breath in. She couldn't move.

"Do you think I care about barley?" he asked.

"I—" She stopped speaking. Her throat was too tight to continue.

"Miri," Caleb said, "thank you for inviting me. I'll see you tomorrow." His fingers slipped from hers, and he opened the gate.

Miriam watched him walk away until she could no longer see him as the sky grew darker. Then she realized she had no idea what he meant by seeing her tomorrow. Something tingled through her. Was he going to ask her father for permission to court her? She stared into the dark, wondering what had just happened.

CHAPTER TEN

MIRIAM

CHILDREN SCREECHED PAST MIRIAM, LAUGHING as they tried to catch each other. She turned to the side, lifting the rug she carried out of the way. The last thing she wanted was for the rug to be soiled before she presented it to Deborah. The woman was getting on in years, and her eyesight was too dim to do much more than take care of basic needs. The last time Miriam had visited Deborah with her mother, she'd noticed the threadbare rug on her friend's floor.

Deborah lived on the other side of the market, and as it was market day, Miriam found herself greeting the many people she passed. Yoseph ran his usual stand of fish, with his daughter standing out front calling to passersby to purchase the fresh fish. Yoseph really was an excellent fisherman and had prepared fish when he'd invited her family to his home for supper.

She hadn't spoken to him since the evening Caleb had come to supper at her home. Had he known Caleb had come, and had he simply fallen away in his interest? Miriam crossed the market area, skirting around Yoseph's stand. It was simpler that way.

Once a month the Hebrews were given a half day in which to run their market and do trades. They were able to travel more freely and often went between villages. Because of the general comings and goings, if Miriam came across an Egyptian, she wouldn't be questioned. It was always the best time for her to steal away to try to spot Moses. It had been weeks since she'd seen him.

Just before she reached Deborah's hut, someone called out to her. She grimaced before turning around because she easily recognized Reuven's voice—the man said to be the most handsome bachelor in the village.

Reluctantly she turned around. Reuven was definitely handsome, with his easy curls and large dark eyes. His eyelashes were longer than those of any woman's Miriam had ever seen. But as he approached, walking with his usual swagger, her stomach clenched. She couldn't believe her brother's excuse that Reuven was nervous around her. Maybe if she told Aaron what Reuven said to her, he would change his mind.

"You put the rising sun to shame, Miriam," Reuven said, smiling his white-toothed smile.

She wondered how he managed to keep his teeth so white. "You flatter me too much," Miriam said.

He stopped in front of her, close enough that she could detect his acrid scent. She didn't know why he always smelled unwashed; he didn't look dirty. It was a sharper smell, though, than she'd expect after a day's labor. Besides, today was market day.

She must have let her guard down because she wrinkled her nose without meaning to.

"Oh, you smell it, then?" Reuven said, looking very pleased. "I thought you might." He winked, and Miriam could only stare at him in confusion.

"Smell what?"

"The scent of a leopard." Reuven leaned toward her.

Miriam caught a full whiff, and she was sure it singed the inside of her nose. "A leopard? How did you manage that?" What she really wanted to ask was *why?*

Reuven grinned. "That's a secret I cannot reveal, pretty lady." He leaned even closer. "I knew you would like it. All females do. With this scent, every woman will want to be my betrothed."

Miriam didn't know if she wanted to gag or fall to the ground laughing. She forced her expression to remain neutral. "I must get back to my errand."

Reuven nodded, still smiling. "You are a hard worker." He winked at her. "And will make a good wife for a lucky man."

Miriam wanted to disappear. Maybe it would be a good time for a sandstorm. "Thank you," she barely managed to say.

"You're welcome," Reuven said in a serious tone. "I won't keep you any longer, although I know it will be hard for you to forget me today."

Miriam forced herself to not smile. "Good-bye," she said simply and turned away. She hurried to Deborah's hut, trying not to appear as if she was hurrying. When she reached Deborah's door, she knocked, and the woman's voice called for her to enter. Miriam stepped into the dim interior, where Deborah was situated on a cushion, stitching something that looked like a cloak.

"Welcome, my dear," she said upon seeing Miriam. Her eyes nearly disappeared into her crinkled face as she smiled.

"I've brought you a gift," Miriam said, unrolling the rug and positioning it on the floor.

Deborah's eyes rounded. "You made this for me?" She rose from her cushion on unsteady legs, then walked over to the rug.

"I thought you could use a new one," Miriam said with a smile.

"Oh, my dear," Deborah said, shuffling over to Miriam. She embraced her, then pulled away, her eyes moist with emotion. "You've treated me like a queen."

Miriam was standing in one of the most plain and humble huts of the village, but she didn't contradict Deborah. Miriam wished she could do more. Since Deborah couldn't work for the Egyptians, she was completely dependent on her neighbors.

"You deserve every good thing." She kissed Deborah on the cheek.

As Miriam drew away, Deborah said, "Have you accepted a proposal yet?"

Miriam's face heated. It seemed there were no secrets in this village. "I am not betrothed."

Deborah grasped her hand and squeezed. "You won't last much longer. Not once everyone sees what a beautiful rug you gave me."

Miriam laughed. "That's what I do all day long. There's nothing special about my weaving. Now, if I were an excellent cook—"

"Food is food, and living in these conditions makes us grateful for even the scraps," Deborah interrupted.

Miriam wasn't sure whether she should feel comforted or not, but Deborah was right. She said good-bye to the woman and left the hut. Miriam paused on the threshold. Across the market square was Caleb. He hadn't seen her yet, and she was grateful. If he knew where she was heading, he'd try to stop her. She moved quickly around the hut and found a roundabout way to the main road without having to pass through the market again.

She walked quickly, greeting those she passed along the road. Most people were carrying goods either to trade or sell. The sun was fierce today, but Miriam didn't mind. It meant she'd have a good chance of seeing

Moses at the riverbank. She wouldn't stay long, and there were plenty of people about. She wouldn't be alone.

She turned off the main road as she neared the river. Her heart sank when she heard someone call her name. *Caleb.*

She stopped, holding her breath and listening to his footsteps through the dead palms littering the ground. How had she not seen him following her? She folded her arms, refusing to turn around even though she could hear him approaching.

He stopped, and she could almost feel his breath on the back of her neck, he was standing that close. She waited, but he said nothing.

After several seconds of him being just as stubborn as she and not speaking, she turned around.

"Where are you going, Miri?" he said as soon as she looked at him.

It wasn't a demand for an answer; she heard the concern in his voice. His brown eyes studied her, making her feel a bit breathless. "I'm taking a walk," she said.

One side of his mouth quirked. "Alone?"

They both knew what she was doing. "Caleb, you can follow me if you want, but don't try to stop me. It won't do any good."

"I know," he said, his voice quiet. He was still staring at her.

The shade of the trees above her did nothing to cool her skin.

"I wanted to talk to you alone," he added.

Her pulse sped up another notch, and she took a couple of steps back until she felt the trunk of a tree behind her.

Caleb raised his hands. "I'm not going to drag you home. And you know I'd never force anything on you that you don't want."

"Then why did you follow me?" she asked.

He glanced away, then his gaze was back on her. "I'd like to talk to your father to request your hand in marriage, Miri, but not if you don't want to marry me."

Her breath stopped. Had he really said those words? "You wouldn't . . . ask . . . if I didn't . . ." She couldn't finish. She wanted Caleb to speak with her father; she wanted him to propose. Yet even as she realized it, another part of her fought against the idea of being married. She liked her freedom, but she also knew that the day would come when her parents would be gone and she'd be alone.

"Miri," Caleb said, stepping close enough to touch her, "I would never change you. Is that what you're afraid of?"

It had been what she'd been afraid of, but not anymore. "No," she said. "I'm afraid because I *do* want to marry you."

His eyebrows shot up, and then he smiled. This time he closed the distance, his fingers linking through hers. The warmth of his touch encompassed her entire body. "I can help you with that fear," he whispered.

She closed her eyes because she knew he was going to kiss her. And she surprised herself because she wanted him to.

His lips were warm and soft, and his hands stayed linked with hers, his body not moving any closer. It was like she was too fragile for him to hold. But she didn't want to be fragile. She slipped her hands out of his and wrapped her arms about his neck, tugging him closer.

Then he kissed her harder. The sensation running through her body was unexpected, and she was glad he'd finally wrapped his arms around her because she needed to be held upright.

When he drew away, catching his breath, Miriam said, "I think you should speak with my father."

He let go of one of her hands and ran his fingers along her cheek. "I'd love to."

"Are you sure?" She leaned into his touch. "I'm not the easiest woman to get along with."

His smile was crooked. "Good thing I love you, then."

She might have guessed it if she'd really thought about it, but the words shot into her soul.

"Don't worry," he said, his eyes filled with amusement. "I know you love me too, even if you won't admit it yet."

"Caleb . . ."

He chuckled at her hesitation, his gaze warm, his smile teasing.

The sound of footsteps crashed through the trees, and Miriam moved away from Caleb. If her heart had been pounding before, it was thundering now. Had someone seen them kissing? But what she saw next was even worse.

Three Egyptians came into view wearing military tunics. Miriam inhaled sharply. She and Caleb were close to the palace and too far from the road to confidently explain why they were here. Caleb stepped in front of Miriam, and she was grateful for his act of protection, but it only increased her fear.

The soldiers stopped cold when they saw them. "You didn't get far, did you?" the lead soldier sneered in broken Hebrew.

"Seize him!" the one on the lead soldier's left side said.

Confusion shot through Miriam. "No," she cried out, knowing she might be making things worse, but she couldn't help it. "He's done nothing."

Caleb simply stepped forward with his head bowed. Miriam wanted to grab on to Caleb, hold him back, and never let him go. Her stomach went hard as two of the soldiers tied Caleb's arms behind his back. He only looked at Miriam and gave a small shake of his head, indicating she wasn't to interfere.

Once his arms were bound together, Caleb asked the soldiers, "What is my crime?"

The lead soldier barked out a laugh, but the second soldier answered without thinking, "Theft from the palace." His broken Hebrew was filled with disdain.

Heat burned into Miriam's chest at the false accusation. "But he didn't steal anything," she said, speaking Egyptian to them. "He's been with me."

One of the soldiers laughed again and grabbed her. He latched on to her arm and twisted it painfully. "We'll bring her as well. The thief was said to be a tall man, but perhaps the information was wrong." The soldier tugged her against him and leaned close to Miriam. "She looks fresh and unspoiled. We reached her just in time, before this brute of a Hebrew could have her."

The soldier's breath on her skin was hot and moist. She wanted to scream and fight him off, but Caleb's dark eyes were on her, warning her to stay quiet. Hebrew women captured by soldiers never returned in the same condition they'd been in when captured.

Fire pulsed through every vein in her body, but she forced herself to breathe slowly.

"What is your name, little one?" the soldier asked, his fingers digging into her arm, causing her to wince.

"Miriam," she said. It would do no good to give a false name. Egyptians had been known to kill one person after another in order to learn someone's name.

"You have my confession," Caleb said in a loud, clear voice. "I am the thief."

Horror spread through Miriam. Execution was the punishment for stealing from the pharaoh. Caleb had just given himself a death sentence.

"Caleb—"

"Leave the girl," Caleb said in a dismissive tone. "She's been despoiled, and I was about ready to abandon her anyway. Take me to the pharaoh, and I will confess my crime. He must be waiting for news of my capture."

The soldier holding Miriam hesitated, and she silently pleaded with Caleb with her eyes, but his jaw was clenched firm.

"Yes, leave the girl," one of the other men said. "If we make haste with the thief, our reward will be greater."

Miriam gasped as the soldier released her and shoved her to the ground. Then, just as she thought he'd turned away and left her, the soldier grabbed her hair and pulled her partway off the ground. The pain seared through her scalp, and her eyes burned. "Wait here. I'll return for you soon," he hissed.

If Caleb heard, he didn't give any indication. Through tears, she watched in helpless disbelief as the soldiers led Caleb away. This couldn't be real; this couldn't be happening. Caleb was not a thief, and now he'd be executed because he'd been trying to protect her.

But it had happened. The soldiers had led Caleb away through the trees, his hands tied behind his back, his tall, strong body submitting to Egyptian masters.

Miriam knew that leaving the village today in order to catch a glimpse of a brother who didn't even know she existed had been foolish. It was because of her that Caleb was this close to the palace; it was because of her that he had been in the wrong place when the soldiers were on the hunt for a thief.

She waited only a few moments before she followed the soldiers who were leading Caleb away. She needed help, but she had to see where they were taking him. Would they present him to the pharaoh right away, or would they imprison him first? She'd never heard of any Hebrew coming back to the village after being imprisoned.

The soldiers moved quickly through the underbrush, and Miriam did her best to keep them within hearing distance, even as she tried not to make a sound. The men were talking, even laughing from time to time. When one voice rose above the others, she knew they were arguing. Then their voices grew closer, which meant they had stopped.

She crept forward, staying low to the ground and keeping as silent as possible. As she listened to their conversation, a chill raised the hair on Miriam's neck. They were talking about her. The soldier who had grabbed her wanted to turn around and bring her with them. Caleb was protesting, then Miriam heard a thud, and someone groaned. It had to be Caleb. There were sounds of slapping, beating, and then Caleb went silent.

Miriam covered her mouth to stop herself from crying out. She scooted back, then turned and started running toward the river. She would follow it as far as possible, then cut over to the road, a good distance from the soldiers. She had to find Aaron or even Mered.

She didn't know how badly the soldiers had beaten Caleb or even if he was still alive. Her breathing came in gasps, but she forced her legs to move forward, to find someone who could help. She neared the road, then stopped at the sound of more shouting. She crouched near to the ground and moved forward slowly, staying hidden behind brambles.

Several dozen soldiers were standing in lines. Each man held a sword aloft, moving forward in unison. A commander was giving orders, and the soldiers were following. Were they going to march on the village? She watched the soldiers, and they kept doing the same maneuvers over and over. Her pulse calmed as she realized they were training. Perhaps this was not the start of a battle after all.

She settled onto the ground, knowing she was stuck here until they moved on. She couldn't head back toward the palace, and she couldn't get around these soldiers without being spotted.

She waited until the sun set, and only then did the soldiers continue down the road. Her throat dry, she rose on shaky legs. She could rely on the advancing shadows to conceal her from passersby. Whenever she saw an Egyptian on the road, she crouched and waited until they passed.

The time wasted tore into her. What was happening to Caleb right now? Had he survived the beating? Was he in a prison? She rose from her crouch and hurried around a group of trees but immediately ran into someone. She stumbled back. A tall Egyptian stood over her—had he been following her? She scanned his tunic; it wasn't a military one.

Then her eyes settled on his face. *Moses.*

She couldn't think. Not when her brother was staring down at her.

"Aren't you far from your village?" he asked, his Hebrew worse than the soldiers'.

It was nearly dark, but Miriam had paid little attention to the time. Voices sounded from a distance, and Moses looked behind him. When he turned back around, Miriam had scrambled to her feet. "You shouldn't be out here alone. It's not safe."

He was letting her go, but she hesitated, wanting to talk to him.

His gaze ran over her. "You are lucky you ran into me and not one of my friends. You wouldn't be left alone so easily." He stepped closer to her, his face looking puzzled over her silence. "Are you mute?"

"No," Miriam gasped. *You are my brother*, she wanted to say. "They took my friend Caleb. He's done nothing. He stole nothing. He was only trying to distract them from capturing me, so he confessed."

Moses stiffened. "The law will make the right decision. If he is innocent, he will be freed."

Dismay pulsed through Miriam, and before she could stop herself, she said, "Have you ever seen a Hebrew slave set free?"

"I . . ." Moses was looking at her, a thoughtful expression on his face. "I'm sure I have."

"You haven't," Miriam said, her voice quiet. "There's never been a Hebrew slave returned to our village after being captured."

Before Moses could answer, they both heard a shout, then laughter.

"You must leave now," Moses said in a fierce whisper. "Go back to your village. I will see about your friend."

Miriam stared at him. He was not like the other Egyptians. She'd never heard of such kindness.

"Thank you, Moses," Miriam said. She wanted to throw her arms around him and tell him who she really was, but the voices grew closer.

"How did you know my . . . ?" Moses started, then stopped as a man crashed through the brush.

"There you are!" someone said.

Miriam didn't wait to see who it was. She ducked away and kept herself hidden as Moses talked to his friends.

"They've caught the thief already. Haven't you heard?"

"I heard he turned himself in to protect his woman," Moses said, his voice clear and strong.

Miriam hugged her knees as she crouched, listening closely. Would the others believe him? Would Moses truly be able to free Caleb? She'd seen him in action when he'd bargained for Pentu with Ramses. But Caleb was a Hebrew slave.

The men moved away, and their voices faded. Miriam forced herself to stand and return to her village, but all she wanted to do was run to the palace and plead for Caleb's release.

When she reached home, she told her parents what had happened to Caleb, then she walked to Aaron's hut. Aaron was silent as she relayed the details, and when she came to the part about running into Moses and what he'd promised to do, Aaron shook his head.

"No matter what Moses said, he's still an Egyptian," he said. "No Egyptian risks anything to help a slave."

"He's different, Aaron," Miriam insisted. "He didn't even try to harm me; he just told me to return to my village."

"I don't know why he did that; perhaps the Lord was looking out for you. But Moses doesn't believe in our Lord."

Adonai had to protect Caleb. If He didn't, Miriam didn't know what she'd do. "Then our belief will have to be enough."

CHAPTER ELEVEN

MOSES

W HY HAD THE WOMAN SEEMED familiar? Moses wondered as he hurried back to the palace with Pentu and a few of their friends. And she had called him by his first name. Was she associated with the palace in some way? There were Hebrew slaves there. Perhaps she was related to one of them or had even worked at the palace in the past.

Still, he couldn't get her soulful eyes out of his mind. She had looked so frightened, desperate even, ready to risk her own life to save the man who'd risked his life for her. Pentu had laughed when Moses had told him the Hebrew the soldiers had dragged to the palace was innocent.

"Someone will have to pay for the crime, and it might as well be him," Pentu said, a smirk on his face. "Why he would be way out here . . . He was seeking trouble, if you ask me."

Moses wondered the same thing. Why had the two Hebrews been so close to the palace? Again he pictured the woman's large, dark eyes beseeching him. He sensed she blamed herself for her friend's capture. And she would even risk asking an Egyptian like Moses for help, as if someone of her low station could ever expect to have a man like him on her side.

When they reached the west courtyard of the palace, a crowd had gathered in the late afternoon. Moses was surprised to see Ramses dressed in full regalia. It seemed the pharaoh wanted his son to take on more responsibility, and petty theft was a good place to start.

The pharaoh sat on the outdoor throne, surrounded by harem women holding palm fronds over his head, while Ramses strutted about the courtyard. It was an almost festive mood, not an atmosphere Moses expected when a man's life was on the line. Typically Pharaoh was very sober when dealing with matters of court judgments, even when they had to do with slaves.

Pentu's betrothed, Beset, had found him and latched herself to him almost immediately. Where Beset was, Cena was always close behind. Sure enough, in a moment, Cena found Moses and grasped his hand.

"There you are," she said, looking him up and down. "You've been running?"

"Not exactly," Moses said. "But I was in a hurry."

"Why?" she asked.

Her questions grated on Moses. She was always seeking out minute details. She'd already stirred up several contentions among the women at court, revealing private confidences. Moses knew she was asking an innocent question, but it seemed that with Cena, nothing was ever innocent. "I wanted to make it back in time for the court hearings today," he said.

She nodded, her eyes narrowing. "Oh, there's Beset. I must speak with her."

And then Cena was gone. It had almost been too easy. Moses looked around for the Hebrew prisoner. Moments later he saw the man named Caleb shackled at the top of a dais in the center of the courtyard where everyone had a full view. He'd been stripped, and his skin was already marked by the whip. Moses tore his eyes away from Caleb and scanned the crowd. Several dignitaries were there, as well as the usual court members who seemed to be at every court proceeding, gossiping and trying to procure favors from the dignitaries.

Female servants walked among the gathering, serving drinks and sweets like this was a celebration. Moses spotted Mered, the Hebrew scribe who worked at the palace. He was with the other scribes, already writing down the proceedings. Moses walked over to the man, trying to figure out how he might question him in private.

Moses stopped one of the female servants who was carrying a platter of sweets. "Tell Mered the scribe that he is needed in the side courtyard." Then Moses slipped to the courtyard to wait for the Hebrew.

When Mered saw that it was Moses waiting for him, his eyes widened. He scurried over in his usual hurried fashioned and bowed his head. "I was told to come here."

Moses didn't waste time on explanations. "How well do you know the man on the dais?"

"Caleb?" Mered looked surprised but wary at the question. "He lives in my home village, and I know him as an acquaintance."

Moses read the uncertainty in Mered's eyes. Perhaps the man knew Caleb quite well but didn't want to associate himself with him. "You can trust me with information about Caleb." Strangely enough, Moses wanted to help the man. He also wondered what Mered the Hebrew was made of.

"Caleb is a hard worker, and he stays out of trouble," Mered said. "He's not married yet, but there is a woman. He is close to becoming betrothed."

Moses nodded, thinking of the woman he'd met who'd begged for his life. She had to be Caleb's intended. "Is he a thief?" Moses asked. The scribe's next answer would tell Moses whether or not Caleb was worth standing up for.

"Can a man truly know another?" Mered asked. "Perhaps only the Lord can, but Caleb is not a man who would put himself or his village in jeopardy. His loyalty is too strong."

It was the right answer, even though it referenced the Hebrew god. "How strong does his loyalty extend toward the woman he is thinking of marrying?"

Mered was quiet for a moment, his eyes shifting from Moses to the scrolls he carried in his hands. "On my honor, he is very loyal. He'd give his life for her."

The oath impressed Moses. "Thank you for telling me this."

Mered then held Moses's gaze in an uncharacteristically bold move. "Thank you, Moses, for believing that a Hebrew slave's life has value. If you need someone to speak for Caleb's character in front of the pharaoh or the prince, I will do it, despite what it might cost me."

Which could very well be my life, Moses thought. "With Prince Ramses presiding, I may need your help, depending on how he receives my plea." Moses then left Mered in the side courtyard and joined the growing crowd in the outside court.

As he moved through the people, he heard the chatter about the silver the Hebrew had stolen from the treasury room. Moses recognized the treasury guards, who were standing near Ramses, speaking to him.

He walked up to the group, and Ramses grinned at him.

"I'm glad you could make it," Ramses said. "Father is letting me do all the judging today. When I suggested we have it outside in order to enjoy the day, he agreed." His tone was triumphant, and if Moses wasn't so worried about asking for concessions from the prince, he would have laughed.

"It certainly brings a bit of festivity to something that is typically a serious undertaking," Moses said, unable to help himself. He smiled at Ramses to let him know he was giving him a hard time, but the meaning wasn't completely lost on the prince.

Ramses snapped his fingers at a hovering servant girl. "Moses needs some wine."

Moses took the cup with a laugh. "It seems I do." Because what he was about to do next was already creating doubts in his mind. Perhaps Mered was right; Moses did see the Hebrews as people. Yes, they were slaves, but he couldn't get rid of the image of the Hebrew's woman's haunting eyes when she was pleading with him. It had stirred his heart, which had rarely been stirred by much of anything lately.

Moses sat among the dignitaries' cushions, and servants held shades made of palm fronds over their heads to stave off the western sun. The court proceedings started, and Moses waited as people approached Prince Ramses one by one to air their grievances.

For the most part, Ramses fared well. He handed down judgments much as his father would, not deviating from the established royal laws, and his father nodded with approval at the end of each sentencing. But it was clear everyone was waiting for the sentencing of the slave on the dais.

Moses glanced over at the Hebrew. His hands and feet were tied, and the whip marks on his back had swollen. But he looked far from beaten down. In fact, he was watching all of the proceedings with interest.

As the sun settled beyond the horizon, the air began to cool, and torches were lit. At last Caleb was brought forward, and Ramses took his time looking the man up and down.

"What is his crime?" he asked the magistrate.

"Theft of silver from the treasury," the magistrate proclaimed for all to hear.

Ramses scoffed as if he couldn't believe a Hebrew would dare steal from the treasury. It was all a show. He knew very well why this man was here. "How did a Hebrew slave enter the royal treasury?"

The magistrate nodded to the treasury guards. One of them stepped forward, prostrated himself, then rose and said, "He timed it during the changing of the guards. He was disguised as a guard, and before we realized what had happened, he had fled."

Ramses gave a short nod. "Is this the thief standing before you?"

Moses was surprised to see the guard hesitate. Whether or not the guards recognized Caleb, surely they'd accuse him—after all, he was Hebrew.

"The man I remember was not as large," the guard said. "He was shorter and thinner."

The second guard stepped forward and interrupted. "Everything happened so quickly and unexpectedly. This is the man."

Moses had seen the hesitation in Ramses's eyes. But did the prince care if the wrong man was sentenced? It was time for Moses to step in.

"The thief was shorter and thinner than this man?" Moses addressed the first guard.

The guard looked from Moses to Ramses, then back to Moses. His face reddened, but he straightened his shoulders and said, "Yes." Then he amended, "I don't care how many Hebrews are sentenced today, but the thief might strike again if we don't capture the right one."

Moses hid a smile. This had been too easy.

But Ramses was frowning. "The Hebrew has already confessed. How can we argue against that?"

Moses knew he had to be direct. This time he addressed the slave. "Tell him why you confessed to a crime you didn't commit."

The crowd started to whisper amongst themselves at Moses's interference.

Ramses threw him a sharp look. "Why the interest in the Hebrew, Moses?"

Moses swallowed against a dry throat. "I would like to see the true thief caught. He might return and steal again." Ramses didn't disagree with that, so Moses looked over at the prisoner. "It's time to speak the truth."

Caleb held Moses's gaze, then he looked nervously around at the other Egyptians.

"Yes, tell us the truth," Ramses said, leaning forward. "Why are you willing to die for another man's crime?"

When Caleb spoke, his Egyptian wasn't refined, but it was understood. "I was walking with a woman—"

Ramses barked out a laugh. "Say no more. I know enough that if there was a woman involved, someone lost their senses."

Caleb reddened as the crowd joined in with Ramses's laughter.

The pharaoh rose from his throne, and everyone prostrated themselves. "Silence. I would like to hear the rest of his story."

So Caleb began in stilting Egyptian to relate the events, entrancing those attending the court. By the time he finished, Ramses had a smile on his face.

He clasped his hands together and straightened, then gave his sentencing. "You will be released tonight, Hebrew. But you will discover who the true thief is, or you will pay for his crime."

Caleb looked both relieved and terrified, the dilemma plain on his face. As the bindings were removed from his hands and feet and a kilt was handed to him, his gaze met Moses's for a brief second. Gratitude.

Moses gave a very slight nod of acknowledgment.

CHAPTER TWELVE

MIRIAM

HER PARENTS HAD TRIED TO convince her to go inside and get some rest, but Miriam knew she wouldn't be able to sleep until Caleb was safe.

The entire village had gathered that evening and offered a community prayer for him. But the consensus was that Caleb had no chance. He'd confessed, and the punishment would be swift.

Even Aaron had returned to his home and wife, leaving Miriam to wait alone at the road leading into the village. Finally she saw a man hurrying along the road. He was smaller than Caleb.

Mered.

Miriam could hardly stand waiting for him to draw closer, but she wanted to remain near the short-cut path to the village in case Mered wasn't alone. And in case those soldiers came back for her.

When the palace scribe was within speaking distance, Miriam rose from her crouch and softly called out his name. He startled and turned toward her.

"What's the news?" Miriam said, rushing to meet him. "Is Caleb alive?"

"He's been set free—"

"Oh, thank you," Miriam cut off his words with an enthusiastic hug. "Where is he?" She drew away and peered down the road in the moonlight.

Mered took a step back, straightening his robe. "I don't know."

And then she saw him. It had to be him. Same height and build, though he was walking with a slow gait.

Miriam's heart thundered with excitement, but she drew back toward the path. She wouldn't know if it was safe to approach Caleb until he grew closer.

Mered spoke in a quiet voice. "It looks like he's arrived. The Lord has blessed him on this day."

Miriam nodded, hardly listening to Mered. She watched Caleb instead. He walked with a limp and seemed to be favoring his left arm. She scanned the area surrounding him. He appeared to be alone, with no soldiers following him. Mered said something to Miriam, but she hardly paid attention again as the scribe continued down the road toward the village.

She waited as long as she could stand it, then she was running to Caleb. He stopped when he saw her, but it was too dark to see his expression.

When Miriam reached him, he held out his hand, warding her off. "You should not be here. It's not safe."

"I want to be where you are," Miriam said, grabbing his hand. Her eyes burned with tears. "I thought—" A sob tore through her, and she covered her mouth.

"Oh, Miri," Caleb said, pulling her into his arms. "I was fine."

"You were *not* fine," she cried. "I told Moses—"

"You spoke to *Moses?* Prince Ramses's cousin?" Caleb drew away, staring at her.

"Yes, he found me," she said, the tears coming fast, "and I begged him to spare your life."

Caleb tugged her hand and pulled her off the road until they were standing in a copse of trees. "You did *what?*"

Miriam let out a shaky laugh. "I told him you were innocent. I pleaded with him to set you free."

Instead of smiling, Caleb's eyebrows drew together. "What did he ask for in exchange?"

"Nothing. I think he felt sorry for me."

Caleb released her hand and placed his on her shoulders. "Egyptians don't do favors to slaves for *nothing*. Think. What did he say exactly?"

"Nothing." It came out as a whisper.

Caleb blew out a breath. "Your life could be in danger," he said. "Both of our lives. I'm to find and turn in the thief, or I will pay for the crime. Prince Ramses gave me a chance. But it will require turning in one of our own."

"Find him, then," Miriam insisted. "Even if he's Hebrew, he's still a thief."

Caleb nodded. "That might be so, but the Egyptians are the bigger thieves; they stole our lives."

"I won't let you pay for a crime you didn't commit." Miriam raised up on her toes and wrapped her arms around Caleb's neck, drawing him close. For a moment, he relaxed in her arms, then he pulled her tightly against him, holding her as if he never wanted to let go.

"The soldiers who captured me and threatened you didn't look happy that I was released," Caleb whispered against her ear. "They'll be on the lookout for you. They might even follow me to find you."

Miriam clung tighter to him. "Then find that thief, Caleb." She felt him nod against her hair.

"As soon as I find him, I'll speak to your father about our betrothal."

Warmth traveled all the way to Miriam's toes at the thought of marrying Caleb, of not having to bid him farewell at night, but she didn't want to wait for the promise to be secure between them. "Ask my father tomorrow."

Caleb pressed his lips against her neck, and she closed her eyes at the sensation. She had never thought she could feel so secure in a man's arms yet want so much more. His mouth moved up her neck, kissing as he went, then his lips were on hers. She kissed him back, and with each kiss, she grew more confident in her ability to show affection. She released a small sigh as Caleb cradled her face and slowed his kisses so that each and every one became a memory. If only tonight could last forever and tomorrow didn't have to come.

He released her all too soon, but Miriam realized it had to be after midnight.

"You need to stay close to home and always be with someone else," Caleb said, grabbing her hand as they took the shorter path back to the village.

"You sound like my brother," Miriam said.

Caleb stopped her and squeezed her hands. "Are you listening to me?"

Miriam nodded. "I am."

Caleb leaned forward and brushed another kiss on her lips. "I don't want anything to happen to you, all right?"

He was very convincing, Miriam decided.

"Moses might not have asked for something, but that doesn't mean he'll not come and take it for himself," Caleb said.

He didn't understand. He didn't know who Moses truly was and that if she told Moses the truth, she'd never have to fear. Miriam took a deep breath. "There's something I need to tell you."

Caleb's eyes flashed. "Did he touch you? Hurt you?"

"No," Miriam said. "Moses is . . . my brother."

Caleb's brows drew together. "Miri, you've been through a lot. It's very late now, and you need to get home." His hand threaded through hers. "Come on."

But Miriam pulled back, keeping him in place. "I need to tell you a story about something that happened eighteen years ago."

Caleb was still for a moment, looking like he didn't know whether or not to believe her, then he said, "All right, Miriam, tell me this story. But let's walk back to your home while you talk. I want you safely tucked away at home."

She allowed him to lead her by the hand. As they walked, she told him about her mother's grief when Pharaoh had handed down the terrible pronouncement and sent an edict throughout the land. "Our neighbors were hiding their children. Some women took their own lives. Others tried to run away. A couple of women tried to hide the gender of their child. Whatever the case, there was never a good outcome. The infant sons ended up dead, and many times so did the mothers trying to protect them."

Caleb's hand tightened around hers. "I heard that some of those things happened in my village as well."

"My mother was frantic. She argued with my father over and over. She told him she would rather die than part with her babe." Miriam's eyes burned at the memory. She had been young, but she hadn't forgotten. "She said all of this in front of Aaron and me. It wasn't until my father reminded her that she had two other children to live for that she fell quiet. It was like that for hours. She didn't speak, didn't look at any of us. She stayed huddled in the corner of the hut, holding her babe, rocking him all day and all night."

Miriam shuddered at the thought of her mother's grief and desperation. They were close to her home now, and Caleb stopped, facing her in the moonlight. His eyes were wide.

Miriam continued. "It was when word came that the Egyptian slayers had entered our village that Mother seemed to wake up. She bundled Moses and grabbed one of our baskets, hiding him in it. Then she ordered me to come with her. Before Father or Aaron could say anything, my mother and I were running toward the river." Miriam paused for a moment, trying to gain control of her trembling voice.

"When Mother said we were going to send Moses down the river, I started to cry. 'He'll fall in the water,' I said. 'He'll be eaten by a crocodile.'

But my mother hushed me and said I would need to follow the basket and watch over my brother." Tears spilled onto Miriam's cheeks as she recalled the fear and uncertainty she'd felt. She was afraid to see the baby in the basket floating on the river, but she was even more afraid to follow and see what might happen to him.

Caleb touched her cheek, wiping away tears. "What did you do?"

"I followed, of course," Miriam whispered. "And what happened next was a miracle from Adonai. Only He could have orchestrated it." Her tears came faster, and her body trembled. She knew without a doubt that the Lord had watched over her infant brother that day. "The pharaoh's daughter was wading in the water, and when she saw the basket, she reached for it and drew it near. It was then that I realized my mother had wrapped Moses in one of her blankets—a Hebrew blanket."

Miriam's voice choked. "I could see that the princess knew by the blanket alone that Moses was a Hebrew baby." Caleb's arm came around her, and Miriam leaned into him. "He started crying, and I started crying. The princess hugged him to her breast and kissed the top of his head. I couldn't believe it. Then she smiled down at him."

Miriam took a steadying breath. "I wanted to cry out for him, tell her I wanted him back, that he was my brother. Instead, I watched and waited. One of the princess's handmaids called to her, and the princess quickly removed his blanket and hid it among the reeds. It was at that moment that I knew the Lord had saved my brother." Miriam fell silent, unable to continue with the emotions taking over her voice.

"Does Moses know?" Caleb asked quietly.

"No," Miriam whispered against his chest. "Only my family knows. But that's not all. I spied on the princess until she was near the river again and her handmaids weren't watching. I told her I'd heard she'd found an abandoned babe and that I knew of a nursing woman who could feed him."

Caleb stroked his hand over Miriam's hair as she spoke, and she let her eyes close. "My mother breast-fed Moses for three years, and I went with her. I don't know what was harder, putting him in that river or saying good-bye to the small boy when he was weaned." The tears were back but not so fierce this time. She let Caleb hold her, feeling relieved that she'd been able to share the burden she'd carried for so long.

No one in her family would talk to her about Moses, not even her mother.

"Your brother saved my life," Caleb said.

Miriam nodded. "He's a good man."

"Do you think he has any idea that he's Hebrew?" Caleb asked.

"I don't know," Miriam said. "But he's different from the other Egyptians, though he was raised as one of them."

Caleb pulled back and looked down at her. "I agree. But we still need to be careful. If he doesn't know, he could be in danger if it's discovered."

"Some nights," Miriam started, "I miss him so much and wish my whole family could be together. It is why I find myself going to places he might be."

Caleb slipped his hand into hers. "Moses will always be your brother, and in order to save his life, you had to make a great sacrifice. It was the only way." He started toward her home, still holding her hand. "I understand why you seek him out, but you also have to think of your own safety. Now come. You'll need sleep before the morning comes."

Miriam walked slowly with him, in no hurry to release his hand. What would it be like when they were married and didn't have to say good-bye to each other at night? Her face flushed as she allowed her thoughts to wander.

Caleb had stopped and said something to her, but she'd been too lost in her thoughts. "Sorry," she whispered. "What did you say?"

He just smiled, then leaned down, close enough to kiss her. She let her eyes shut. Kissing Caleb was a new sensation, but she'd quickly realized she no longer feared marriage. She certainly wouldn't put it off any longer than necessary. She just had to help Caleb find the thief.

CHAPTER THIRTEEN

MOSES

"YOU *ARE* EXPERIENCED, AREN'T YOU?" Cena asked, her eyes half open as she gazed at Moses. "I mean, you are part of the royal family, even if you don't know who your father is."

Moses pulled his arm away from Cena's grasp as gently as he could. They sat at the banquet honoring the birth of a son to one of Pharaoh's consorts. By "experienced," Cena was asking if he had ever been with a woman. And the question made him uncomfortable, especially since they were surrounded by people who were all eyes and ears when it came to anything to do with royal gossip.

"Your questions never cease to surprise me," Moses said, hoping his jest might conveniently change the subject.

But she only pressed closer to him, her Nubian wig brushing against his arm. "So many things about you are mysterious, Moses," she said in a low, sultry voice. "And I plan to find everything out about you. So you should tell me." Her long, elegant finger traced the contour of his upper arm.

Moses knew that if anyone was watching them, they'd think he and his betrothed were having an affectionate moment, but the truth was that he wanted to be anywhere but sitting on a cushion with her.

"Don't tell me you're a virgin?" she whispered in his ear.

Her warm breath shivered down his neck. He'd seen the way Pentu acted around women who spoke in sweet whispers to him, but Moses couldn't bring himself to enjoy Cena's whispers—they were anything but sweet.

"Oh." She giggled breathlessly. "That is divine. To think you have never"—she laughed—"You must come to my room after the banquet. Or I can come to yours. It's a shame you've lived this long without experiencing—"

Moses tugged away from her as a servant approached carrying a wine jug. The Hebrew girl seemed nervous as she poured, and Moses didn't blame her with the way Cena was watching her so closely. The girl couldn't be more than ten or eleven years in age.

"Make haste," Cena said to the young girl. "We're thirsty."

The servant girl's hands shook more, and she overfilled the wine cup, causing the red liquid to seep onto the floor.

"Clumsy girl!" Cena flung her hand out and knocked over the whole cup, sending the rest of the wine onto a nearby cushion. No one was on that particular cushion, but Cena acted irate enough that Moses could only stare. "Now there's something for you to clean up, you miserable thing. Go back to your cave, or wherever you people live."

The servant girl didn't say anything, just started to clean up the spilled wine with her tunic.

"I apologize, but I need to attend to something urgent," Moses said, climbing to his feet before Cena could pout and make more of a scene. It seemed whenever he was around, she went to extremes with her actions and emotions. And if there was anything he couldn't stand, it was when she pouted publicly. The spilled wine wasn't a good omen, and Cena had made it clear how she felt about servants, especially the Hebrews. Even though they were there to serve her, it seemed they were all a large inconvenience.

Cena was fast. She was on her feet and following him out of the banquet before he could make his escape. "Where are you going?" she asked, her voice sounding gentle to anyone who might overhear, but Moses heard the sharpness in it. It seemed he'd gotten to know his betrothed very well over the past few weeks.

"I forgot to finish preparing the gift for my mother's upcoming birth date," he said, thinking fast. It was true his mother's birth date was in a couple of days.

"Oh, may I help you?" Cena said, reaching for his hand. "I can help you in other ways too, you know."

He stopped at the entrance to the banquet room and actually gave her a smile. He hoped it looked genuine. "It's a surprise for you as well," he said.

Her smile was slow and seductive. She was gazing at him like she wanted nothing more than to be alone with him.

He had to leave before she got her way. "I won't be long. Enjoy yourself at the banquet."

Before she could reply, he walked into the corridor. With relief, he realized she hadn't followed, but that didn't mean she wasn't still watching him. If he turned around, he was sure he'd find her amber eyes on him.

He turned the corner, pleased to be out of her line of vision, when he nearly bumped into someone.

"Moses, there you are," Pentu said.

Moses snapped his head up, surprised to see Pentu out in the corridor. Hadn't he just seen him moments before at the banquet? Of course, Moses's mind had gone a bit dim when Cena had started questioning him.

"Were you looking for me?" Moses asked. He'd left the banquet only moments before; surely no one had missed him already.

Pentu smiled a sloppy smile, and Moses realized he'd had too much wine. "I'm escorting some of the visiting dignitaries to the harem after the banquet," Pentu said with a wink. "Would you like to join us?"

Moses took a step back from Pentu's leaning form. "I . . . we're betrothed, Pentu." He didn't exactly expect Pentu to be faithful, but he thought the man would at least honor his betrothal for a little while.

Pentu laughed, then wiped his face. "Beset will be my wife, not my master." His hand latched on to Moses's arm. "Come with me. We'll return to the banquet and gather the others."

"I have some things to do right now," Moses said, knowing his excuse was flimsy. Perhaps Pentu wouldn't even remember this conversation in the morning. "I will see you later."

"You must come—" Pentu started, but Moses had pulled away and started down the corridor again.

Once in his bedchamber, he crossed to the doors leading to the courtyard. He needed fresh air, even if it was the hot dusty night air of Mennefer. Where had the carefree days of his youth gone, when he, Pentu, and Ramses had swum in the pools and learned from their tutors?

Now he was betrothed to a woman he didn't trust or love, Pentu was turning into a man who only cared about merrymaking, and Ramses was being given more and more royal duties.

Moses walked into the courtyard from his bedchamber. The soft darkness was welcoming. It was familiar, unlike the recent events of his life in which tempers were short, lusts were strong, and everyone was watching everyone else.

He gazed up at the moon and the stars, reaching as far as he could see as he thought about the kind of woman his mother was. Why couldn't

Cena be more like her? Moses shook his head and crossed the courtyard. He went through the gate and walked along the perimeter of the courtyard toward the pools. If they were empty, perhaps he'd take a swim and wash away the memories of the evening.

The pools glimmered in the moonlight, and no one was strolling about. Moses waded into the first pool and swam across it, then back again. He swam for over an hour, resting every so often. The water was cool and invigorating, and by the time he stepped out of the pool, he felt better, stronger, more able to face the intrigues of court life.

He sat next to the edge of the pool, dripping wet but satisfied.

It was then that he heard laughter coming from the nearby courtyard. This particular courtyard was filled with benches and statues. Moses decided he didn't want to be discovered sitting at the edge of the pool after his swim. He didn't want to answer for not being at the banquet and fulfilling his new role of being more involved in the royal court.

He rose to his feet and started back toward the palace, but the laughter sounded again, this time closer. Instinctively he looked in the direction it had come from and was surprised to see Cena walking out of the courtyard toward him. A man was following her, and Moses stilled.

Cena hadn't seen him yet but would do so at any moment. There was nowhere to turn, nowhere to hide; he was in the open, standing plainly beneath the moonlight.

And then she saw him. Her eyes widened, and she brought a hand to her mouth and giggled.

The man came to a stop as well and looked panicked, whereas Cena just seemed to find everything amusing.

Moses wondered how much wine Cena had drunk and, more importantly, what she was doing alone with this man. Anger and embarrassment flooded through him, and even though he knew he should return to his chamber and think everything through, he strode toward his giggling betrothed.

The man stepped back, raising his hands. "I did not touch her." But the man's voice was full of guilt.

"Moses! How wonderful to see you," Cena said. "I was looking for you, but I found the commander instead." She laughed and winked at the man backing away from her.

It was then that Moses realized who the man was—Commander Thoth, who was to be Pentu's future father-in-law. And he was here . . . with Cena . . . alone?

Moses didn't know who he was more angry at. He stepped forward, and Cena reached for him. "Remember what we talked about at the banquet?" she said with another giggle.

Moses ignored her and continued past, striding toward the commander. Moses also ignored the fact that the commander was taller and broader than he. The man took a few more steps back but then stopped when he backed into a statue at the entrance of the courtyard.

With his hands still raised, he said, "She brought me here. I was reluctant, but she—"

Moses drove his fist into the commander's face, and the man's knees buckled, then he toppled sideways, clutching his face and screaming. Moses knew the man's nose was broken, and it would be a moment before he'd be back on his feet and striking back.

He turned and strode to Cena, grabbed her arm, and pulled her with him.

"Why did you do that?" Cena said, her laughter now fading. "You think you can get away with hitting a commander of Pharaoh's army?"

Moses shook his head and continued to pull Cena with him toward the palace.

"Let me go," Cena said. "I need to see if Commander Thoth is all right." She pulled against Moses, but he had her in his firm grasp. "He only kissed me. Nothing else happened." A giggle bubbled up. "Well, other things happened, but that was before tonight."

Disgust swept through him; so she wasn't denying anything. That would make what he had to do much easier. He escorted her into the palace and started down the corridor.

"Where are you taking me?" she said, her voice rising in pitch.

"We're going to visit with your father," Moses said. "And then I'm going to petition to have our betrothal broken on the grounds of infidelity."

She tugged against him hard enough that Moses stopped and turned to look at her. Her eyes were dark with fury in the torch-lit corridor. "*My* unfaithfulness? What about you? You turned down all of my offers."

"It was because we're betrothed, not married yet," Moses said.

"Our betrothal is as if we are married," she spat out. "If you hadn't continued to ignore me, I wouldn't have had to turn to the other men."

"*Men*? There's more than one?" He stared at her, disbelief pulsing through him. How could he have been so oblivious? Moses let go of her arm. He didn't even want to touch her now.

She looked away then. Some of the fire in her eyes had dimmed. Her next words cut into his heart, and even though he wasn't in love with her, they still hurt. "You are not good enough for me and never were. You don't even know your father, and your mother has shamed the royal family. It might all be forgotten now, but I don't want my future children to have a father who is a nobody and an embarrassment."

"How will you know which of your lovers is your children's father?" Moses stared at her as she turned and walked away, back down the corridor. He didn't know where she was going or what she would tell people.

When she was out of sight, he exhaled. The disbelief, confusion, and anger blended together and made him feel exhausted. Slowly he walked to his bedchamber. Once inside, he lit an oil lamp and picked up a piece of papyrus.

Carefully he began to write his request to the pharaoh—the request to formally put an end to the betrothal with Cena, daughter of Vizier Amon. When he finished, he reviewed the lettering. Instead of relief and elation, he only felt disappointment.

His mother would be so disappointed. Pentu and Ramses wouldn't understand.

Moses realized the older he grew and the more he learned, the more he felt distance between him and those he cared about the most.

CHAPTER FOURTEEN

MIRIAM

THE RUMORS HAD SPREAD THROUGH their village as well as surrounding villages that Caleb's life had been spared, for now. Miriam was desperate for the treasury thief to be caught. She wasn't happy that one of her own people would have to pay for the crime, but the fact remained that another man had committed it. And it wouldn't be fair that Caleb would have to pay.

Her face heated each time she thought of him and the way he'd held her and kissed her. He'd asked her father for permission to marry her, and of course that had been granted. On one hand, Miriam couldn't believe she was finally betrothed; on the other, she worried about Caleb.

Just as he worries about me, she realized. This morning Miriam had determined to make inquiries at the building sites. Her main task was to weave rugs and cloth, but today she planned to bring water to the Hebrew men and women who labored on the various projects commanded by Pharaoh. Someone knew something.

Miriam set off early, before her parents woke. She'd told them the night before of her plans. Though they hadn't been too happy about her traveling to various locations, they'd understood the need. They were just as anxious to learn the thief's identity.

The first building site she visited was being dug out. It would be an arena used for games during Egyptian festivals. Miriam made her rounds with the water she'd brought. After each person had a drink, she'd speak to them in a quiet voice. "Have you heard about the hunt for the thief of Pharaoh's treasury? It is said there is a great reward, even greater than what was stolen."

The thin man she spoke to now shook his head. "It will be too much of a risk for someone to give out information. That person will be ostracized by his village."

Miriam tilted her head to study the man. She kept her voice soft and innocent as she said, "Some may believe that. But even though the thief is a Hebrew slave like we are, it is not right that another man should pay for his crime."

The man didn't look convinced. "The Egyptians have taken everything from us—are a few silver and gold pieces from the pharaoh's treasury really theft?"

Miriam blew out her breath, focusing on keeping her tone even. "The Egyptians haven't taken everything from us." The man narrowed his eyes as he listened. "They have not taken our belief in the true Lord, who wants us to be honest and truthful. The Egyptians can't take away our honor if we don't let them."

She turned away from the man, afraid she may have said too much, may have let too much of her emotion show. Another man came up to her, and she offered him a drink. She didn't talk about the thief. Just before he turned away, he said, "Do you know Reuven, son of Abram?"

Miriam drew her brows together. She didn't know the man who was speaking to her, but she did know Reuven, who lived in her village. Her nose wrinkled as she remembered Reuven wearing a leopard scent because he thought the women would be attracted to him. She hadn't talked to him since that market day. In fact, she'd avoided him when she could.

"Why?" Miriam asked, but the man was already making his way back down the sandy slope to continue digging.

As more Hebrews approached her for water, she continued to tell them about the reward for turning in the thief, making sure she spoke as if she was gossiping and not desperate to save her betrothed. Were there others who feared that the villagers would think less of them if they turned in one of their brothers for a crime?

When Miriam ran out of water, she walked to the nearest well to refill her jug, then she made her way to one of the fields of crops. Slaves by the dozen were working beneath the merciless sun. As she approached, the taskmaster walked over to her.

"Who are you?" he asked.

"I'm the weaver, but while I'm waiting for the next delivery of yarn, I'm bringing water to those who need it." She lifted the jug up for him. "Do you need a drink, sir?"

He scrunched his nose as if he couldn't stand the thought of touching anything meant for a Hebrew slave. Stepping back, he waved her on. She bowed her head to him, grateful he wasn't giving her further trouble. She approached a woman who was loading rocks into a cart. As Miriam handed her the jug to drink from, the woman gazed at her with open curiosity.

"I haven't seen you in this field before."

"I'm Miriam, from north village."

"Ah, the weaver. I've heard your name."

Miriam smiled. The woman seemed more friendly than most. "I'm also passing along the information about the reward for catching the thief—"

"Yes," the woman said, bending to lift another rock. "I've heard of the reward. The person who refuses to turn in the thief is a fool."

Suddenly Miriam wanted to confess to this woman that she had special interest in finding the thief. "Have you heard anything?"

The woman peered up at her as if she was wondering whether she could trust Miriam. "You are betrothed to Caleb, are you not?"

Miriam's face flushed, but she said, "Yes."

"So you are very interested in what I might have to say."

Miriam crouched next to the woman and helped her free a stubborn rock. "I am. I would be happy to repay you in any way I can."

"I don't know who it is," the woman clarified. "No payment is necessary. But as a woman to another woman, you might consider any man who is seeking to raise his station, perhaps attract a certain young woman to become his betrothed."

Miriam exhaled. "But wouldn't it be obvious to the young woman and her family? If someone were suddenly living at a higher means?"

"I didn't say it was a smart decision." The woman flashed her a smile, and Miriam returned it.

Miriam knew she'd delayed too long with the woman and needed to move along. "Thank you," she said in an earnest voice. "You've given me a new direction to think about."

The woman nodded. "Being so recently betrothed yourself, you might know of the men who are eligible, who might be currently seeking a bride."

For the next few hours, Miriam continued to fetch water, bringing it to the building sites or fields and speaking with as many people as she could. The more who knew about the reward, the greater the chance that someone who knew the thief would be tempted to turn him in.

In the late afternoon, she walked back home, still needing to put in a full day's work of weaving. Those she'd talked to had given her a lot to think about. Between the thin man at the first building site who'd asked her if she knew Reuven, the woman in the field who was sure the thief was a man who wanted to raise his living standard in order to attract a wife, a young man who said he knew Reuven's family and confirmed they'd had hard times, and others Miriam had spoken to, she now had some ideas.

But she had to wait until evening fell to see Caleb and tell him.

Her mother was in the side courtyard, working at the loom, when Miriam arrived. When she told her mother all that had happened, she was surprised when her mother said, "We should visit Reuven's home. I know his mother well enough that I could bring her a gift."

Miriam's eyes widened at the thought. "Won't she wonder at your visit?"

"Not if you come with me."

"Me?" Miriam was interested in hearing what Reuven's mother would say. "What would we say to her?"

"Don't worry," her mother said. "We'll be very discreet and, of course, very observant. Did you know her husband was recently crippled?"

That might explain Reuven's desperation. Without the father of the home working, the family's grain allowance would be cut back. "Will her husband recover?"

"It's unlikely he'll make a full recovery and return to his position," Miriam's mother said. "He fell from the top of one of the edifices he was carving. Both of his legs were broken. By the time he heals, someone else will have taken his position."

Miriam shook her head at the tragedy. "Should we wait for Father? Or Aaron? They could come with us."

"That would be too much. This visit will be just to gather information. And to plant a few seeds as well."

Miriam followed her mother into their hut, and they searched for something they could take to Reuven's mother and not make it look like they had planned anything too specific.

"What about a basket of beans?" her mother asked. "We can say we have an abundance and need to give them away before they rot. We could sympathize with her husband's misfortune."

The whole situation was a misfortune, Miriam thought as she set out with her mother. It was the time of day when most of the slaves were returning from the worksites, allowing Miriam and her mother to blend in with the others traveling about the village. Miriam hoped they'd be able to visit with Reuven's mother before Reuven returned from wherever he worked.

The hut was typical, nothing different in appearance from the other dozens they'd passed. Reuven's mother opened the door after they knocked. She was a small woman and, thankfully, didn't smell of leopard stench.

"Jochebed!" she exclaimed, clearly surprised.

"Hello, Anna. I've brought Miriam," Jochebed said.

The woman nodded. "Come in out of the heat. I've just returned from the fields, so I'm preparing a meal for my husband."

Inside, Anna gestured toward some fur-covered cushions for them to sit on. Before taking a seat, Miriam's mother held out the basket. "We are sorry to hear about your husband. We had a surplus this week and didn't want the beans to go to waste."

"That's kind of you," Anna said. "We have plenty to eat, but I will put the beans to use."

Miriam wondered how they had plenty to eat; no one had plenty to eat. The inside of the hut was well kept, and nice rugs hung on the walls—not ones Miriam had made, she noticed.

"Would you like a drink?" Anna asked.

"We are only here for a few minutes," Jochebed said, "and we wouldn't want to trouble you. We just wanted to see how your family is doing."

Anna sat across from them and clasped her hands in her lap. "We are praying for my husband's full recovery." Her eyes shifted away. "It's almost like I'm a widow, and my son isn't married, so there is no family to rely on in that way."

Jochebed nodded with sympathy. "What are your son's skills?"

"Carving stone, like his father." Anna exhaled. "I hope I don't end up with two crippled men. But I suppose someone needs to do the work."

"Is your son working on the temple site?" Jochebed asked.

"Oh, no. Not since my husband's accident. The past two weeks he's been working right inside the palace, repairing and recarving."

Miriam's heart tripped on a beat. Working inside the palace put Reuven near the treasury.

"Miriam, can you wait outside for me?" Jochebed said, turning to her and smiling with a knowing look.

"Of course," Miriam said. "It was nice to meet you, Anna, and I wish your family well." She couldn't hurry outside fast enough. Her mind was spinning with possibilities, and she knew her mother would ask Anna more direct questions in order to gather more information. But her mother had to do so without Miriam present so Anna could be more open.

Miriam walked around the courtyard, wondering, if Reuven was the thief, where would he keep the pharaoh's treasure? It was likely buried, and as she waited, she scanned the ground, then the areas near the courtyard trees and along the stone wall. Then she stopped. A patch of dirt against the wall looked as if it had been recently dug. She considered the meaning behind the disturbed earth.

Her mother stepped out of the door, bidding farewell to Anna. Miriam crossed the courtyard to join her, and Jochebed linked her arm with Miriam's.

They walked for a few moments in silence, passing other villagers, then Jochebed said, "Anna said Reuven is actively seeking a wife. He recently learned that you were betrothed to Caleb." Jochebed paused as they passed yet another person. "Anna confided that Reuven is pursuing an Egyptian girl, one who is part of a former dignitary's family, one whose father fell out of favor with the pharaoh."

Miriam looked over at her mother. "But Reuven is Hebrew."

Jochebed gave a small shrug. "Yet it's not unheard of. Reuven's family would move to the Egyptian village and adopt their ways."

Miriam still couldn't believe it. "But what about *our* faith? Our traditions? All of those would have to be given up."

"Yes," her mother agreed. "Anna was mortified at first, but now with her husband's injuries, she is getting desperate."

"How would an Egyptian family accept one of our own?" Miriam asked.

"Reuven and his father are highly skilled laborers. They spend a lot of time with architects, and I'm sure they've formed friendships." Jochebed paused as one of the villagers passed by them. "Why would Reuven steal from the treasury and jeopardize his family?"

Miriam absorbed all that her mother had told her as they neared their home. "Unless he is angry, more angry than most of the Hebrews. And now this girl he wants to marry has been hurt by the pharaoh as well."

"Revenge?" her mother suggested.

"I believe it might be," Miriam said, then hurried to add, "We have no real proof, of course. Only speculation."

"How many days are left before Caleb has to turn in a name?" Jochebed asked.

"Only two more days."

"Then something needs to be done," Jochebed said. "Whatever it is, I will support you."

Miriam knew what she had to do, and it would be something her parents or brother most likely wouldn't approve of, but her mother had essentially given her permission. She just had to get Caleb to agree to her plan.

After supper and long after dark had fallen, Miriam walked to where Caleb lived with a family who had taken him in when he'd first come to the village. He was surprised to see her.

He stepped out of the hut and led her to the side courtyard where they could speak without being overheard. "What are you doing here?" he asked, reaching for her hand.

Warmth shot straight into Miriam at his touch, but she didn't have time to think about being alone with Caleb. Miriam told him about how she'd spent part of the day taking water to the Hebrews, and then had gone with her mother to visit Reuven's home. She explained her suspicions and how they fit the fact that Reuven had been working in the palace recently in close proximity to the treasury.

"And he's a smaller man than me," Caleb mused, his dark eyes speculating in the moonlight.

"What does that mean?" she asked.

"It was observed by one of the treasury guards during the court session," Caleb said. "What are you planning, Miri?"

"I want to dig up Reuven's yard tonight, but I need you to come with me and help."

.

CHAPTER FIFTEEN

MIRIAM

Miriam watched for Caleb from the side courtyard. She'd sneaked out of the hut moments ago and had been waiting for a while. She startled at every sound and every movement, whether they were caused by the wind or by an insect.

Finally she saw Caleb's form beneath the moonlight, walking toward her hut. She stepped out of the courtyard and wordlessly joined him. He grasped her hand and gave her a dagger.

"What's this for?" she whispered.

"Things might not go so well tonight, and we need to be prepared."

Caleb's words both thrilled and scared her. He was including her, taking her suspicions seriously, but he was right—this was dangerous. She smiled nervously at him, then threw her arms around his neck. He pulled her tightly against him, holding her for a moment.

Miriam wanted Caleb to be free from the threat of the pharaoh, and she'd do anything to ensure it. Even if it meant trespassing and carrying a dagger. "Did you bring the digging tools?" she asked.

Caleb released her. "Yes." Their gazes met in the moonlight, Caleb's expression serious. "Thank you, Miri. I don't know what tonight's outcome will be, but know that I'm grateful for your help."

She reached up and touched his cheek. When had Caleb become so dear to her? When had she realized that the more she expanded her heart, the more it was filled?

She smiled at him, although her eyes stung with emotion. "Let's go fight for your freedom," she whispered.

Caleb took her hand again and squeezed. Then they walked to Reuven's hut, careful to walk to the side of the main paths in case they should come across anyone. The moonlit night provided enough light for them to be easily spotted and even recognized.

Once they reached the proximity of Reuven's home, Caleb motioned for Miriam to stay absolutely silent, then released her hand and crept forward until he reached the side courtyard. He climbed over the stone wall, then turned and held out his hand to Miriam.

After he helped her over, they both stood for a moment catching their breath. "The earth looks freshly dug up next to that wall," Miriam whispered, pointing.

Caleb nodded and crossed to the wall. He motioned for Miriam to start at one spot, and he started a few paces away.

So it was that Miriam found herself kneeling in the dirt, quietly digging into the soil of Reuven's courtyard. At each location, she dug down about two handspans, then, when nothing was found, she carefully covered up her hole with dirt. She moved a few handspans farther and started again.

Every so often, she'd glance over at Caleb, who was digging much faster than she and making greater progress. Miriam wiped her forehead with the back of her hand. The night was pleasant, and the work not too intensive, but her nerves were on high alert.

Hearing Caleb make a soft hissing noise, Miriam turned toward him. He pointed to where he'd been digging, then motioned for her to join him. She scooted over the couple of paces and crouched to look inside the hole Caleb had dug. The moonlight revealed a wooden box.

Miriam looked up at Caleb, her eyes wide. He gave her a nod, then reached into the hole and removed the box from the earth.

Miriam found that she was holding her breath. It could be anything—something buried long ago and forgotten, Reuven's mother's dowry, treasures handed down within the family, the stolen goods from Pharaoh's treasury. Whatever it might be, by the effort Caleb had to make, Miriam knew it was heavy.

Caleb lifted the lid, and Miriam had to stifle a gasp. Several thick gold armbands shone in the moonlight, accompanied by two heavy necklaces.

Miriam didn't know the exact items that had been stolen from the palace treasury, but these items were definitely royal Egyptian jewelry. Both excitement and dread pulsed through her—excitement that they'd made the discovery that would exonerate Caleb but dread for the Hebrew family whose lives were about to be ruined.

"What do we do now?" Miriam whispered, reaching out to touch one of the gold pieces.

"You stand up and turn around," a deep voice commanded.

Shock jolted through Miriam at the sound. Caleb grabbed her arm and pulled her to her feet, making her stand behind him.

Reuven had somehow discovered what they were doing and had crept up on them. His expression was hard, his eyes narrowed.

"Caleb?" Reuven spat out. "I should have known you'd come around." He took a step forward, and that was when Miriam saw that he held a sword.

"Who's that behind you?" Reuven asked.

Miriam stepped to the side of Caleb, even though she knew he didn't want her to. "It's me, Miriam."

"Ah." Reuven studied her, his sword raised. "My mother said you had visited this evening." What might have been surprise on his face turned into a scowl. "So you've come to turn me in in order to save your beloved betrothed."

Miriam's stomach turned sour. She hadn't thought this far ahead—about what Reuven's reaction might be when confronted. Had she expected him to confess and let them lead him to Pharaoh for his sentencing?

"Reuven," Miriam said, "you can't let another man pay for your crimes."

"My *crimes*?" Reuven said with a scoff. "There is no proof of my crimes."

Caleb cut in. "The box—the gold, we know it's from the royal treasury."

"You know nothing," Reuven said, stepping closer, his sword level with Caleb's chest. "If you are loyal to our people, you will leave this alone. You will return to your homes and not speak of this."

"You expect us not to speak of your thievery?" Miriam said, her voice rising in pitch. "If we don't turn you in, Caleb will be executed. Is that what you want? His death on your soul?"

Reuven barked out a laugh. "I can't believe I ever thought to court you, Miriam. I even wasted expensive scent to impress you," he scoffed. "I'm giving you a chance to leave in peace. Will you take it?"

Miriam grasped Caleb's hand and held on tightly.

Caleb moved in front of Miriam again, shielding her from Reuven's sword. "You are coming with us to the palace."

Even though Reuven was one person against the two of them, Miriam wished they'd brought Aaron to help. Miriam had no doubt Caleb could beat Reuven in a skirmish, but what would be the cost? Reuven was armed with a sword.

"Drop your dagger, Caleb," Reuven said, "or this will not end well for Miriam."

At that threat, Caleb released his dagger, and Miriam heard a soft thud as it hit the earth. Secured inside her belt was her own dagger, hidden now from Reuven since Caleb stood in front of her.

Her mind raced as she thought about using it to fight with Reuven.

He smiled now that Caleb was unarmed. "You will rebury that box, and you'll forget you ever saw it."

Caleb crouched, put the box back in the hole, and began to push dirt over it. He worked slowly, and Miriam's spirits sank with every movement.

"I'm sure you can work faster than that," Reuven sneered. He lunged for Miriam and wrapped a strong arm around her shoulders, pulling her against him. Miriam yelped and struggled to get away, but Reuven brought up his sword, holding it against her neck.

Caleb was on his feet in an instant, his eyes fiery.

"Finish your job, or you'll both be sorry," Reuven hissed. "If you want to marry your precious Miriam so much, then turn in Crazy Simone. He won't even know what's happening."

Caleb stared at Reuven in disgust. "You're worth less than a dog, Reuven. You're a criminal and a shame to your family."

With her back pressed to Reuven's chest, Miriam felt his breathing quicken. "My family are slaves to foreigners. They've disgraced themselves. I've found a way to free us, and I'm not going to let you take it away from me."

Miriam tried to wriggle free of Reuven, but he only tightened his grip.

"Don't hurt her," Caleb said, his gaze boring into Miriam, pleading with her to keep still.

"Then finish the job," Reuven said.

Caleb bent again to work on moving the earth over the box. It was nearly covered now, yet he continued to work slowly.

"You *are* a sweet thing," Reuven whispered in Miriam's ear.

His hot, moist breath against her neck made her want to punch him in the mouth, and his lingering musk made her want to gag.

"Close your eyes Miriam," Caleb suddenly called out.

It took her a second to obey, and as soon as she did, dirt struck her face.

Reuven cried out, then was violently jerked away from Miriam, causing her to lose her balance.

Her eyes flew open, and she tried to stop her fall.

Caleb had thrown dirt into Reuven's face and then had charged the thief, diving against his torso and knocking Reuven backward.

The men were wrestling, and it looked like Caleb had the upper hand. Miriam scrambled to her knees and grabbed the sword, then stood up.

Caleb had pinned Reuven to the ground, but he was struggling fiercely to get away. Reuven arched his back, then twisted, but Caleb held him tight.

She lifted the heavy sword, keeping it steady as she backed away. Then she saw a flash of metal in the moonlight; Reuven had a dagger.

"Caleb, watch out," she cried just as Reuven sliced Caleb's shoulder.

Caleb groaned, and his injury gave Reuven the advantage. Moving out from under Caleb, Reuven scrambled to his feet. His gaze found Miriam, and he started walking toward her, limping as he moved.

"Hand over the sword, Miriam," he said. "You don't want anyone to get killed, do you?"

Miriam shook her head, taking another step back. She glanced from Reuven to Caleb, who was still on the ground, holding his bleeding shoulder.

"This can be over now," Reuven said, holding his bloodstained dagger in front of him. "Give me the sword, then take Caleb home." His smile was crooked. "Say nothing about tonight and turn in Simone tomorrow. Our village would be better off without him. Our mothers are friends; you don't want to tear our families apart."

Miriam couldn't move, couldn't speak. She could only stare in horror as Reuven drew closer and closer. Her hands shook as they tried to keep the sword in place, pointed at Reuven.

"Caleb," Miriam whispered.

"Use the sword if you have to," Caleb said as he moved to his knees, still clutching his shoulder.

"I-I can't," Miriam said. She couldn't believe she'd ever feel threatened by a Hebrew man in her own village. Fear was for the Egyptians and the taskmasters, not one of her own people. Reuven was vile, and tonight he was desperate, but Miriam was desperate too. Desperate that Reuven be brought to justice and her innocent Caleb be exonerated.

"Save your betrothed," Reuven said. "Don't make this hard, Miriam."

Behind Reuven, Caleb had climbed to his feet. He looked as if he was about to faint, but he was slowly moving forward, his eyes on Reuven.

"No," Miriam said, lunging toward Reuven with the sword. He dodged her easily, but it gave Caleb the chance to charge Reuven.

The men grappled with each other for dominance, and when Reuven punched Caleb in the face, Miriam screamed. Caleb's head snapped back, and he lost the hold he had on Reuven. Reuven flipped Caleb over and straddled him, holding his dagger at Caleb's throat.

Miriam dropped the sword she couldn't wield and removed the dagger from her belt. She crept behind Reuven, then said, "I have a dagger at your back. And this, I know how to use."

"Miriam, no," Caleb said just as Reuven turned and grabbed her leg, pulling her off balance.

Her head hit the ground hard, and her breath left her body. She was vaguely aware that Caleb had a hold of Reuven and they were fighting again. And then a voice bellowed above her somewhere. Another man was there, shouting.

Miriam peered at the newcomer—it was Reuven's father, and his mother had come out too. Two other men arrived on the scene. Neighbors. And before Miriam could climb to her feet, Reuven was facedown on the ground, his hands tied behind his back.

CHAPTER SIXTEEN

BITHIAH

SHOUTS RANG THROUGH THE LONG corridor, and Bithiah hurried out of her chamber into the muted sunlight. The guard who was stationed outside her door turned as she exited.

"What is it?" Bithiah asked him.

"The treasury thief has been caught," the guard said.

Bithiah brought a hand to her chest. "Oh? So it wasn't that Hebrew called Caleb?"

"No," the guard said. "They are holding court as soon as the pharaoh arrives."

Bithiah knew the pharaoh had been involved with the new building site that morning. He'd taken his scribes with him in order to record his observations, and Mered had been among them. If she hurried, she'd catch a glimpse of Mered before he went into court.

She rarely attended any court proceedings, and to do so now would raise questions. By the time she reached the courtroom, the doors had already been shut and she'd missed the opportunity to see the pharaoh's entourage. She continued walking past the guarded doors as if she'd intended to walk down the corridor.

She'd missed her opportunity to see Mered. It was just as well. Nothing good would come of her following the man about. Her royalty and his heritage would never be compatible in this life. She continued along the corridor and walked toward the records room as if that had been her destination all along. During the daylight hours, it was typically filled with scribes on one assignment or another, but because court was in session, the place was empty.

Bithiah had been educated as a child, along with the other royal children, but most of the learning in the records was beyond her. Still, she visited on the occasional evening, lit an oil lamp, and read through some Egyptian history. She had always been fascinated by the succession of the kings and, in some cases, the queens.

One particular story had always drawn her in—the story of Hatshepsut, the she-pharaoh. She'd been discussed in their history lectures, but since Hatshepsut's stepson had destroyed most evidence of her life, there weren't many records about her.

Moses had alerted her to a few scrolls that talked about Hatshepsut, and Bithiah had read over them a few times, finding any bits of information about the queen fascinating. Today she removed the scrolls from their assigned basket and spread them across one of the long tables. She settled on the cushion and started to reread the history of the woman's many building accomplishments. Pharaoh Hatshepsut had been a fine architect. She'd brought Egypt into a golden age that her father, Thutmosis I, had started and that her husband, Thutmosis II, had continued. Hatshepsut had taken the role of pharaoh so seriously that she had even worn a fake beard and the royal regalia.

Bithiah heard voices in the outside corridor, accompanied by the shuffling of sandals, and she looked up, surprised to see how late in the afternoon it had become. The room had shadowed, and she realized she'd been squinting to read in the dimming light.

Court must be finished, and the scribes were on their way back to finish their record keeping of the day's events. She began to roll the scrolls she'd been reading from. The voices grew closer until she could distinguish them. One belonged to Mered, and he was bidding farewell to someone.

Bithiah hurried at her task, replacing the scrolls in the basket, then putting the basket on the third shelf. Before she could slip out of the room, Mered was standing in the doorway. And he was alone.

Surely another scribe would be arriving soon, but for now, Bithiah was alone with Mered for the first time.

Mered made a move to bow, but Bithiah held up her hand. "There's not need to pay obeisance to me," she said, her voice quiet.

He lifted his head, his expression holding a note of surprise. If they had been surrounded by others, he would have looked away by now, but it was as if he too understood what a rare moment this was.

At least, Bithiah hoped he was seeing her as she saw him, though there was no possibility of any relationship between them.

She approached him, and instead of standing aside as he ought, he remained fixed in his stance, watching her. It was more than watching her, Bithiah decided. He was absorbing her.

Her breath caught, and she stopped, simply standing there, not moving. He was within arm's reach, but there might as well have been the River Nile between them for all of their differences. Bithiah extended her hand toward him, not able to think a reasonable thought except that this opportunity might never come again. "I'm Bithiah."

Mered blinked as if he was coming out of a dream. He grasped her hand, bent over it, and kissed her palm. "My name is Mered, son of Ezra," he said, raising his head but keeping hold of her hand.

She let a smile form. Each of them well knew each other's names. They were speaking introductions, not in order to meet but to reaffirm that they had met many times, just not verbally. His strong hand still clasped hers, and warmth trailed along her skin at his touch, her hand feeling delicate enclosed in his.

"Court is over for the day?" Bithiah asked. Every part of her was on alert for the sound of a footfall from the corridor or a voice or even a whisper of someone coming.

Mered released her hand. "The treasury thief has been sentenced to death."

Even though he didn't show any sorrow in his voice, Bithiah could read it in his eyes. "I'm sorry," she said.

"For a thief?" Mered asked.

"I'm sorry that one of your people was desperate enough to steal and has now been sentenced to death."

"Thank you." His voice was quiet. "Your son Moses did a kind thing for Caleb, the Hebrew who was innocent. It is good that the true thief was caught so an innocent man could be free."

Bithiah nodded. She was proud of Moses for standing up for justice, yet she was worried that he might be seen as different from the other young royals. He might be seen as Hebrew loving, which didn't bode well since Bithiah had already brought enough grief to her parents.

"What were you reading?" Mered asked, interrupting her thoughts.

"The pharaoh—Hatshepsut," Bithiah said. "Moses told me where to find the records on her, even though there isn't much to read. I've gone over them many times."

Mered smiled, and Bithiah realized she'd never seen him smile. Apparently there was little humor in being a scribe for the pharaoh of Egypt. It was a smile that made her heart flutter.

"I know her story well," he said, his fingers now threading through hers as he once again grasped her hand.

"Is there more information than what is found on the scrolls here?"

"Bits and pieces are scattered in other texts," Mered said, tilting his head and allowing his gaze to scan her face. "Why are you so interested in Hatshepsut?"

Bithiah found herself blushing as Mered studied her so closely. She'd only caught fleeting glances before, but now there were no barriers between them. She looked down at their linked hands.

It seemed to dawn on Mered that he was holding her hand again. Slowly he released her, and the cool air surrounded her skin once again.

She grappled for a response, one that would express why she'd been so drawn to Hatshepsut's story—a female ruler who felt it necessary to take on the appearance of a male ruler in order to have her people support her. "I suppose it's because she lived two lives: one life in which she was just herself; the other life in which she was in front of the people of Egypt . . ." Her voice trailed off as she realized what she had said.

With that comparison, Bithiah was not much different from the she-pharaoh. Bithiah was an Egyptian princess on the outside, but on the inside she was in love with a man who could never be hers.

"I've never thought of it that way," Mered said, his tone low and thoughtful. "You're right. She did live two lives."

"Like many of us, I suppose," Bithiah said. She smoothed the ends of her Nubian wig out of habit.

"Is that the case with Egyptians too?" Mered asked. "I know it is with the Hebrews. They work as slaves for the pharaoh during the day, yet in the evenings, they unite as a covenant people." His face paled, and he stuttered out, "I-I didn't mean—"

Bithiah put a hand on his arm. "It's all right. I'm not like the other royals. You can speak of these things to me with no fear of censure." His muscled forearm relaxed. "I am interested in learning more about your people."

His brows lifted, and the edge of his mouth rose. "I would be happy to answer any of your questions."

"That would be wonderful," Bithiah said, her voice falling to a whisper. They hadn't been interrupted yet, and she marveled that she could talk to him so easily. Of course, he was highly educated, like all scribes were, but their classes and cultures were so different. Perhaps she'd thought that once she actually spoke to him, he'd repel her in some way. As it was, she was even more fascinated.

His eyes locked with hers. "Would you like to hear more about Hatshepsut sometime?"

"I would." She could hardly keep the smile off her face. "But how will that be accomplished? I mean—" She motioned between them, indicating that they were not often in each other's company.

Mered leaned down close to her ear. "The records room is empty on the first evening of each week. That is the time when the scribes are allowed to go visit their families."

"And you do not return to your family?" Bithiah whispered, well aware of his closeness.

"I return to my village to update my people on the politics of the land, but there is no family to spend time with."

She knew it was so, that Mered wasn't married, and he seemed to be parentless. But to hear him confirm it made it suddenly real. Mered was offering his only free time during the week to spend in her company . . . answering her questions.

He was close enough that she felt his warm breath brush against her cheek, her neck.

"I will be here on the first night of the week, Mered," she said.

He drew back and smiled. "I'll be here too," he said before turning and leaving the room.

She watched him walk down the corridor; apparently he'd forgotten why he'd come to the records room in the first place. That was fine with her. As he walked farther away, only one word came to Bithiah's mind: *fire.* She was touching fire.

* * *

Bithiah walked along the corridor to the records room on the evening of the first day of the week. She hadn't been able to think of much else since her conversation with Mered. It seemed the time had dragged agonizingly slowly, yet whenever Bithiah thought of what she was about to do, her heart raced like she was running as fast as a horse.

Evening had fallen, and torches had been lit and placed along the corridor walls. Tonight there was a large banquet taking place at the other end of the palace. It centered on Nefertari and her extended family—no one would miss Bithiah's absence. The scribes weren't needed at such banquets since Pharaoh didn't want the dignitaries' drunken declarations recorded. It was all better summarized the morning after.

Bithiah had chosen her clothing with care. She wore a linen tunic that draped from her shoulders to her feet and soft animal-skin slippers. Her Nubian wig was short and swayed softly against her neck as she walked. Beneath her cautiously selected clothing, her nerves thrummed wildly. Questions and doubts ran through her mind. Would Mered come? Would someone else be in the records room and thwart their meeting? Would someone discover them?

Even if a servant came inside to clean, seeing them together would be enough to create plenty of gossip.

The main corridor leading to the records room was guarded, but beyond that, the guards wouldn't know if she went inside the room or walked past it to one of the courtyards. She nodded to the two guards as she passed. Their uninterested acknowledgment told her they registered that she was royal but one of the lesser royals, so not a person to raise much interest.

When she reached the records room, she stopped in the doorway. A man sat inside, bent over a few scrolls on one of the tables. Several oil lamps had been lighted, creating a warm glow in the room. The man looked up, and Bithiah found herself smiling.

Mered stood. "Welcome," he said in a hushed voice, giving her a bow.

"Good evening," Bithiah said, stepping forward. Then she pulled the door mostly closed behind her, being sure to leave a gap so she could hear any footsteps approaching.

When she turned, Mered was still standing and watching her.

"What are you reading?" she asked.

One side of his mouth lifted into a smile. "I found several references to Hatshepsut that I think will be of interest to you."

Bithiah walked slowly toward Mered, knowing each step that brought her closer to him also became a step across the division between them.

"Show me," she said, settling onto a cushion across the table from him. If someone did enter suddenly, it would be much easier to explain her presence *across* the table from Mered than it would be to explain her sitting right next to him.

"Here," Mered said, turning a scroll so she could see the sketches. "This first one talks about her father, King Thutmosis I, and his chief wife, Queen Ahmose. Hatshepsut was the oldest child born to the couple."

Bithiah followed along the places he was pointing to. "Too bad she was born a girl," she said. "It seemed she had to work so much harder in order to achieve anything."

"Yes," Mered said, moving the first scroll aside and picking up a second scroll. "She lived a life of privilege already, but that wasn't enough for her."

Bithiah looked up at Mered. "It might seem selfish, I suppose," she began. "But all great leaders have never settled for what life has handed them. They want more than whatever their assigned lot is. They aren't happy with the circumstances into which they are born."

Mered seemed to consider this. "You are a wise woman, Bithiah," he finally said.

The sound of her name was soft and gentle when he spoke it. Bithiah looked down at the second scroll, needing to breathe, which was hard to do when she looked into his eyes and saw the way he was looking at her in return.

"For Hatshepsut," Mered continued, "being born a royal female was not enough."

"Or perhaps it was too much."

"What do you mean?" he asked.

Bithiah stole a glance at him, then smoothed out the scroll in front of her. "Do you think our spirits are given a choice of where we're born?"

"I haven't thought of it. I can't say that I know."

"If I was given the choice today, I'd not choose the life of a princess." She felt Mered staring at her. "My life is constantly monitored. I have to live within the confines of how a royal person should live. If I agree to marry, it will be an arranged marriage."

Mered nodded, listening closely.

Bithiah continued. "My son has been brought up to see everyone and everything as a competition. His future is always in question. If I married and had more children, they would be caught up in palace intrigue as well, always afraid to say or do the wrong thing."

Finally she looked up.

Mered's eyes were nearly black in the lamplight. "If you could choose right now," he said in a soft voice, "what would you choose?"

"I would choose to be free of the palace."

His brows drew together. "You would want to be an ordinary Egyptian citizen?"

"Perhaps," she said. She could see that she'd surprised him.

"Surely you can't mean you'd rather be a Hebrew?" he asked. "Working as a slave from first light to last, always feeling hungry, working under the taskmasters . . . A woman like you could never be happy in that life."

Mered created a grim image, but life could be hard in any circumstance. "I've seen the Hebrews in their villages, with their families," she said. "They seem happy."

Mered's eyes widened. "We must find happiness no matter what we are born into." He clasped his hands together, and Bithiah noticed the ink stains on the ends of his fingers. "You are meant for better things than a slave. And if we were given a choice before we were born, I'm glad you were born a royal so you could be well taken care of and protected."

He patted her hand, and Bithiah turned her hand over. Their palms brushed, and Bithiah looked down, Mered's ink-stained hand holding her smooth hand that had never labored a day. Even their skin was different.

"Tell me about your Hebrew god," she said in a quiet voice as warmth flowed through her at his touch.

Mered began to pull his hand away from hers, but Bithiah wrapped her hand around his so it was cocooned. "I want to know what's in your soul, Mered."

He allowed their hands to remain together, his eyes on her, soaking her in. "I-I can't. It's too dangerous for you. If it's known that you've been taught the Hebrew ways, you'll be an outcast. "

"Is that what you fear for me?" she asked.

"Do you have no fear for yourself, Princess?"

Did she fear? If so, what? That she and Mered would be discovered in the records room together? That her son, Moses, would someday reject her? That Mered would never know how she felt about him? She feared all of that, but she also feared something greater. She feared that she'd never find her true soul. "What I fear is that when I enter the underworld, I will discover that the stones and statues I've been taught to worship are nothing more than rocks and gold."

Mered withdrew his hand from hers. She had most likely struck fear in him, asking him to put his own life in danger by teaching her the forbidden.

"The Lord of Israel is the true one. He is not a statue or a tree. He is a living being in a spirit form." Mered's voice washed over her, warm and sure.

"Our Lord is a jealous god, and He wants to be recognized, revered, and worshipped. We make animal sacrifices for peace offerings and sin offerings," he said.

She saw that his smile was sad, his eyes moist. It was costing him a lot to trust her. Bithiah rested her head on her hand as he told her the story of Joseph and how he was abandoned by his brothers. Joseph rose to prestige and title in Egypt, and he also predicted the seven-year famine. So when Joseph's brothers came to Egypt seeking help for their starving people, Joseph forgave his family and helped them.

The brothers remained, raising families, and the Hebrews multiplied in strength and in number, so much so that they eventually became a threat to the Egyptian government. Bithiah let the words wash over her. This part of the Hebrews' history she knew well, but she could listen to Mered's voice for days.

"An entire generation was lost," Mered said, his tone regretful. "My son was killed."

Bithiah stared at Mered. "You had a son?" Emotions battled within her. This man had been married? He was a slave to those who had taken his son's life. Yet Bithiah didn't sense any bitterness.

As if reading her thoughts, Mered said, "It was many years ago now, and I know my son is with God. If he'd lived, he would have been worked nearly to death."

Bithiah took a steady breath. She had thought Mered unmarried. And here she was alone with him . . . "And your other children? Your wife?"

"Abram was our first child," he said. "My wife died in childbirth two years later, taking our daughter with her."

Bithiah blinked back hot tears. The Mered she knew worked day after day in the palace, never complaining, yet he carried a heavy burden. As did all the Hebrews, she realized, no matter whom they served. If she hadn't fetched Moses out of the River Nile, what might have become of him? "I am sorry for your suffering, Mered."

He met her gaze, his eyes rimmed in red. "We all have burdens. It's how we bear them that fashions our true character."

Bithiah's throat tightened, and all she could do was nod. She wanted to tell him about Moses—how she'd saved a young Hebrew child and how he was being raised as a royal right under the pharaoh's nose. But what would that prove? That she'd taken pity on the poor infant? She was still living a privileged life. One she didn't want. What kind of selfish person did that make her?

Mered went back to their task and pointed out a few other notes that referred to Hatshepsut. The more Bithiah learned about the she-pharaoh, the more Bithiah realized she had no courage at all. As a woman and as a princess who'd displeased her parents, her only chance at survival was to obey. Much like the Hebrews. Yes, they were slaves, and they might be trapped, but she was a slave in another sense.

Bithiah read through the recording of Hatshepsut's marriage to her half brother who became the next pharaoh. "Do you think Hatshepsut cared for her husband?"

Mered raised his eyebrows. "I don't know."

"I mean," Bithiah tried to explain her question, "they probably knew they were intended for each other and had to marry in order to keep the royal blood strong, but it seemed she had ambitions beyond being merely a chief wife."

A smile played on Mered's lips. "I don't think she would have been a *quiet* chief wife."

Bithiah laughed. "I agree. With what she did after her husband's death, it seemed she'd planned to rule all along."

Mered nodded. "She was just biding her time."

"Yes," Bithiah said. "Her patience paid off in the end."

They were silent for several moments, then Mered stood. "I'm afraid I must make my farewell. If we are here too long, someone will surely come by."

Bithiah knew he was right, but she was reluctant to end their time together. She stood and followed him to the door. He paused, glancing a final time at her. The glow of the lamps cast a soft light about them, making it feel as if they were the only two in the palace, perhaps in the world.

As he walked away from her, down the corridor, she wished she had asked him what kind of life he would have chosen.

CHAPTER SEVENTEEN

MOSES

"WHAT IS THE MEANING OF this?" Pharaoh demanded as Pentu hurried into the throne room, interrupting his counsel with Ramses.

Moses was sitting with the scribes, discussing the dedication of the Temple of Seti I in Abydos, a temple that Seti had built in honor of his pharaoh ancestors. They needed extra scribes for the event, and Mered had asked Moses for recommendations of some of the royal students. Since his betrothal to Cena had been broken, Moses had stayed busy.

"The Libyan tribesmen have crossed the western desert!" Pentu cried out. "They invaded the military camp and killed many of our soldiers. They are marching toward Memphis now."

Moses was on his feet immediately. Ramses jumped to his feet as well and stepped off the dais. It only took a single glance between the two to convey they were both ready to fight whether they were soldiers or not. There had been several skirmishes with the Libyan tribesmen over the past few months, but they'd never breached the border or attacked the military camp. The Libyans were barbarous by nature, and they'd been known to send their own women as diversions in order to trick their enemies.

"How many?" Pharaoh demanded.

Pentu shook his head. "I don't know, but it must be hundreds to get through the camp."

The hairs on Moses's arms stood up. It would be a battle, one close by, one that couldn't be avoided.

Pharaoh was on his feet, pacing. "How many soldiers are at the ready to defend Mennefer?"

At this, Pentu paled. "The commander sent me because his second-in-command rebelled and fled with most of the men who serve Mennefer."

Pharaoh stood as still as a statue, his face a mottled red. "*Most*? How many fled? Give me a number."

Pentu still hesitated until Ramses approached him, leveling his gaze. "How many? We need to know what to expect."

"Almost all," Pentu said. "There are a few dozen remaining, but they won't be able to hold the tribesmen off for long."

Pharaoh's voice was as hard as steel when he asked, "And where did they go? Are they joining the Libyans?"

"They went south, so it's unclear whether they intend to cross into Nubia or veer west and make their way into Libya."

The pharaoh's face darkened even more. "If they dare return to Egypt, every single one of them will be executed." He turned and looked at Moses. "Moses, there's no time to bring in the army that's stationed in the Delta. We need the Hebrew slaves."

Moses stiffened. To fight? Against massive and ruthless warriors who were marching on Mennefer? The slaves would be cut down in moments. But he had no other solution to offer. A woman's scream interrupted everything else, and Pentu ran to the corridor, Moses following right behind him.

A young soldier was running toward them. He looked as if he'd been in the chariot race of his life. His skin was blistered like he'd been in the sun for days. "The Libyans have passed the Southern Oasis and are heading toward the palace."

Pentu grabbed the soldier's arm. "How fast are they moving? How soon will they be here?"

"They'll arrive tonight if no one stops them. They are a half day's march from Mennefer."

The pharaoh started shouting orders while those inside the courtroom scrambled for weapons. Moses headed down the corridor in the opposite direction of the panicked soldier. Once outside, he sprinted through the courtyard, then toward the north, where the final cleanup was taking place at the front of the new temple site. The taskmaster was standing beneath a palm tree, speaking to a Hebrew woman who balanced a clay jar on her head.

Moses hurried to the taskmaster and explained what the pharaoh had ordered. The taskmaster turned away and bellowed his orders, and the slaves moved quickly toward the palace. Pentu had already organized men from the court to gather the slaves for battle.

"They need weapons," Moses said, coming to a stop near Pentu.

Pentu looked over at Moses and shook his head. "We don't want them turning on us."

Moses stared at him in disbelief. "You expect these half-starved men to fight for Egypt without weapons?"

Some of the nearby slaves had slowed, listening to the interchange between the two men.

Pentu scoffed. "Pharaoh's orders."

Moses narrowed his eyes. "Where is Pharaoh now? Where's Ramses?"

"They are on their way to Pithom."

In other words, Moses thought, they were running, which meant they thought the Libyans might have a chance to overtake the palace. Pharaoh would return later with the rest of his army that was currently stationed in the Delta of Lower Egypt.

Moses scanned the pitiful line of thin men passing by and following the taskmasters. Some looked near death. "Which one of you leads this group of people?" Moses called out in broken Hebrew.

A man stepped forward, one Moses recognized as the accused thief. *Caleb.*

"I will speak for this work crew," Caleb said in passable Egyptian.

Moses nodded. He already knew what this man would do to preserve those he loved. Moses replied in Egyptian. "We need to arm your people against the invading Libyans. If the Libyans invade Memphis, your people and your women will not be spared. But I need an oath that you will not turn against the Egyptians if you join the battle." He caught his breath. Most of the slaves had stopped and were listening to him. He knew they didn't all understand Egyptian. Caleb would have to explain later.

"Upon my life, we will not use the weapons against the Egyptians," Caleb said, simply and conclusively.

It was good enough for Moses.

"This will be upon your head," Pentu said to Moses, but the resistance had left his voice. He turned to the court members standing near. "Fetch the weapons."

Moses turned to a group of female servants from the palace who stood huddled just inside the palace's archway. "Bring the slaves food and water. They will need all the strength they can muster."

Pentu whipped his head around and scowled at Moses. "You've gone too far, my friend."

"We have a palace to save." Moses moved to help the men bring out the weapons. They distributed them quickly, and soon the women returned with bread and water.

Moses watched the men eat the bread as if they hadn't eaten anything in days. He marveled that none of them ate more than their share, and when they finished, they formed into the original line, except this time they held daggers, axs, spears, or maces. The women had returned to their shaded alcove, but they stood taller and looked less frightened, as if they were proud of their contribution in feeding the men.

Moses turned to the Hebrew named Caleb. "Do you or any of the Hebrews know how to shoot a bow or drive a chariot?"

"No," Caleb answered. "They will all fight on foot."

What an ill-equipped and unprepared army, Moses thought. He reached for a sword from one of the court members and turned it over. It seemed he would be riding out in a chariot with a stack of arrows that only he and Pentu knew how to shoot.

"Bring all the chariots that are available, even the royal ones."

Once the chariots were brought and Moses and Pentu took their places, along with a dozen other Egyptians who knew how to drive the chariots, Pentu mounted his chariot and guided his horse so that he rode to the front of the line of slaves. "In the name of the pharaoh," he called out, "we fight for our land and people." He urged his chariot forward, and the slaves followed at a half run.

Moses mounted his own chariot and rode to the side of the marching Hebrews. Only a couple of taskmasters had been chosen to take out chariots; the rest would remain behind, shoring up the defenses of the palace itself. Moses focused on the nearly hundred men who would be facing their deaths in mere hours unless the gods and goddesses were feeling generous today.

They passed through a couple of small oases, over dunes of sand, and around ridges of rock. As they crested yet another long ridge, the desert spread out before them like an ocean, and Moses spotted the approaching Libyans in the distance. They were a mass of men moving slowly. They didn't come in chariots though, which brought some relief to Moses. They pulled carts with supplies, but most were on foot. The Libyan tribesmen wore their hair long, plaited and beaded, with animal-skin headbands wrapped around their heads. Bird feathers decorated the headbands, and their robes were made of dyed animal hides.

"Halt!" Pentu called out, and the Hebrews came to a stop.

Moses brought his chariot to where Pentu had stopped at the top of the ridge, his heart thundering at the sight of the approaching army. The Libyans had pressed farther into Egypt's territory than he had suspected. They were literally three hours' travel from Mennefer and the palace.

"We will divide—half will take the right side, the other half the left side," Pentu said.

"Do we have a chance?" Moses asked in a low voice.

"The Libyans look far from slowing down, and they have dozens of horses," Pentu said. "We will lose many today, but we must create a barrier and hold them off."

Moses gave a curt nod, then said, "How will we protect the middle? If there is a break, they could still get through and make it past us toward the palace on their horses."

Pentu looked at the approaching slaves. "We'll give that man named Caleb thirty of the strongest slaves to drop back from us and set up a secondary barrier on the back side of the ridge, one that absolutely must not be breached should our front line fail. Instruct him what to do."

Moses climbed off his chariot and hurried toward the main body of soldiers, knowing he was less skilled than Pentu at military strategy, yet with the pharaoh gone, they'd have to do their best.

As soon as he spotted Caleb, Moses approached. "You're commanding thirty of your strongest men and remaining on this side of the ridge. If the Libyans break over the ridge, you're to stop them."

If Caleb was uncomfortable taking over a commander's position, he didn't show it. "I will gather the men, and we will drop back and hide ourselves."

Moses watched as Caleb moved among the slaves, gathering his group. Then Moses set about dividing the remaining Hebrews into two groups. He sent a portion Pentu's way and then guided his own group toward the right.

"Watch Commander Pentu's signal," Moses ordered. "We'll assemble at the top of the ridge, and when he raises his sword, we will charge. If an Egyptian soldier is already in a fight, help him take down his opponent. You will have to learn fast. Strike at the neck or the heart. Death comes faster that way."

A few of the slaves cowered back, and Moses said, "If you flee, you will be executed with no mercy. Face our enemies and defend our country, or your families will be slaughtered by the enemy!"

Murmuring arose, a whisper at first, then it grew in volume. It sounded like some sort of prayer or plea to heaven—it was most likely to their Hebrew god. Moses didn't mind. They needed any and all help they could get. If the prayers could put courage into his small army, so much the better.

Moses returned to his chariot and climbed inside. He urged his horse toward the top of the ridge. He knew it was somewhere beyond the marching Libyan army. Somewhere beyond the ridge, out there, in the desolation, his Egyptian people lay dead. And it was as if the wind brought the scent of death. It churned Moses's stomach to imagine the brutality of the Libyans as they sliced their way through the Egyptian camp.

Moses turned to watch Pentu, who was moving up the left side of the ridge for the rest of the slaves to reach him. Moments later, Moses reached the top of the ridge about the same time as Pentu. Moses came to an abrupt halt as he caught sight of the scene spread out below. The prayers and chants of the Hebrews went silent. Everyone stared at the mass of Libyans and Egyptians fighting each other below. Man battling against man. Moses sensed the fear from the slaves surrounding him. These Hebrews were men who were abused every day, but now they would use what strength they had to kill others.

Pentu raised his sword and shouted, "Charge!"

Like a wave of locusts, the Hebrews moved forward, running down the slope toward the approaching Libyans.

"Forgive us," a man next to Moses cried out. Then he was off and running.

Moses drove his chariot ahead, pulling up alongside the charging Hebrews. He began to launch a volley of arrows toward the advancing Libyans, joining the other chariots in their attack. The arrows soared into the blue sky, arcing, then bending toward their targets. As the Egyptian and Hebrew soldiers clashed with the Libyans, the sun burned hot on the fierce fighting. Moses launched another volley of arrows, hearing the cries and screams, the weapons clashing, the dull sound of flesh being hit. He smelled the blood and perspiration, but all he could think of was doing whatever it took to save Egypt as the Libyans were defeated one man at a time.

CHAPTER EIGHTEEN

BITHIAH

BITHIAH RAN OUT OF HER bedchamber to find people hurrying through the palace, calling to each other in panicked voices.

"What's going on?" she demanded of a guard passing by her door. She didn't know what had happened to the regular guards who were usually stationed at her room.

"The Libyan tribesmen have crossed the border and are advancing on Mennefer," the guard said, hurrying past. "The pharaoh has fled to Pithom. Protect yourself, and go to the courtroom where the doors will soon be barred."

Bithiah stared at the man. Her father had fled the palace and left her behind?

"Where is his family?" she called after him.

"They've gone with him," he said before turning a corner, intent on being anywhere but standing in the corridor with her.

"They haven't gone with him. I'm still here—I'm still left," Bithiah said. Then she thought, *Moses!* She ran down the corridor, following the guard, calling after him. "Did Moses go with the pharaoh?"

Thankfully, the man stopped. "No, he went out with Commander Pentu to fight. They've taken the Hebrew slaves with them."

The breath left Bithiah. Her son was battling against the fierce Libyans. And who were his comrades? Untrained slaves.

"Come to the courtroom with the others," the guard said. "You'll be safe there."

But Bithiah could only stare at the guard.

"Princess, you must come and save yourself," he urged.

She shook her head, and finally the guard left, running again.

Bithiah blinked her eyes slowly as if she was just waking up from a dream. She turned from the direction the guard had gone and moved through the now-empty corridor toward Moses's room.

As she stood in the entrance of his empty chamber, she knew her son would have never abandoned her like her father had. Only the call of fighting to save her would take him away.

She walked into his room and crossed to the door that led to the west-facing courtyard. She opened the door and stepped outside. If she hadn't known better, she might have thought it was just another hot day filled with sunshine. Yet the courtyard was deserted, and all was quiet. The flowers and bushes seemed motionless, as if they were holding their breath. Even the birds and insects were silent.

"Moses," she whispered as if he was standing next to her and could hear, "don't be foolish. Be careful, my son."

A scream sounded from somewhere within the palace, and Bithiah turned to peer through Moses's room to the corridor. Two men ran down the hall, shouting for weapons.

Bithiah's head snapped back to the courtyard, and she gazed at the ridges that rose in the west. She couldn't see any advancing army, but that didn't mean the Libyans weren't close. Fear crept through her, growing stronger as she considered where Moses was and what he might be doing. Fighting for his life. Fighting for Egypt.

"Oh, Ra, god of the sun," Bithiah said, sinking to her knees. She prostrated herself beneath the orange, round sun. "Protect my son. Bring him home to me safely. Spare our land and preserve Egypt." She stayed in her prostrated position, the sun beating down on her, and prayed until she heard more shouting. Then she heard someone calling her name.

She recognized Mered's voice.

"Bithiah." Mered's voice again. He touched her shoulder.

She rose slowly to her knees and blinked up at him.

"It's not safe here," he said, extending his hand. "You must come with me."

Bithiah reached for his hand, and it clasped securely over hers. He helped her to her feet, and she said, "What's going to happen to us, Mered? Where's my son?"

"He is fighting for Egypt," Mered said. "He would want you to find a safe place so when he returns, he'll find you unharmed."

Bithiah looked down at their clasped hands. "What if *he* is harmed? What if the Libyans reach the palace?"

Mered squeezed her hand. "Moses is a strong young man. He'll be able to take care of himself. And if the Libyans reach the palace, I will keep you hidden and safe." He tugged at her hand. "Come now. We must join the others in the courtroom. They have gathered weapons and food and drink so they can withstand a siege."

Bithiah nodded numbly and let Mered lead her through Moses's room and out into the corridor. The stillness of the place was all wrong.

"Are we too late?" she whispered as they hurried along the corridor. It seemed strange to talk in a normal volume with the palace so deserted.

"We have time," Mered said. "We're almost there." He slowed his step and reached for the door handles. He tugged at the doors, but they were stuck. Locked.

"Aren't they expecting us?" Bithiah asked, trying to keep the panic out of her voice.

Mered pounded on the door. "Let us in!" he shouted.

They waited, but there was no response. Mered pounded again, then called out, "I have Princess Bithiah with me. She needs protection."

Still nothing. The moments crawled by as Bithiah and Mered waited, listening.

"Have they moved locations?" Bithiah finally asked.

Mered met her gaze, his eyes somber, and he shook his head. "They are afraid. They don't trust anyone. We must find another place to hide."

Bithiah stared at him as fear jolted through her. "Where?"

"Let's go to the cooking rooms and gather food and drink to take with us, then we'll find a good place to conceal ourselves until the danger has passed." Mered grasped her hand again and led her down the corridor.

If Mered hadn't been so insistent, Bithiah would have sunk to the floor outside the courtroom, knocking and begging to be let inside.

"We must hurry," Mered said, his voice urgent.

Whatever calm Mered had portrayed before was now gone. They ran until they reached the cooking rooms. Bithiah grabbed a basket, and together they filled it.

"Let's fill one more basket, then we must hide," Mered said. After doing so, they hurried out of the cooking room.

"Now where?" Bithiah asked. She couldn't think.

Mered hesitated, then said, "We'll go back to Moses's room, where we have a view of the western ridge. We'll have first glimpse at the advancing army should they make it past the Egyptian forces."

Or the Hebrew forces, Bithiah wanted to say, but didn't.

They hurried down the corridor, each carrying a basket. When they reached Moses's room, Mered set about blocking the door to the corridor by moving a low table in front of it and placing two heavy statues upon the table.

Bithiah covered the windows with tapestries. Then she stepped into the courtyard, her gaze drawn to the western ridge. Although the air was warm, she shivered. Mered came out into the courtyard too and watched with her.

"The room is secure. We'll keep the door to the courtyard accessible for now, but be ready to block it if necessary."

Bithiah turned to him and focused on his dark eyes. "Thank you for helping me."

His eyes scanned her face, and he opened his mouth as if he wanted to say something, but then he let it close.

"What if the palace is invaded?" she asked. "We can only hide for so long."

"We can hide here until they pass the room, then as they are occupied in the palace, we can leave through the courtyard. I can take you to my village. There will be nothing there the Libyans will want."

Bithiah took comfort in his steady words, but only a little. "What about my family?"

Mered scrubbed his hand through his hair and looked past Bithiah. "There are probably a couple of things that could happen. The royal family could be left alone but be required to pay a tribute. Or they could be captured."

"And executed," Bithiah said, her mind filling with unthinkable thoughts. "Would the Libyans be so cruel?"

Mered gave a slow nod. "They would. War brings out the worst in people, and the Libyan tribesmen are already some of the worst I've heard of." He paused. "Come inside; we don't need to be staring at the horizon."

Bithiah shook her head. "I need to stay here so I can see what's happening. So I can know."

Mered exhaled. Then without a word he went into Moses's chamber and brought out two cushions. He arranged them near the stone wall, beneath the shade, and motioned for Bithiah to sit. She settled into place, then looked at Mered, who stood leaning against the wall.

"Come sit with me," Bithiah said. "Hopefully there will be a victory to celebrate soon."

Mered sat on the other cushion, and they waited and watched together as the sun moved across the sky.

At one point, Mered closed his eyes and mouthed a prayer. When he finished, Bithiah asked, "What were you saying to your god?"

"I asked Him to preserve your son and my people."

Bithiah looked down at her hands clasped in her lap. Moses was more connected to Mered's people than he realized. "Thank you," Bithiah said. "I was praying to the sun god when you found me earlier. Surely Ra will watch over Egypt."

"Look," Mered cut in. He rose to his feet and pointed at the western horizon. "Someone is coming."

Bithiah leapt to her feet, joining Mered. "Are they our people or the Libyans?"

"I can't tell yet." Mered was still for several minutes, watching. As the men advanced, their images became clearer, and the dark animal-skin kilts were unmistakable. "Libyans."

She gasped. "They've broken through our defenses." Her eyes filled with tears as the horror settled into her soul. She stood like a statue, staring at the men approaching the palace. Even though she couldn't hear them at this distance, she imagined their shouting and war cries. She pictured their bloodshot eyes and wild hair. She could almost smell their perspiration and bloodstained bodies.

"Come inside," Mered said.

But Bithiah couldn't move. Not until Mered grasped her arm and pulled her with him did she go inside Moses's room. Seeing her son's things and not knowing if he was still alive brought on fresh tears. She turned toward the windows again. Was Moses out there? Was he alive or dead? Was he injured and needing help?

"Bithiah, we need to hide now," Mered said. He drew her with him to the small storage area concealed by a curtain. Inside, they'd stacked their food and moved several cushions they could hide beneath.

"I can't. What if Moses needs me?" Her tears came faster now.

Mered's arm slipped around her shoulders. "Your son needs you safe. Come into the hiding place."

She nodded, feeling numb, and let Mered guide her to the storage room. She sat on the cushion in the corner and closed her eyes, listening to Mered's movements as he stacked furniture and other items in front of them so the place looked like a storage space instead of a room hiding two people.

Finally, he let the curtain fall, and they were plunged into near darkness.

She heard rather than saw Mered sit next to her. She heard his breathing and his movements as he settled into the small space. Reaching for his hand, she grasped it and took small comfort in the fact that she was not alone, for now. In Mered's other hand, he held a dagger at the ready.

She couldn't stop thinking about her son. There were too many unknowns. She'd happily flee conquered Mennefer if only she could have her son with her. The darkness engulfed her, and she clung to Mered's hand as if that alone could preserve her.

The wait dragged on, and Bithiah's heart pounded double time with each passing minute. Her tears had long dried, replaced by encroaching feelings of defeat.

It was then that she heard a loud crash. She flinched and buried her head against Mered's chest. His arm came around her, holding her tightly. They didn't speak; they hardly breathed.

The sounds grew closer. Banging. Shouting. And then the screams.

Bithiah gripped Mered tighter. "Pray for us," she whispered to Mered. "Someone in heaven must take compassion."

CHAPTER NINETEEN

MOSES

THE SCREAMS WERE DEAFENING AT first, making Moses's skin crawl. He felt like gagging at the smell of death and blood, but he continued to swing at one opponent, then another, barely registering when a man fell before him screaming in pain or gurgling in death.

He just kept going. Kept fighting.

He'd abandoned his chariot long ago and started fighting like a foot soldier. It wasn't until the screaming changed to shouting that Moses realized something had changed. He turned from the newly slain opponent at his feet to see that Pentu was racing across the ridge on his horse. "They've broken the line!" he shouted.

Caleb, Moses thought. *Caleb must hold them back now.* He was relying on the inexperienced Hebrew slave who had kept back thirty of the best men.

Moses didn't need to study the surrounding battle to know Caleb's thirty stood little chance of holding back the fierce tribesmen. The Hebrews had been effective, had held on strong, but the Libyans remained determined and had backed the Hebrews up the ridge little by little.

And now the tribesmen were over the ridge, heading toward the defenseless palace. Moses didn't waste any more time but turned and followed the group of Libyans over the ridge. His muscles ached, and his breath was short, but he could worry about recovering later.

What he saw on the other side of the ridge stunned him motionless. Caleb and his thirty men were valiantly fighting off the Libyans. A group of tribesmen had skirted the Hebrews and was heading toward the palace, yet the rest were in a fight for their lives.

Moses hurried back down the ridge, calling to Pentu that he was chasing after the Libyans. He ordered a few Hebrews who were nearby to go with him and follow the Libyans headed toward the palace. Moses knew he could never catch up to them; he needed his chariot. He would have to leave Pentu in charge of the battle and trust Caleb to keep his promises. Then he turned toward his idle chariot. The horses stood almost motionless.

Not for the first time, Moses wished Ramses and Pharaoh had thought ahead and kept more forces in Mennefer. It would take them most of the day to bring in reinforcements from Pithom.

Moses ordered two of the Hebrews to join him in the chariot. The others would have to run alongside. By the time they crossed over the ridge again, the Libyans were well ahead.

Moses drove the horses against the wind, his breath coming in gasps even though he rode in a chariot. The Hebrews who were on foot valiantly ran, falling farther and farther behind, but they were still advancing. Moses couldn't slow for even a moment. Not when images of what the Libyans might do to those remaining in the palace jumped into his mind. He hoped his mother had left with the rest of the royal family, but if not, his urgency was even greater.

The wind continued to build, pushing against Moses's chest as if it was trying to push him backward. He drove forward for what seemed like hours. He couldn't move fast enough. Finally Mennefer came into full view.

"We're almost there," Moses called out. "We must stop this invasion." Moses calculated it would be about one Hebrew slave to two Libyan warriors. The odds weren't great, but they weren't impossible either. It was better than what it had been on the battlefield.

Finally Moses and his men reached the main courtyard of the palace, and Moses climbed out of the chariot and grabbed an ax. The wind gusted about the plants and flowers, bending them almost to the ground. Sand flew through the air at nearly the level of a full sandstorm. He stopped in front of the palace entrance to look for any sign of the Libyans, but there was no telling where they were now.

"I hear screaming," one of the Hebrews said in broken Egyptian. He pointed toward the left, where the courtroom was located.

The other men started to speak in rapid Hebrew until Moses raised his hands for silence. He pointed to the Hebrew who'd spoken Egyptian.

"We will split up and go to both sides of the courtroom. There is a front entrance and a back entrance."

The Hebrew explained this to the other men, and they nodded, then quickly split up. Moses led his group to the back entrance, and that was when he smelled smoke.

The screaming grew louder, and Moses couldn't bear the thought of people being caught in a fire. He ran to the courtroom doors and pushed against them. They didn't budge. "They're blocked," Moses shouted. "We need to break them down." He didn't know if the Hebrews understood his words, but they followed his actions as he started hitting the doors with an ax.

They hammered and chopped at the doors until they started to give way. Smoke seeped out, and as the doors splintered, the smoke increased.

Finally the doors were broken enough that Moses and the slaves were able to wrench them open. Many people were lying on the floor, coughing. Some weren't moving. Several ran outside, coughing over and over.

Moses pushed his way in, past the exiting Egyptians, and started to drag out those who were on the floor. He didn't know if they were alive or dead, but he wanted to get them out in case they had a chance at survival.

The other door had been barred as well, and surprisingly enough, Moses didn't see any Libyans inside the room. That meant the Egyptians had started the fire on their own.

Moses called for a couple of the Hebrews to slap at the fire near the front entrance, but it proved too large and was growing rapidly, so they turned to the people instead, helping them out of the room. As he worked, Moses tried not to inhale too much of the smoke.

The doors to the front entrance came crashing down, and Moses turned to see that the second group of Hebrews had broken through. Moses stared. Libyan tribesmen were lying in the corridor, not moving. The slaves had defeated them.

The fire raged out of the front entrance, leaping up the walls and approaching the dead tribesmen. Moses ordered several men to start filling jugs with water from the pools in the courtyard.

They had to put out the fire before it spread too far.

While those men worked, Moses fought to get everyone into the courtyard where there was fresh air. But the sky had darkened with the blowing sand.

"It's a sandstorm," someone shouted.

"Everyone to the throne room!" Moses called out. It was the only room big enough to hold this crowd, and since it was on the other side of the palace, it would be safe from the fire.

Those who could walk started to make their way through the courtyard, and others helped carry those who couldn't walk. Moses supported one woman who was wheezing more than she was breathing. He cast a backward glance at several who were lying motionless on the ground. They didn't look injured like those on the battlefield, but the smoke had stolen the breath of life from them.

The woman Moses was helping started to cough. He paused to let her catch her breath. "Thank you," she said, her voice raspy. "Did you find your mother?"

Moses stiffened. "My mother? Didn't she go with the rest of the royal family to Pithom?"

"No," the woman said, then fell into another coughing fit. After a minute, she said, "She knocked on the door to the courtroom, but no one would let her in." The woman shook her head. "Fear changes people."

The woman was right. Fear did change people. It made Moses want to release this woman and run through the corridors, calling for his mother. He gritted his teeth and forced himself to continue helping the woman. Once he got her to the throne room, he told the men, whether Hebrew or Egyptian, to split up. They needed to put out the fire and prepare to defend the palace.

Then he went to search for his mother. He didn't know how long he had—minutes, maybe longer. As he left the throne room, he hurried to the end of one of the corridors that opened into a west-facing courtyard. He didn't know how much longer Caleb could hold back the Libyans, and urgency pulsed through him. Moses reentered the palace and ran to his mother's chambers. He burst through the doors, calling to her while checking every corner and closet.

"Moses," a man's voice called from the chamber entrance, "is it you?"

Moses turned to see the royal scribe, Mered. "Have you seen my mother?"

"She's in your chamber, hiding," Mered said. "Come with me."

Moses followed Mered out and hurried to his chamber. The moment he stepped inside, he called for her. She emerged from her hiding place and wrapped her arms around him.

"You're alive," Bithiah said, sobbing. "Praise the gods and goddesses, my son is alive!"

Moses held his mother tightly, feeling his own emotions surface. He hadn't realized until just now how afraid he'd been. Tears trailed down his face as he inhaled his mother's familiar scent.

"When I saw the Libyans coming, I nearly gave up hope," his mother said, her cheek pressed against his chest. "Mered made me hide. And when I heard the screams and the Libyans running through the palace, my heart wanted to die."

"Oh, Mother," Moses said, stroking her back. "I didn't know you were here. I thought you'd left with Pharaoh."

His mother pulled away. "I didn't know about the border raid until it was too late. I was stuck here, and . . ." She paused, looking over at the scribe. "If it hadn't been for Mered, I might have gone crazy."

Moses reached out to place a hand on Mered's shoulder. "Thank you for taking care of my mother."

Mered nodded. "What can I help with?"

"There's a fire in the courtroom—the dignitaries decided they'd rather die than be captured by Libyans." Moses looked at his mother, then back to Mered. "We need all the help we can get to put it out."

"I'll do it," Mered said.

"What about the Libyans who invaded the palace?" his mother asked.

"The Hebrews who were with me overpowered them," Moses said. "But the battle isn't over. We need the men to defend the palace."

Mered's face was grave, but he nodded.

"What can I do, Moses?" his mother asked softly.

"Assemble some women and fetch drink and food for everyone." Moses eyed Mered, thinking specifically of the Hebrews. "Don't leave out the slaves."

His mother went one way, and he and Mered went the other. They found a line of men transporting jugs of water and dousing the fire. The wind bursting in through the broken doors didn't help, but the fire had been contained enough that Moses could leave and check on the battle preparations.

One of the viziers named Saba was barking orders into the screaming wind. When he saw Moses, he turned and called over the wind, "We need a dozen men to take position behind this wall. It will be our first line of defense against the Libyans."

Moses glanced at the wall. It had several areas where there were open spaces. It would be easy to hide and watch for the approaching tribesmen without being spotted themselves. "I think that will work. I need a few men to take with me to go help at the front line." If the Libyans could be stopped at the front line, they wouldn't make it as far as the others.

Saba narrowed his eyes. "You're royalty; perhaps you should send others."

"Everyone is the same today," Moses said. "We have Hebrew slaves doing an Egyptian soldier's job. I will face what may come regardless of who my mother is." He waved his arm. "The sandstorm will work in our favor."

"Very well," Saba said, then called over several men, Hebrews and Egyptians alike. Six men came over, shielding their eyes from the blowing sand. "These men will go with you."

"Come to the stables first," Moses said, looking at the assembled men. "We'll take horses." The men followed Moses to the stables. By the time they were inside and untying the horses, the wind had increased and the sky had darkened.

Moses stepped outside into the blinding storm. The wind pushed his breath from his body, and he turned and staggered back inside. "We've been delayed. There is no visibility. As soon as the storm lifts, we will ride to see what's left of the battle."

CHAPTER TWENTY

MIRIAM

MIRIAM TUGGED OUT THE THREAD she'd just woven and started over. The wind had increased over the past few minutes, and she decided it was the cause of her clumsiness. It was as if the wind had brought bad luck. Her mother came out of the hut and looked up.

Miriam saw only blue sky. "What is it, Mother?"

Jochebed clasped her hands together and looked over at Miriam. "The wind brings a feeling of foreboding."

Miriam had to agree even though she wished it wasn't true. "What do you think has happened?"

Jochebed didn't have the chance to answer because just then Miriam's father came bursting into the courtyard. Perspiration stood out on his forehead, and he stopped, catching his breath as if he'd run all the way from the brick-making area.

Miriam immediately rose to her feet, weaving and loom forgotten. "What is it, Father?"

Her mother rushed to his side and grasped his hand.

"Hundreds of our men were sent into battle against the Libyans," he said. "I don't know how long ago. Word took a while to reach the brickyard, and then the taskmaster kept us working. I came as soon as I could."

"The Libyans?" Jochebed said, fear in her voice. "They are worse than our own taskmasters." Her voice fell to a whisper. "May Adonai preserve us."

Miriam's father gave a short nod. "The Libyan tribesmen crossed the western border yesterday and have now fought their way across the desert, coming so far that they are threatening the palace."

"Oh no." Jochebed brought a hand to her mouth. She squeezed her eyes shut. "It's bad enough being under the yoke of the Egyptians—the Libyans will extend no mercy, no mercy at all."

Miriam's thoughts were on the Hebrews-turned-soldiers. "Our men have no training to battle against warriors like the Libyans." At least no formal training. She knew there were groups of male slaves who practiced military strategy in secret. "Why are slaves being used? What about the Egyptian armies?"

"The larger portions are in Pithom," her father said. "Pharaoh has fled there with his family. Some say he is bringing back the army to fight the Libyans."

"So the Hebrew men are to defend Mennefer?"

Her father's face went pale. "Yes, and it appears Caleb was among those sent to fight."

Miriam's felt her blood turn cold. "Caleb? He's done enough for the Egyptians. He's been through enough!" Panic rushed through her. They'd just apprehended Reuven and spared Caleb, and now this.

"What about Aaron?" her mother cried out.

Amram's face was grim. "I haven't heard from Aaron yet," he said in a quiet voice.

Miriam met her father's fearful gaze, which mirrored her own emotions. For all her worry over Caleb, she also considered another woman who would be suffering over the news of Hebrews fighting the Libyans. "Salome," she whispered. Her sister-in-law was alone, ill, and with child, and would be worried to death once she heard about the Libyans.

"I'll go to her and find out if she knows anything," her mother said.

"No, I'll go," Miriam said. "You stay here with Father, where I know the two of you will be safe."

"Make haste," her mother said. "The wind is growing stronger."

Miriam nodded, took the scarf from around her waist, and tied it about her head so only her eyes were showing. She set out the short distance to Aaron's hut, but already the wind was intent on pushing against her, making each step an effort. Above, the sky grew dark, blocking out the great sun.

Sand pricked Miriam's skin as if she wasn't wearing clothing. She increased her pace and shoved open the door to Salome's hut without knocking first, then pushed the door shut behind her, gasping for clean air.

"Miriam!" Salome rushed to her and grabbed her hand. "What are you doing here?"

"I've come to see if you've heard from Aaron and to see if you are all right."

"I am fine, but I haven't seen Aaron," Salome said. "I was hoping he'd taken shelter somewhere during the sandstorm."

Miriam caught her breath, then relayed all the news her father had brought about the battle with the Libyans.

Salome grew quiet, then said, "We can't go out in this storm. All we can do is pray."

The two women clasped hands and sent their pleadings heavenward. As they prayed together, the sandstorm raged around the hut, blocking out all light and making it seem that it was the middle of the night. A fine dust began to fill the room.

"Caleb will be all right," Salome whispered after they finished praying.

Miriam tried to find comfort in Salome's assurances. "I can only hope the Lord will preserve him yet again," Miriam said. "I wonder if there comes a time when Adonai tires of His people's pleadings."

"I don't think He does," Salome said. "I think He wants to hear from His people, to know we need Him in all things."

Miriam settled onto a cushion in the main room and pulled her knees up to her chest. The wind continued its eerie pitch. "Aaron will be safe too," she added, hoping and praying he would. "He's a smart man and knows how to stay out of harm's way."

Salome simply nodded, then closed her eyes again, mouthing more prayers.

Miriam stared out the window at the darkness beyond. Where was Caleb now? Had the sandstorm stopped the battle? Were the Libyans still fighting? Was Aaron in the battle as well, or had he found refuge someplace in the village?

She noticed the moment the wind decreased. She rose from her cramped position and crossed to the window. It was early evening now, and the sky was thick with impenetrable dust. But the wind ebbed, and that meant she could go out and seek her brother and Caleb.

Before she could turn around and announce her intentions, Salome was already on her feet. "I'm coming with you to find Aaron."

Miriam was surprised, but she couldn't turn away Salome. She was just as worried about Aaron as Miriam was.

Salome busied herself preparing a basket of dried fish and fruit, then filling a goatskin with water from a storage jar.

"Do you have anything we could use for bandages?" Miriam asked, even though she hated to suggest it.

"There is a tunic I was mending in my bedchamber. We can bring it and tear it up if needed."

Miriam fetched the tunic, then returned to the front room, where Salome was ready to go.

The two women left the hut in relative silence, each lost in her own thoughts and each breathing in the lingering dust. They walked slowly at first, passing the huts. Dirt and sand layered everything. Some huts were damaged, and many courtyards were hardly recognizable. The Hebrews who had made it to their huts before the worst of the storm were just coming out, gazing at the sky, then looking around to assess the damage.

"We should check on the widow Deborah," Miriam said as they neared the village center. She looked over at Salome, who nodded.

They found Deborah in her small hut. The elderly woman had thankfully stayed inside and was doing well. Salome fetched her some water, and Miriam made sure she had something to eat.

When they left Deborah's hut, they hurried to the rock quarry where Aaron worked. Along the way, they received more and more bits of news from the villagers, and by the time they reached the rock quarry, Miriam was completely discouraged, having heard of the pharaoh's flight to Pithom and the fire at the palace.

Several men were working to clear a drift of sand when the women reached the quarry.

"Aaron," Salome cried out.

At the same time, Miriam spotted Aaron. He was covered in sand and was leaning over an older man, who was obviously hurt. He straightened to embrace Salome, then his gaze found Miriam's.

An unspoken understanding passed between brother and sister, and Miriam knew Aaron had heard about Caleb. He crossed to her, Salome clinging to his hand.

"I'll come with you to find out news about Caleb and the battle," he said.

Miriam embraced her brother and kissed him on the cheek. "Thank you, Aaron."

He turned to his wife. "Are you all right?" With her nod, he said, "Check on your parents and my parents. Miriam and I will be back by nightfall."

With good news, Miriam hoped.

Salome embraced her husband again, then bid them farewell.

Miriam felt the exhaustion in her body as she and Aaron set off toward the palace, but she completely ignored it. She had to find Caleb.

CHAPTER TWENTY-ONE

MOSES

As soon as the piercing cry of the wind lessened, Moses prepared the horses and chariots, instructing the men with him to do the same. He told them all to fetch the whips for the horses. It would be a hard ride ahead. "It's all right," Moses said to the horse he was leading from the stable. The animals were jittery, and with good reason. The worst of the storm had passed, and it was now possible to see the sky, but the wind was still strong.

Moses waited until the other men and their chariots joined him. None of the Hebrews had ridden in chariots before, and their eyes were wide with nervousness. "We'll ride toward the western ridge until we encounter the first line of Libyans—wherever that might be. We need to stop them from advancing on the palace."

One of the horses reared back, jerking against the chariot, and the chariot's rider said, "The horses will tip the chariots. They're terrified of the storm."

"Use the whip," Moses said. "We have no choice but to try to reach the Libyans before they get closer. If they are still waiting out the storm, we'll have the better advantage. Their horses will be spooked as well."

The man nodded and delivered a single strike to the horse, which reined the beast in, but only barely. Moses urged his horse forward, taking off into the dying storm. The others followed, shouting and using their whips to get their horses to pull the chariots.

They rode west, past the barricade Saba and his men had constructed. The sand stung Moses's face and torso. He could make out palm trees, and the farther they went, the more the sky cleared. The sand twisted and turned where it hadn't before, pushed into high drifts, and circled trees, making the terrain look foreign.

Moses slowed his chariot when he spotted a swath of cloth in the sand. He knew that in storms like this one grown men could be buried by the sand. He stopped the chariot and climbed out. Approaching the cloth, he scanned the rest of the area. Seeing no other patches of clothing, he knelt and started digging around the cloth. His worst fears were confirmed when his hands touched a body.

The man wasn't moving, wasn't breathing.

"Help me!" Moses called out. Two of the other men had already arrived, and they climbed out of their chariots and started digging frantically next to Moses. By the time the other men had caught up, Moses and the first two men had mostly uncovered the body.

Moses sat back on his heels, wiping the perspiration trickling down his face. The man wore a coarse linen kilt, the identifiable clothing of a Hebrew slave. Moses turned the man over. It wasn't someone he recognized. "Do you know this man?" he asked, turning to the Hebrews who were with him.

"His name is Hosea," one of the men said in broken Egyptian, his voice raspy, whether from emotion or from riding in the wind, Moses didn't know.

"Tell me about him," Moses said. They didn't have much time, but this man deserved recognition for his sacrifice.

"Hosea was a quiet but strong man. He was faithful to God. He leaves behind a wife and two young daughters."

Moses nodded. "His posterity will be blessed for his sacrifice."

The men around Moses nodded, not all of them understanding his words, but they sensed his reverence.

Moses rose to his feet. "We'll return his body to his village after we finish our battle."

The men rose as well, and they climbed into the chariots. Again they pressed forward. The wind had slowed to a steady breeze, and the sky was now clearly visible, just in time to display the setting sun. Moses urged his horse to go faster, wondering why a lone Hebrew was lying dead in the sand. Why was he separated from the others? Had he defected? Was he running to warn those at the palace?

As they rode west, the golden sun splashed its warm rays across the new mounds and dips of sand. The land was beautiful, forgiving, but too much blood had been spilled today. Moses's pulse drummed as he rode; he didn't know what they might stumble upon next.

Then he saw dark forms moving in the sand ahead of them. He slowed his chariot and indicated for the others to do the same. They were Hebrews, that much Moses knew, and they appeared to be walking toward them. That should be good news.

As they grew closer, Moses saw that some of the men were injured. A couple were helping others as they limped through the sand. He scanned the faces for Caleb, the one Hebrew he would recognize. His heart soared when he saw him trudging along, supporting another man who had a gash on his arm.

"Caleb," Moses called out. The man snapped his head up, and Moses was surprised the Hebrew hadn't heard the chariots and horses approaching. Although they had only the glow of the half moon, there was still plenty of light for the men to see each other.

Caleb helped the man he was supporting sit on the ground, and then he strode to where Moses was climbing out of his chariot. Caleb began to prostrate himself, but Moses reached out to stop the Hebrew. "We don't need formalities on the field of battle," he said. "What is your report? Where are the Libyans?"

"The storm drove them back to behind the oasis." Caleb straightened. "We holed up here and are waiting for more instructions."

Relief coursed through Moses. The Libyans had retreated. For now. It was giving the Egyptians more time to prepare and fortify. Moses clapped Caleb on the shoulder. This man had been more loyal than many Egyptian soldiers.

"How long do you think we have until they try to attack again?" Moses asked.

Caleb shook his head. "It could be tomorrow or could perhaps be days or weeks. Your commander would have a better idea. He and the other men are on the other side of the ridge, preparing to camp through the night."

"They'll need food and drink," Moses said. He assessed the men who'd fought with Caleb. There were about ten missing from their numbers. "Your men need nourishment as well, and it looks like we need to tend to several injuries."

"The Lord has blessed us today," Caleb said, then he quickly corrected himself. "We have been fortunate."

Moses stared at Caleb. How could this slave feel he was blessed today? He'd been sent to fight in place of the Egyptian soldiers who'd fled, yet he was *grateful*. He'd defended Egypt at the cost of his own people's lives.

"How many of your men have been lost?" Moses asked.

Everyone was quiet as they listened to Caleb speak. "Nine have perished." His gaze flicked over to a man who was groaning while being supported by another Hebrew. "Boaz's injury is grave."

Moses gave a curt nod and turned to the men who'd ridden with him. Pointing at three of them, he said, "Return with your chariots to the palace. Bring back food, drink, and a healer. There will be a great many injuries to attend to. We need all the help we can get."

The three men departed, and Moses turned to Caleb and the remaining men. "Set up camp here tonight while we tend to the injured. If we can transport any of them back to the palace, we'll do that."

He looked directly at Caleb. "Thank you for your service. I now need you to come with me to speak with Commander Pentu and decide how we will continue to keep Egypt free from the Libyans." Moses motioned for Caleb to join him in the chariot. "Come with me."

Caleb didn't hesitate but climbed into the chariot alongside Moses.

The ride to the ridge was short as they rode up the slope, and Moses steeled himself for what he was about to see. The last time he'd been on the other side of the ridge he'd been fighting fiercely against the Libyan warriors, defending his life and others' at all costs.

Those memories burned in his mind as he crested the ridge. Moses and Caleb brought the chariot to a stop. Spread below them was the valley of the Southern Oasis. The Egyptians and Hebrews were setting up camp, and on one side of the camp, bodies had been collected and the burying had started. From his position, Moses couldn't tell if the bodies were Egyptian, Hebrew, or Libyan. He winced at the number of the dead. The Libyans had been ruthless.

Well beyond the Egyptian camp, the Libyans had retreated, but they were still in sight. They camped as well to rest their weary bodies and try to care for their wounded. The descent of the sun had made it impossible to continue fighting.

They started the chariot down the ridge, and Moses scanned for Pentu, hoping the commander still lived and had escaped injury. At the bottom of the ridge, Moses and Caleb climbed out of the chariot. Moses approached the closest Egyptian soldier. "Where is Commander Pentu?"

"I haven't seen him since the storm," the soldier said. "He commanded us to all band together in order to shelter ourselves."

The news was not good. Moses looked at Caleb to see if he understood the soldier's words.

"Perhaps he became disoriented in the storm," Caleb said.

"We must find him," Moses said, not only thinking about what a great loss it would be to lose Pentu but that it would be a blow to the royal family as well, especially Ramses. The two fought and argued, but they were as close as brothers.

Caleb stayed with Moses as he walked through the camp, where the soldiers were settling in for the night. Fires burned and ragged-looking men had gathered around them, staring into the flames.

Moses asked other soldiers if they'd seen Pentu, but the responses were all the same. They'd not seen him since the sandstorm.

"Where would he go?" Moses said, mostly to himself. He couldn't imagine Pentu going far during such a fierce storm. It was nearly impossible. "We must look among the bodies of our enemies," Moses said.

Caleb followed after him, not saying a word.

The Libyans had left their dead strewn about the desert ground. Many of them were partially buried by the shifting sand. Moses's stomach churned at the sight of so many corpses lying motionless from the last pains they'd suffered. The desert ants and flies had already discovered the bodies.

Some of them were lying facedown, and it would be impossible to identify them if it weren't for the distinction of their robes of antelope hide and the feathers decorating their headbands. Pentu had been wearing the royal white kilt, and his head was shaved, which would set him apart from the Libyans, and he'd been wearing gold armbands—which might be missing by now if he was killed by a tribesman.

Caleb used his tunic to cover his mouth and nose against the stench of death, and Moses found himself covering his nose as well with his hand. There was some movement among a few of the men who were not quite dead, but they were too far gone to have a healer help them. The battle wounds had been cruel.

And then Moses saw a man with a white kilt. "There," he said to Caleb, pointing. Moses hurried over to the man, but as he approached, his heart sank. It was Pentu all right, but he wasn't moving.

Moses scanned for any signs of a fatal injury but couldn't see anything. He knelt by Pentu and turned him over. Pentu groaned, and relief flooded through Moses. He was alive, at least for now.

"Can you hear me, Pentu?" he asked, and the man groaned again. "We're going to get you to a healer." He examined Pentu's body briefly; nothing seemed to be broken. Moses wasn't sure what was wrong with him.

"Help me carry him to the camp," Moses told Caleb.

They heaved Pentu up off the ground and began to carry him, side-stepping around the deceased. When Pentu moaned, Moses talked to him, telling him again that they were getting him help.

It was nearly dark by the time they reached the makeshift camp. Moses quickly ordered men to make a place for Pentu to rest, and Caleb set off over the ridge to see if a healer had arrived on the other side yet.

While Moses waited, he knew Egypt had been spared tonight. But tomorrow, when the sun rose in the bright blue sky, only reinforcements would save them.

CHAPTER TWENTY-TWO

MIRIAM

THE JOURNEY TO THE PALACE was slower than Miriam wanted it to be. Aaron stopped multiple times to help people, and Miriam found herself helping as well. They dug out front doors and rounded up straying goats. They even helped one little girl rescue her pet lamb, which had become stuck beneath a partially crumbled wall.

By the time the palace walls came into view, it was nearly dark. "No," she whispered when she saw the smoke coming from the palace, pluming against the sunset.

"Miriam," Aaron said, putting his hand on her arm, "perhaps you should wait here for me and hide along the walls. Even though Hebrew men have been fighting for Egypt, you are still a single Hebrew woman walking into a dangerous situation."

"I have to know where Caleb is," Miriam said. "No matter the outcome." Aaron's gaze searched hers, and she met it with confidence. "I'm coming, Aaron."

He gave a small nod. "All right, but stay with me. We might need to say you're my wife." He ran his hands through his dusty hair. "If we come across any Libyans, you need to leave me, run away, and not look back. No matter what you might hear."

Miriam's throat tightened, and she could only nod in response. She didn't want to think about what might happen if they found the Libyan tribesmen had invaded the palace—not only what might happen to her and her brother and what a Libyan takeover might mean for Caleb and Moses but also what might happen to all of Egypt.

She followed Aaron into the wild brush that led to one of the outer courtyards. The closer they walked, the stronger the smell of smoke was until Miriam could taste it in her throat. Her heart sank when she saw a slain man lying next to one of the courtyard walls.

"Aaron," she whispered, grabbing his arm and pointing.

Aaron stilled, looking at the man. "It's a Libyan warrior."

"Who do you think killed him?" Miriam asked.

Aaron shook his head. "It's hard to know, and it's hard to know whether this is a good thing or a bad thing. Does a dead Libyan mean they were defeated? Or is he just one casualty on their side, and we have hundreds of casualties on ours?" He looked over at Miriam. "Do you want to return home?" he asked. "It would be safer."

"No," she said. "I just hadn't expected to see death so soon."

Aaron's lips tightened. "You will see a lot of death if you continue."

Miriam let go of her brother's arm and walked over to the fallen man. His head was twisted at an odd angle, and blood stained his robe. There was no weapon in sight—whoever had killed him must have confiscated it. She knelt before the dead body and bowed her head. "May the Lord preserve your soul."

Aaron touched her shoulder. "We must go. We are too much in the open here."

She rose from her knees, sorrowed at the death before her. This one man's still body was only a small part of the suffering Miriam expected to see. She followed Aaron to the road that led around the palace, and they created their own parallel path to the road, cutting through bushes, skirting around palms, and pausing often to watch and listen.

From their vantage point, Miriam hadn't seen any activity or heard any voices. Except for the fallen Libyan, there had been nothing. The silence made Miriam more uncomfortable than screams or shouts would have.

"Why can we not hear anything?" Miriam asked.

"I don't know," Aaron said in a hushed tone. They reached the outer wall that surrounded the palace. There were several entrances, ones usually manned by guards. Today, there were no royal guards to stop a Hebrew slave from entering.

They moved slowly and quietly, keeping their eyes open, their senses alert. Darkness was quickly descending, and the half moon was glowing now. As they passed through the entrance and crossed the courtyard that led to the palace, Miriam noticed a barricade and several men sitting behind it. The men weren't Libyans; they were Egyptians and Hebrews.

She motioned for Aaron to look. "Is Caleb among them?" she whispered. Seeing the armed men prepared for battle sent a shiver along her back.

Aaron studied the men, then shook his head. "I don't see Caleb, but it looks like they've defeated any Libyans who have reached the palace."

Just then, a man came out of the palace and rushed toward them. Miriam tensed, and Aaron stepped ahead of her. "Mered," he said as the man grew closer.

Relieved, Miriam moved from behind Aaron to greet the man, but he spoke before she had a chance to.

"Are you here to join the soldiers?" Mered asked, looking between the two of them. "We need all the help we can get until Pharaoh's reinforcements arrive."

"What's happened at the palace?" Miriam asked. "What about the smoke?"

"A group of Libyans broke our defenses and reached the palace. The people hiding here had barricaded themselves in the courtroom. They set the fire themselves."

Miriam brought a hand to her mouth. "How awful."

"Moses and his men arrived in time to get them out and defeat the Libyan group," Mered said. "Caleb is at the western border fighting with the other Hebrews the Egyptians recruited."

Miriam tried to comprehend it all.

"Has there been any news about Caleb or the battle from the border?" Aaron asked.

A shout went up among the men at the barricade, and they stood and called out to someone Miriam couldn't see.

"Hurry inside," Mered said. "It sounds like soldiers are coming."

Miriam followed Mered, with her brother following after her. They entered the dark corridor, absent of torchlight.

Mered started to lead them deep inside, but Aaron said, "Wait. It sounds like the soldiers are Egyptian, not Libyan."

Mered stopped and turned, then he crept outside. Miriam's fear thundered in her ears as she waited in the dark corridor with her brother for Mered to return. When he arrived, Miriam exhaled in relief.

"You were right," Mered said. "The soldiers were sent back by Moses to fetch food and drink and to bring back healers for the injured."

"I can help," Miriam said immediately.

"I will go," Aaron said. "You stay here and help at the palace, Miriam. Or return home and comfort our parents. The battlefield is no place for a woman."

But Miriam didn't want to return home and hide in her hut, not knowing whether Caleb was safe. "I can clean and bandage wounds."

Mered shook his head as well. "Your brother is right. There's no place for a woman in this type of battle. Pray for the return of Pharaoh and his soldiers, and do as your brother asks: go be with your family. There is no reason to put your life at risk."

"I have to see Caleb," Miriam said, turning to Aaron. "If something happens to him, what happens to me won't matter."

"No, Miriam," Aaron said. "I'll go, and I'll find Caleb and make sure he has what he needs. I'll fight by his side against the Libyans if necessary."

Miriam stared at her brother, both of them knowing there was a lot more at stake than just Caleb and the land of Egypt. They also had to worry about their parents and Aaron's wife and unborn child, and their younger brother, Moses, was also in harm's way.

"Either I have your blessing or I don't," Miriam said. "I am going to help our men. There is nothing for me to do here."

Aaron exhaled and rubbed his face. "I don't know how you even made it this far in life. You are always taking risks without thought to your own life or the consequences to your family."

"That's all I think about," she retorted. "And if I don't do anything but stay behind and wait for news, I'll find another way to get into trouble."

"If you're willing to say good-bye to all you know—"

"I am," Miriam said, her eyes pricking with tears. Caleb had become more important to her than anything.

Aaron walked out of the palace, not saying another word, which Miriam decided signified his permission, however grudgingly he'd given it.

Miriam went outside, Mered next to her, and they all hurried to the barricade. The men who had come to make requests explained that they'd gone with Moses to find out how close the Libyans were, but they'd come across a small band of Hebrews.

Miriam crossed to one of the Hebrew soldiers. "Was Caleb among them?"

The soldier nodded. "He was, and he was unharmed."

Miriam wanted to sink to her knees and thank the Lord for preserving Caleb. "Is he staying out there, then? Are all the men remaining?"

"The Libyans retreated due to the sandstorm," the soldier said. "Many were killed, but they've camped within sight and will probably strike tomorrow."

Miriam let that news settle. "I will come and bind up wounds and help wherever I'm needed."

The soldier frowned, but Miriam turned from him and spoke to Mered. "Can I bring any cloth that's available so I might make bandages?"

"I will go too," a woman's voice cut in.

Miriam looked over at the newcomer in surprise. A woman wearing a dark cloak and holding an oil lamp stepped forward. She wore a Nubian wig and a fine linen tunic beneath the cloak. Miriam recognized her—Bithiah, adoptive mother of Moses.

Miriam started to prostrate herself, but Bithiah said, "We are all working together tonight. There is no need for us to stay with tradition." Her dark eyes studied Miriam as she spoke to Mered. "Is it my understanding that this Hebrew slave woman wants to help on the front lines of the battle?"

"Yes," Mered said. "And her brother, Aaron. They've just arrived to see what they can do to serve Egypt."

Bithiah's smile was faint. "Impressive." She motioned to Miriam and spoke in broken Hebrew. "Come with me. We'll collect healing herbs and cloth for bandages. Then we'll ride out to help the men."

Miriam's mouth almost dropped open. She didn't know if Bithiah remembered her as a small girl, but it wouldn't be wise to bring it up. She followed the princess into the palace. Bithiah led the way with her oil lamp, saying nothing as she traversed the expansive corridors. Finally she arrived at a door and pushed it open.

Inside, the room was filled with looms and wheels meant for constructing cloth. "Gather as much as you can carry," Bithiah instructed, pointing to a stack of cloth on top of a low table.

Miriam crossed the room and picked through the cloth. It was much finer than anything her loom could create. The silk and wool and linen felt luxurious in Miriam's fingers. It would be a shame to create bandages out of such fine cloth. "This is beautiful," Miriam marveled.

"We must make haste while we have the moon's light to accompany us," Bithiah said.

Miriam nodded and sorted the linen from the other fabrics. She rolled it into a large bundle, then crossed back to Bithiah.

The princess nodded her satisfaction and led Miriam into the dark corridor. They walked until they reached the cooking room. Torches lit it, and several palace servants worked inside. They bowed to Bithiah as she entered and explained they were gathering food to be taken to the battlefront.

Miriam had never seen such an expansive room, and she couldn't stop staring at the baskets of grains, legumes, fruits, and jugs lining the shelves. Bithiah opened a door set in one of the walls and ducked inside.

Miriam followed and immediately wrinkled her nose at the dank smell inside. The room was packed in earth. As her eyes adjusted to the deep darkness, Miriam saw the herbs hanging from the ceiling in varying stages of drying.

Bithiah set her oil lamp on one of the shelves and grabbed a basket, then started filling it with roots, herbs, and plants. When the basket was full, she set a poultice bowl on top. Then she balanced the basket on her hip and picked up the oil lamp again. She gave a short nod, and Miriam knew Bithiah was ready to leave.

Miriam led the way out, crossed the cooking room, and returned to the corridor they'd come from.

When they exited the palace, Bithiah went to the stables. Both men and women were there loading baskets and bundles of supplies onto chariots. Miriam added her rolled linen to the pile, and Bithiah handed over her basket of herbs to be secured.

Aaron and Mered were nowhere in sight, but Miriam didn't have time to worry about where they were or what they were doing.

Bithiah turned to Miriam. "Have you ridden in a chariot before?"

"No," Miriam said, but the opportunity thrilled her.

Bithiah offered one of her rare smiles. "You can ride with me." She turned to one of the servant girls and commanded her to fetch a cloak. The girl took off running, and Bithiah turned again to Miriam. "Come this way."

Bithiah climbed into a chariot, then indicated for Miriam to join her. Miriam climbed in and looked around for a place to brace herself before the chariot started moving.

"Hold on to the front, and you will be safe," Bithiah said. She asked for one of the other servants to bring over a satchel of supplies and a couple goatskins of water. Then the young servant girl who had been sent to retrieve a cloak came running up to the horse. She handed the cloak up to Bithiah.

"For you," Bithiah said, giving the cloak to Miriam.

Miriam was astonished. "Thank you." She'd never held or worn something so fine before. She tugged it over her shoulders, reveling in the softness of the weave.

"Hold on," Bithiah said just before urging the horse forward.

Suddenly Miriam was riding in a chariot through the desert beneath the moonlit sky.

CHAPTER TWENTY-THREE

MIRIAM

WIND PUSHED THROUGH MIRIAM'S HAIR as she stood next to Bithiah in the chariot, riding across the dark desert. It was an exhilarating feeling, and now Miriam understood why the royal family owned so many chariots and used them for pleasure in addition to battles. Battle was one thing, but just riding created a freeing feeling Miriam had rarely experienced. It was almost as if she had no worries or troubles plaguing her. It was just Bithiah and her, the wind, and the chariot and horse.

She was impressed with Bithiah, who seemed to be an expert chariot driver. Or perhaps she was just doing what she had to do, what they all had to do at a time like this. If Miriam had been told when she woke up that morning that she'd be riding in a chariot to the battlefront, she would have said it was a fable. But the desert wind and the motion of the chariot was no fable. She wondered what she might experience tonight, what sights she might see, and how she would be able to help. She was grateful that Bithiah was beside her and that the others had accompanied them in this journey. Miriam wouldn't be the only woman after all, and that should make her brother happy.

She pushed back the seed of worry about Aaron. She hadn't seen him since she'd gone with Bithiah. The farther they traveled across the sand, the harder Miriam's heart pounded. What would it be like to see Caleb? He'd been fighting in a real battle, for the Egyptians, and now he seemed to be part of their army.

Bithiah slowed the chariot, and Miriam was pulled out of her thoughts. Up ahead, fires burned, and men were sitting around them. Some were cooking over the fires, and the pungent smell drifted in their direction.

"The scribe Mered said you were looking for someone," Bithiah said in broken Hebrew.

Miriam was surprised and impressed that the princess knew her language. "His name is Caleb, and I'm betrothed to him."

Bithiah looked over at Miriam. "The man who was freed after being accused as a thief?"

"Yes," Miriam said, the memory of her fear returning. "I'm grateful the real thief was caught." She didn't say anything about her role in apprehending Reuven.

"I was grateful when I heard too," Bithiah said. "My son, Moses, hated to see an innocent man pay for another man's crime."

Miriam swallowed against her parched throat. It was strange yet comforting to hear the princess speak of her brother. She had been a brave woman to adopt him during such a tumultuous time.

"Climb out first," Bithiah said. "Then I'll follow."

Miriam did so, landing ungracefully in the sand. She scrambled to her feet and held out her hand to Bithiah, since it seemed the most natural thing to do. Bithiah let Miriam help her down, and then they walked toward the cooking fires. "The others should be arriving soon with the supplies," Bithiah said. "We'll ask questions and assess where the greatest need is. We only have one satchel of supplies, but it will have to do until the others arrive."

Miriam pulled her cloak tightly about her as she walked with the princess. It wasn't cold, and the wind caused only a slight tug, but the cloak somehow made her feel more secure and protected. She'd never been in a military camp before, and she didn't know what to expect.

Half a dozen men surrounded the first fire they approached. Miriam was surprised to see Egyptians and Hebrews sitting side by side, staring into the flames. They looked exhausted and seemed mesmerized by the orange glow.

"Do you have any injured among you?" Bithiah asked.

The men looked up. A couple of them started to prostrate themselves, but Bithiah waved them off. "We're here to help. Food and drink is coming soon."

An Egyptian cleared his throat and said in a raspy voice, "We traveled here with Moses after the battle. Only thirty Hebrew soldiers are holding this side of the ridge. Nine perished, and there are only a few injuries among those who remain. We've heard there are many injured on the other side."

Miriam found she was able to understand most of what he was saying.

"Where are the injured Hebrews?" Bithiah asked. "We'll tend to those first, then go to the other side of the ridge."

Miriam wanted to ask about Caleb but decided to wait until they'd visited the other fire circles.

"The injured men are at that fire over there. We bound their wounds as best we could, and they are now resting," the Egyptian said.

Bithiah thanked him, and she and Miriam left, walking toward the fire the Egyptian had indicated. With each step, Miriam's fear intensified. Would she find Caleb among them? She scanned the faces of the men as she approached. None of them was Caleb. She exhaled, not realizing she'd been holding her breath. Bithiah walked to each man and asked him about his injuries. It seemed the princess was a natural healer. Miriam followed after her, and whatever Bithiah asked her to do, she did.

One of the Hebrews had a terrible gash on his leg. Miriam didn't recognize him but realized he probably knew Caleb. She was touched to see the princess helping Hebrews, men who were only slaves and whose lives the Egyptians rarely valued. Bithiah handed the goatskin of water to Miriam and asked her to clean a wound. Her stomach rolled at the sight of the torn flesh. She did her best to not let it affect her. The man moaned as she worked.

"It will be over soon," Bithiah soothed the man in passable Hebrew. She then took out a large plant leaf and broke it open, then squeezed the substance that leaked out onto the man's wound.

The man didn't move but kept his eyes closed as Bithiah took over the care. When she finished, she said to Miriam, "Use a strip of the cloth from inside the satchel and wrap his leg loosely."

Miriam nodded and grabbed the satchel, finding the rolled-up cloth inside. She ripped off a long piece and turned to the man. His eyes were open.

"We must bandage the wound," she said to him in Hebrew.

He nodded. "You are a saving angel."

"I'm not that at all," Miriam said. "I came to help though." Bithiah had moved on to another man and was speaking with him about his injuries, so Miriam was on her own to wrap this man's leg. She lifted it gently and winced as the man moaned. "I'll try to be gentle."

He only nodded; it seemed he was in too much pain to talk.

She wrapped the cloth about his leg and tried not to cause him any more pain. When she finished, she lowered his leg carefully.

"Thank you," the Hebrew said, his eyes open only a slit now. And then he let his head fall back as if he'd spent all of his strength enduring Miriam's ministrations.

"I need your help," Bithiah said, capturing Miriam's attention. The princess was on the other side of the fire now. The man Bithiah knelt by wasn't moving.

Miriam scrambled over to her. "What's wrong with him?"

"There are no visible injuries, so his must be internal," the princess said.

Miriam furrowed her brows and studied the man. She moved around him so she was near his head. She pressed her fingers gently against his scalp.

He flinched, and Miriam startled, lifting her hands. The man still didn't open his eyes. "He's unconscious, but that hurt him."

Bithiah let out a long breath. "I don't know if we can help him."

Miriam picked up the satchel and sorted through the few herbs they had inside. She removed a collection of them and held them beneath the man's nose. His eyes flew open, and Miriam jumped back.

"What's your name?" Bithiah rushed to ask him.

The man closed his eyes again and seemed to be asleep. But Miriam knew better. She held the herbs to his nose again. Once more, his eyes opened. This time Miriam was prepared. She patted his cheek and said, "Do you know where you are?"

The man blinked a couple times and moved his mouth. He seemed to have heard Miriam, but he wasn't looking at her.

"Where do you hurt?" Bithiah pressed, moving closer to the man's face so he could see her.

"Chest," he whispered so faintly that Miriam wasn't sure she'd heard right. She'd assumed it was his head by the way he'd reacted when she'd touched him there.

Bithiah placed her hands on his chest. "Here?"

"Yes," the man whispered.

"What happened?"

The man's eyes were fully open now, and his gaze cleared as if he was completely awake. "I'm leaving this earth," the man said slowly, as if each word pained him. "And my heart is broken because I'll never see my family again."

Miriam stared at him. This man was a slave, yet his heart broke not for the years of slavery he'd endured or the fierce battle he'd fought but for his family. Her eyes filled with tears.

Bithiah lifted her hand and settled back, staying quiet for a moment. Finally she said in a quiet voice, "He has given up."

Miriam could only nod.

"Miriam?" someone said behind her.

She turned and looked up. *Caleb.* She'd know his voice anywhere. He was walking toward her. She wiped the tears from her face and stood to greet him. He came into the fire circle, the light bouncing off his tanned skin. He looked healthy and uninjured. Miriam's heart hitched. Caleb was whole. He was all right. He was here.

She stepped toward him and wrapped her arms about his waist, pressing her face against his warm chest. His arms came around her tightly. He smelled of perspiration, sand, and hard work. *Battle*, Miriam realized. What had he endured this day? What more would he have to endure?

"What are you doing here?" Caleb asked. "This camp is no place for a woman—" He broke off, having seen Bithiah. "Your Highness."

"Do not prostrate yourself," Bithiah said. "We are on a battlefield and defend the same soil."

Miriam reluctantly raised her head and let Caleb go. He moved around her and knelt by the man they'd been treating. Caleb placed his fingers on the man's neck. "His breathing has slowed. I don't think we have much longer."

Miriam knelt beside Caleb. "Do you know him?"

"Not very well. His name is Ariel, and he worked alongside me many times," Caleb said. "This battle has made us brothers."

Miriam stared at the dying man, tears in her eyes. She was sure to see much suffering and death tonight, but this man had spoken to her not long ago. He was leaving a family behind. And he had fought with Caleb.

Caleb reached for Ariel's hand and held it as Ariel took his final breaths. Bowing his head, Caleb whispered the words of a prayer. "O Lord, receive his soul."

As Caleb prayed, Miriam added her own silent prayers for the man's soul and for the family he left behind. She wondered what Bithiah thought of their Hebrew traditions. But Bithiah remained quiet, her head lowered as well.

When Caleb finished, he blinked back the moisture in his eyes and reached for Miriam's hand. She took comfort in his warmth and strength, but she didn't feel settled at all. There was still a lot of suffering to deal with, and the Libyans could be attacking again in the morning.

"That was a beautiful prayer," Bithiah said.

Miriam looked over at her, surprised by Bithiah's words. She hadn't expected the princess to pay attention or to completely understand their Hebrew words. Bithiah rose to her feet and set a piece of cloth over Ariel's head. The other men surrounding the fire had been watching, and they remained silent with their heads bowed.

Bithiah moved to the next man and began to ask him questions in a quiet tone.

"There were no visible injuries," Miriam whispered to Caleb. "What do you think happened?"

"I think he was hit on the head too hard," Caleb said. He stood and pulled Miriam up to her feet. They remained close together, gazing down on Ariel's body. Scars ran up and down his legs and arms, and if Miriam had to guess, they were whip marks. This man had endured much in his short life.

"How are you?" Miriam asked, turning to look at Caleb. "Have you been injured?"

"Just some bruising," Caleb said. "Nothing to complain about." His dark eyes searched hers. "I really wish you hadn't come. I want to think of you back in the village with your parents and brother, where you'll be safe."

"There is no safety anywhere, so I want to be with you," Miriam said. "The princess came with me. And Aaron is coming out with other soldiers."

Caleb pulled her into his arms and embraced her tightly. "You are a remarkable woman, Miri. You amaze me."

She practically melted against him. "We have to get out of this alive and whole," she whispered. She was beginning to realize Ariel was right. The small challenges in life, even in slavery, weren't as important as having family with her.

Caleb drew away and ran his finger along her cheek. "I'll help you while I can."

"You should be resting," Miriam said. "We don't know what tomorrow might—" She stopped to avoid the tremble in her voice. She took a deep breath and grasped his hand so he'd enclose hers. "We must pray that Pharaoh is on his way with more soldiers."

Caleb nodded but remained quiet.

Miriam looked over at Bithiah and saw that she was applying a poultice to a Hebrew's shoulder. She crossed to her and helped support the man as he groaned with pain. Caleb followed and offered the man water.

When they finished binding the man's shoulder, Bithiah stood and said to Caleb, "Do you know where Moses is?"

"He's on the other side of the ridge. He came through here at sunset."

Bithiah nodded. "He is well, then, and made it through the sandstorm?"

"The battle was over when he reached us," Caleb said. "He was seeking out Pentu, the commander."

Bithiah looked toward the ridge, its form dark against the sky. Miriam followed her gaze, wondering what they'd encounter there. There were only a couple dozen men on this side, but there had to be hundreds on the other side.

"I will take you to him," Caleb said.

"I am most grateful for your offer," Bithiah said, "but I only need to know he's all right. I have my own work to do among the injured."

Miriam's attention shifted to the sound of approaching chariots and horses. She turned in the direction of the palace and saw several chariots heading toward the camp.

"The supplies are here," Miriam said, hoping to see Aaron among those traveling. Caleb joined Miriam and Bithiah as they walked over to greet the new arrivals.

Relief flooded through Miriam at the sight of Aaron and Mered. Those who'd come with them climbed out of the chariots. The new arrivals bowed to the princess, then Aaron crossed to Caleb, and they started talking in hushed tones.

"We've attended to the injured in this camp," Bithiah said to the new arrivals. "We need to hand out some food, but then we will go over the ridge where the rest of the army is camping."

Aaron nodded and helped unload some of the baskets of food. Miriam took one of the baskets from him and set out toward the first fire. She passed out the flatbread, figs, and fresh dates to the grateful men, and when her basket was empty, she walked back to the horses in the cooling sand, steeling herself for their next destination.

CHAPTER TWENTY-FOUR

Moses

Moses kept vigil by Pentu, trying to get him to drink a little at a time. Pentu had spoken a few words but had been sleeping a lot. His breathing was shallow and erratic, and that worried Moses. He prayed to the god Horus more than once, but there was no improvement on Pentu's part.

Moses looked up at the bright stars against the black sky. Was heaven listening tonight? With all the prayers from the Egyptians, and most likely the Hebrews to their own god, would they receive their miracle? Were the Libyans praying too?

Moses looked toward the ridge and hoped Caleb would return soon with a healer. Everything seemed to move so agonizingly slow. So much was unknown. Would a healer be able to help Pentu? Or was it too late for his friend?

Moses studied the man in the light of the moon. Pentu groaned from time to time, and his skin was cool to the touch. Too cool?

Moses snapped his head up and scanned the ridge again. He sensed something had changed before he saw it. Sure enough, someone was coming—several chariots and men. He rose to his feet and started toward them. Others in the camp had seen them too, and a few of them met Moses at the base of the ridge.

When Moses saw his mother in one of the chariots, he hurried forward and helped her down. "You've come," he said. He was both elated to see her and worried that the Libyans might strike again. He didn't know if he would be able to protect her.

"Bring us to Pentu," Bithiah said. "I've brought others to help. And we've brought food."

Moses led his mother and the Hebrew woman with her, who his mother introduced as Miriam, to where Pentu was resting. Moses recognized the woman, but it took him a few minutes to realize she was the same woman who'd begged for Caleb's life. She didn't speak to Moses but cast a few quick glances his way. He was impressed that she'd come with his mother to help the soldiers.

Bithiah knelt by Pentu and touched his face. "Pentu, can you hear me?"

When Pentu didn't respond, Moses knelt on his other side. "He's said a few words but has mostly slept."

Bithiah moved her hand to his chest. "His breathing is very shallow."

Miriam handed over some sort of herb to his mother, and Bithiah placed it under Pentu's nose. He startled and opened his eyes.

"Pentu?" Moses immediately said.

Pentu's eyes closed but then opened again, and his gaze slid toward Moses.

"Drink this," Moses said, putting the goatskin to his lips.

Pentu drank, and relief flooded through Moses. It was the most he had done since Moses had found him.

He looked over at his mother. "Thank you." And then to the Hebrew woman, "Thank you."

Miriam finally spoke. "We have only made him alert, but we still need to assess his injuries."

As Bithiah prodded his limbs, Pentu's eyes remained open, which Moses took as a good sign, although his breathing was still too shallow.

"There may be internal injuries," Bithiah said, her tone somber. "Ones that will require a lot of rest. We'll burn a bit of incense to keep him alert for a while longer so we can get him to drink some broth and hopefully build his strength."

The Hebrew woman placed a plant on a clay dish and lit it on fire. It flamed quickly, then smoldered. She placed it on the ground near Pentu's head. Bithiah helped Pentu eat while Moses held up his head.

After Pentu had eaten several small bites and closed his eyes again, Moses asked his mother, "What are his chances?"

She exhaled. "He looks better than the man we treated on the other side of the ridge."

Moses let that information sink in, and then he reached across Pentu to grasp his mother's hand. "Thank you for this." He looked over at Miriam. "Thank you for coming with my mother."

The Hebrew woman nodded and blinked rapidly as if she was trying to hold back emotion. He'd sensed her gaze on him multiple times.

"Look," Bithiah said, pointing at the ridge.

Moses looked up. Dozens of chariots surrounded by hundreds of soldiers had appeared on the top of the ridge.

Next to him, his mother gasped. "We're saved!" A cry went up around the camp.

"Ramses," Moses said, climbing to his feet. It was an incredible sight. The soldiers continued to pour over the ridge, and Moses scanned the men, searching for the prince. Moses chuckled. In all the hours since the battle had begun, he finally felt at ease. Even if the Libyans were to come at them full force at sunrise, the Egyptians would easily be able to set them down.

"Moses!" Ramses's familiar voice sounded above the commotion.

The soldiers separated so Moses could make his way through the crowd.

Ramses climbed out of his chariot and embraced Moses. "You're alive, thank the gods and goddesses. Where is Pentu?"

"He's resting," Moses said. "He's been injured, and we've given him food and water. Now he sleeps."

Ramses's expression was somber. "We will avenge Pentu and all others who have suffered this day at the hands of the Libyans."

"Is Pharaoh safe?" Moses asked.

Ramses nodded. "He remains in Pithom. He wanted me to stay back as well, to protect the throne, but I couldn't bear the thought of you and Pentu out here without me, having all the enjoyment of fighting Libyans."

Moses laughed and clapped Ramses on the back. "We saved a few for you to battle with tomorrow."

Ramses grinned. "Thanks for your generosity." He assessed the camp and all the death that lay beyond. "We need to bury those bodies. They'll attract the jackals and hyenas."

"The soldiers were already doing that when you arrived," Moses said.

Ramses only seemed to half hear him; he was looking past Moses. "Who is that?" Ramses asked.

Moses turned to see Miriam. "She belongs to Caleb, the Hebrew who was freed after being accused of stealing from the treasury."

"Wife?" Ramses asked.

"No," Moses said. "They are betrothed." He watched Ramses study Miriam, and for some reason, it bothered Moses. Ramses had his run of the royal harem, and he would be married soon, but this woman, who was so obviously devoted to the man she was about to marry, didn't deserve to be a plaything of Ramses.

Ramses crossed to Bithiah and asked her some questions about the injured, but Moses noticed he kept looking over at the Hebrew woman.

Moses found Caleb in a group of soldiers. The man didn't seem to notice Ramses's attention to his betrothed. That might be good or bad. There had been more than one death of a Hebrew husband when an Egyptian royal was interested in the wife. The Hebrews were always on the losing side of that battle.

But now they were fighting together for a single cause, and Moses didn't want to see Miriam harmed in any way. He walked over to where his mother was still speaking to Ramses.

"I'll take you to see Pentu now," Moses offered Ramses. The two of them crossed to their friend. He was still and quiet, sleeping, and Moses hoped it was a healing sleep. Ramses knelt by Pentu and looked at him for a long time. Then he shook his head. "Those Libyans will pay dearly."

Moses nodded, glad Ramses's focus was back on the war.

"Will you retain the Hebrew volunteer soldiers?" Moses asked, treading carefully.

Ramses scoffed. "*Volunteer* soldiers? Is that what you call them? They're hardly soldiers, and they hardly had a choice."

"They've made a lot of choices since they've been fighting for Egyptian soil," Moses said, then realized it was probably the wrong thing to say.

Ramses snapped his head up and looked at Moses. "What kind of choices? Whether to fight and live or abandon and die?"

Moses felt his face heat up. "They could have fled. They could have joined the Libyans."

Ramses narrowed his eyes. "What's going on? You want that Hebrew woman for yourself? She does look familiar; have I seen you with her before?"

"No," Moses said. "She's too old for me."

"Age isn't always important," Ramses said with a laugh.

Moses didn't know how the conversation got to this, but he had to change it. "All I meant was when I asked Caleb to hold back with thirty of his men on the other side of the ridge, they did an admirable job of slowing the Libyans. He lost ten men, but they stopped the major break that would have happened if the Hebrews hadn't been willing."

"That was more likely due to your excellent command, Moses," Ramses said. "Which, I must say, was well executed, although I'm not too happy about all of this Hebrew loving you seem to be doing lately." The prince rose to his feet and brushed off his kilt.

Moses rose as well, taking another look at Pentu.

"Let's get some sleep," Ramses said. "We might have a battle in a few hours."

The soldiers who'd come with Ramses were already organizing into camps and settling down for the night. Moses followed Ramses, keeping his eye out for Miriam. He finally spotted her next to Bithiah as they talked to another injured man.

Moses waited until Ramses was speaking with a soldier before he slipped away and joined his mother, who was giving a drink to a man who could barely lift his head. Miriam was applying an ointment to his injured hand.

"Mother, may I speak with you when you are finished?" Moses said.

Bithiah glanced up at him. "In private?"

He nodded, and Bithiah drew her brows together, but she didn't say anything else as she finished helping the soldier. Then she stood and followed him a few paces away. Moses kept his voice low. "Ramses has his eyes on the Hebrew woman helping you."

"Miriam?" Bithiah asked.

"Yes," Moses said. "He noticed her right away, and I know she's betrothed to one of the Hebrews—Caleb."

"They have a close relationship," Bithiah mused. "She is devoted to him, and it seems she will do anything to make sure his life is preserved."

Thinking of how she'd begged him to speak for Caleb when he'd been put on trial, Moses couldn't agree more. "She . . . she doesn't deserve to be assaulted. Or worse."

Bithiah nodded, but there was curiosity in her gaze. "Are you fond of her?"

"No," Moses said. He certainly recognized her beauty and strength, but it was only appreciation, not attraction. "Caleb has been a good soldier. He's sacrificed a lot already, and something happening to her would be tragic for him."

A smile lifted Bithiah's mouth, and she placed a hand on his arm. "You are a good man, Moses, and a good son. I don't know what I'd do without you." She stepped closer to him and whispered, "I'll watch over Miriam, but you had best not voice your concerns to anyone about her safety. It wouldn't be safe for you to be seen favoring the Hebrews."

Moses knew she was right, but it was already too late for him to erase what he'd said to Ramses about the Hebrew soldiers deserving some respect. "Will you tell . . . Miriam?"

His mother straightened and looked behind her. When she faced Moses again, she said, "I will. I think she needs to know, and that way she can be more careful. If she inadvertently gives any encouraging signals to Ramses, there will be no chance for her."

Moses thought about his mother's reasoning. She was right, but he also didn't want Miriam to act like a fearful kitten around the prince. That might draw his attention even more. "Tell her to avoid his presence if possible."

He looked past his mother to where Miriam had moved on to another injured man. She was bandaging his upper arm. He hoped his mother's warning would be enough.

"There's movement in the valley," someone shouted, and the words rippled through the various camps.

Moses hurried to his chariot and climbed in, then he picked up his bow. Several others were heading toward chariots, including Ramses.

"I need three scouts to ride ahead and see what's going on," Ramses said.

The men quickly assembled themselves, waiting for more instructions from their prince.

"Ten will ride with me behind the scouters."

Moses didn't have to be asked twice. "I'll come with you."

Ramses gave a curt nod. "Aiyah!" he shouted, and his horse leapt forward, pulling the chariot toward the valley.

Moses urged his horse into a gallop, keeping up with Ramses, whose royal cape billowed behind him.

They kept their eyes on the scouts riding ahead of them. Ramses stopped his ten chariots short of a few scrubby bushes and let the scouts ride ahead. When they returned, the lead soldier said, "They are moving their dead. No battle preparations that we can see. No advancing army."

Ramses gave a curt nod. "We will return to camp, then." He wheeled his chariot back around.

Moses turned his chariot around and matched Ramses's pace. It was a relief that the soldiers might be able to secure some rest before the morning.

Ramses looked over at Moses on the ride back to camp. "I'm looking forward to tomorrow," he called out with a grin.

Moses couldn't quite match the prince's enthusiasm.

CHAPTER TWENTY-FIVE

Miriam

Miriam could barely keep her eyes open as she and Bithiah worked. They'd been at it half the night, treating the injured as best as they could. Other healers had arrived, but there was still much work to be done.

When Aaron had joined the other soldiers, Miriam had been nervous for him, though she was grateful to see Caleb with him. But it had sent shivers down her back as the Hebrews had worked on battle moves, enacting fighting with Egyptian spears and swords. Each time she'd been drawn in to watch, she'd eventually turned away.

The injuries she was treating had been caused by that sort of brutality. The work was overwhelming, and that was only after one battle cut short by a sandstorm.

"We can take a break now," Bithiah said next to her. They had been cleaning a man's arm that looked as if it could not be saved. Bithiah insisted that they clean it regardless and apply a healing ointment.

"Where will we sleep?" Miriam asked, looking about them. Areas had been organized into sleeping sections, the Hebrews separated from the Egyptians. From her vantage point, she couldn't see where Aaron or Caleb were, though she didn't know if she should find Aaron and sleep in the middle of a group of men.

"We'll find our own place," Bithiah said.

Relief shot through Miriam. She hadn't thought of all the complications that coming to help with the injured might entail. As far as she could see in the moonlight, the men were sleeping on the ground, most of them surrounding the dying fires kept burning low to ward off snakes and scorpions. The smoke rose against the dark sky, dissipating to nearly nothing in the darkness.

"Come," Bithiah said in a soft, tired voice.

Miriam's exhaustion was great as well, and she suspected the princess was nearly beyond her endurance. She'd experienced more than Miriam, with the Libyan raid on the palace. Besides, Miriam was used to hard labor, and the princess wasn't. And Miriam felt they had gone beyond even a normal slave's duties.

Miriam followed Bithiah as she wound her way through the various camps. She stopped near the base of the ridge. Not far from the place Bithiah had chosen was what appeared to be the royal camp. Three chariots were lined up next to each other, and thick rugs had been laid out on the ground. Miriam couldn't see the men who were sleeping on them, but she assumed one was Ramses and another perhaps Moses.

Bithiah surprised Miriam by lying on the ground with nothing but her cloak between her and the sand. Miriam had never thought an Egyptian princess would sleep in such conditions. Miriam lay a couple paces away from her, not wanting to be too far away yet not feeling like she could get too close either.

"Sleep well," Bithiah said.

Miriam's heart tugged at the kind words from this woman who was impressing Miriam more and more. "You too," she said, and then she closed her eyes.

She expected sleep to claim her within moments, but with her eyes closed, the sounds of the camp and the desert grew more distinct. The wind was gentle now, like a swaying reed on the River Nile. Male voices rose and fell, quiet for the most part, but audible enough to cut into the silence. Someone laughed in the distance. Another cursed. Someone coughed. The distant barking of a hyena made her shudder.

"Miriam?" Bithiah's voice again. "I must give you a word of warning. Please don't attract the attention of the royal men, especially Ramses."

"Why?" Miriam asked, even though she was afraid she wouldn't like the answer. Aaron had been worried about her coming, had been set against it. He'd said she'd be the only woman in a camp full of soldiers. But since Bithiah had accompanied her, Miriam hadn't worried.

"Just be wise," was Bithiah's reply, and then she was quiet again.

It was a long time before Miriam closed her eyes. The sounds of the night returned, and it was as if the slumbering men were mimicking the sighs of the desert as the wind pushed through the sand and the beetles settled into their night song.

Miriam turned onto her side, using her lower arm to cushion her head. She decided that if she was tired enough, she'd fall asleep eventually. But for now, she'd completely rest her body and keep her eyes closed so she could continue her work in the daylight.

She found herself praying, unconventional as it was, lying in the sand surrounded by an army of men. Just as she was almost asleep, she heard what sounded like a cry of pain from somewhere within the camp.

Bithiah's quiet voice came. "I'll go find out what I can do," she said. "You stay here and rest."

Miriam turned over and sat up, about to protest, but Bithiah had already risen and was on her way across the camp.

Miriam pulled her knees up to her chest and hugged them against her. She felt very alone. She thought about her parents and Salome and hoped they were well and safe, and she hoped that wherever Caleb and Aaron were, they were getting the rest they needed. She yawned, wishing it would lead to sleep, but with Bithiah gone, her mind was alert again.

"Can't you sleep?" a man's voice said from somewhere behind her.

Without turning around, Miriam knew it was an Egyptian soldier. His Hebrew was broken, but she understood it enough. Instinctively she pulled her cloak tightly about her, then looked over her shoulder.

"Are you injured?" she asked, speaking slowly. She couldn't see the man's face because he stood above her on the ridge, but she hoped that if she didn't stand to speak to him, he would leave her well alone. Unless he needed her help. She didn't know how much she could do since Bithiah had taken the satchel with her.

"I'm not injured, but thank you for your kindness," the man said, his voice deep and caressing.

She stiffened at his tone. He was paying her more attention than she wanted. It was the middle of the night, and if she shouted, those in the royal camp would hear her. She didn't want to wake the prince or his men unless necessary.

She nodded and turned forward again, squeezing her eyes shut. She hoped he would go away. Walk back along that ridge. Return to wherever he'd come from.

Bithiah, where are you?

But the man didn't leave. She heard his footsteps as he came down the slope, each step growing closer than the last.

Please leave. Turn around. Go away.

His hand brushed her shoulder as he came around her.

Miriam's eyes flew open.

"Are you cold?" he asked.

Her body had never been so cold. With nervousness.

She looked up into the Egyptian's eyes. Recognition dawned. "Your Highness." She moved to her knees and then prostrated herself.

He said nothing as she finished her prostration. He continued studying her as she rose to her knees, then her feet. She couldn't very well sit on the ground in front of the prince of Egypt. This was a man whose very order could put someone to death. His father's orders had put hundreds of Hebrews to death. His grandfather's command had put thousands of male infants to death.

She didn't know where to look, what to say, or if she could say anything. What did the prince want? She hoped he was looking for Bithiah. She was his aunt, after all. "Bithiah is helping another man," Miriam said, not sure if she should speak without being questioned first.

But he continued to stand there and watch her. Then he stepped closer, and she felt the heat of his breath on her forehead. He was taller than she but not as tall as Caleb. Still, Prince Ramses was a more powerful man, from his muscled shoulders and lean torso to the way he carried himself and commanded others like they were tiny insects under his feet.

Miriam didn't move, and she didn't dare speak any more. At least not unless he asked her a question first. She kept her eyes down.

"I'm not looking for Princess Bithiah," he said, his voice low and quiet.

Warning knotted in her stomach. Perhaps it was his closeness, perhaps the heat of his breath against her skin, or the fact that she was standing alone before the prince of Egypt.

"You are cold," he stated.

Before she knew it, he'd wrapped something about her shoulders. The weight and dry scent of it told her it was an animal fur. His own. She looked up at him and regretted it immediately.

His lips were turned up, and his eyes were intent on hers.

She'd seen that look on an Egyptian before, from the men who prowled the roads and watched the Hebrew women walking home from their labors. Not all of those women made it back home.

Miriam moved to take a step back and put some distance between them, anything between them, but his hand lifted and cupped her chin. She was locked into place and had nowhere to look but into his face.

Her feet wouldn't move, and her mind tumbled, her confused thoughts knocking against each other.

He gazed at her until she wanted to scream. What did he see? Her dark eyes? Her Hebrew face?

"Are you married?"

"No," she said, but it came out as a whisper. "I am betrothed." She hated that she'd told him. Egyptians had killed Hebrew husbands who'd protested the use of their wives. Egyptians had killed Hebrew fathers who'd protested the capturing of their daughters for the royal harem.

What did the prince intend? Why was he here offering her his fur coat, touching her face?

His smile widened; his brows lifted. "Then you are a virgin."

Miriam opened her mouth to answer, but his fingers brushed against her lips slowly, stopping any words.

She wanted to collapse. She wanted his hands off her face.

"You are untouched." His breath was warm against her skin. "You are unspoiled. Beautiful and unspoiled. This is an unexpected surprise out here on the desert battlefield."

Miriam couldn't bear the way he was looking at her any longer. He lowered his head and chuckled. And that was when she knew. He was playing with her. He was the predator . . . and she was his prey.

"I'd like to see you in my harem," he said, his hand dropping to her shoulder. His touch was no longer gentle but firm upon her shoulder. His hand then slipped down her arm, and he grasped her hand and turned it over. Then he brought her hand to his mouth and pressed his lips against her palm.

Not the harem. Anything else.

Caleb. Aaron. Where are you? Wake up. Bithiah!

Maybe the prince of Egypt hadn't asked her to join his harem. Maybe she was dreaming and would wake up with the rising sun. Maybe this wasn't truly happening.

"*Please, Lord.*"

"Lord?" Ramses said with a scoff, still holding her hand close to his mouth. "Who's that?"

She'd spoken aloud without realizing it. "Do you not already have a harem full of women?" she asked, her voice trembling.

One side of his mouth turned up as he appraised her. "I do." He wrapped his arm around her shoulders and pulled her close against him. His whisper was hot against her ear. "You will be cherished by me. You'll have fine clothing and spend your days in luxury. The servants will bathe the desert from your skin, and they will oil your hair. I will come visit you, and then I'll take you someplace you've never been."

Tears stung her eyes, and she blinked them back rapidly.

His hand slid down her arm again slowly, as if he was memorizing every curve of her skin. She wanted to move away so he couldn't touch her, but she was unsure of what he'd do, and she feared what the consequences might be of rejecting the prince of Egypt.

Her breathing came fast, and he seemed not to care that she wasn't speaking, that tears were dripping down her cheeks.

"Yes," he whispered, his voice low and full of meaning. "Your life will change for the better. You will love being taken care of."

His mouth was closer now and his whispers soft. Miriam could only think of one thing: getting away, running as far as she could, hiding someplace, anyplace.

"Ramses," a woman's voice called out.

At first Miriam thought she might be imagining the other voice, but then the prince released her and stepped away.

"Bithiah?" he said, his tone sounding strained and annoyed about being interrupted.

Miriam gulped for air and tried to breathe normally. Bithiah walked toward them, but instead of waiting for her to join them, Ramses crossed to her. They started speaking in low voices, turning away from Miriam.

She wiped the tears from her cheeks, wondering if Bithiah had seen what had been happening and wondering if the princess could help her. Miriam's heart pounded as she watched the two talking.

She knew she couldn't face Ramses again. She couldn't look at him or let him touch her. She couldn't go into his harem. If she did, she'd never see her family again. There were horrible stories about the Hebrew girls who were taken, used, then turned out. They became beggars, ostracized by all. No one wanted a harlot in their village. Most of the harem girls took their lives after being cast out.

Miriam took a step back, then another. Ramses and Bithiah weren't looking at her or paying attention. She continued to move back, hoping, praying Ramses wouldn't look over. Wouldn't speak to her. Wouldn't remember her or the words he'd spoken just moments before.

When the thought crossed her mind, Miriam at first dismissed the idea. Then it came again. *Flee. Flee now.*

How could she run from an entire army and escape? What would Ramses do? Chase after her? She'd come to help the injured. If she left now, more men would suffer. Bithiah and the other healers weren't enough, especially if there was more fighting in the morning.

The desert was vast, the night dark, and on the other side of the ridge were more soldiers. Danger was present at every step. And what about Caleb and Aaron? What would they do if they found out she'd run during the night? When Ramses found out their connection to her, their lives could be in danger. Would they be punished in her place, just as Caleb had nearly been punished for Reuven?

Miriam exhaled. She was a marked woman. She faced two choices: remain and become part of the royal harem, losing Caleb forever, or run and hide and by God's miracle find a way to stay safe in her village.

She took another step back, then another, and then she turned and started up the ridge, keeping low to the ground so her silhouette would blend with the hillside.

Don't turn around, she begged in her mind. *Don't notice me.*

She stepped on something sharp and cold. She didn't know if it was an insect or a rock, but it startled her into a run.

She pushed up the ridge, moving her legs as fast as she could, her muscles burning already, even though she hadn't gone far. There was no turning back now. There was no asking for mercy. She'd made her choice.

And that choice was to run.

CHAPTER TWENTY-SIX

BITHIAH

BITHIAH WATCHED AS MIRIAM SLIPPED away, moving up the ridge. She continued to talk to Ramses about what the injured soldiers had told her about the Libyans and how the Libyans thought. Ramses listened to her every word, which Bithiah was grateful for. It told her he would be a good commander and a good pharaoh—listening to others and making decisions only when he had all of the information possible.

Miriam had reached the top of the ridge now, and Bithiah was torn between going after the girl before she made a mistake that couldn't be repaired and letting her continue. It had been obvious what Ramses was interested in when Bithiah had arrived and seen the two of them together. Miriam looked like she was ready to die of fright, which meant Ramses had made his intentions clear.

Bithiah didn't think her half brother would assault the slave girl, so he must have offered her the harem. Moses had been right. Miriam had captured the crown prince's interest. For a slave, being part of the harem wasn't a terrible life. They were fed and pampered, and then they were expected to please their male guests—whether they were men from the royal family or occasional visiting dignitaries. But from the moment Bithiah had met Miriam, she'd sensed something different about the girl. And it appeared that Moses had as well.

"I will leave you to get some rest before the sun rises," Ramses said. He turned from Bithiah and walked a few steps away from her as she desperately tried to come up with something else to talk about, but it was too late.

"Where did the slave girl go?" he asked, turning back to Bithiah.

The sky was no longer as black as night; it was a dark gray now. Dawn was a couple hours away.

"She needs her rest, Ramses," Bithiah said, making it sound like she was teasing him a bit and not censuring. "We have a lot of work to do tomorrow."

Thankfully, he just nodded and looked a bit thoughtful. He didn't have the terrible temper of his father, but he was his own force to be reckoned with, nonetheless. Bithiah let out a breath of relief as Ramses walked back toward the royal camp. It seemed he believed Bithiah's claim that Miriam had found a place to sleep for the rest of the night.

With Ramses back in his camp, Bithiah returned to where she'd been before. But now she was left alone to contemplate whether or not she'd made the right decision in letting Miriam disappear down the other side of the ridge.

Where had the slave girl gone? Miriam's brother was with the Hebrew soldiers on this side of the ridge, as well as her betrothed. It seemed Mered knew Miriam as well. Bithiah sat in the sand and pulled her cloak about her. The air had chilled enough to make her wish she had a rug to sleep under. She thought of Mered sleeping somewhere across the camp from her. She'd been both surprised and impressed that he'd come out with the soldiers. He was a learned man, valued as a scribe in the royal court, and, like the other slaves, not trained in military strategy. Yet he was here with his Hebrew people, ready to defend the land of Egypt.

Bithiah wished she could ask his advice about Miriam. Should they try to go after her? Where did the Hebrew girl think she could go on her own? The journey back to the palace would take the better part of the early morning, and the desert was never a safe place to travel alone.

Lying down, Bithiah finally decided she'd let Miriam chart her own course and destiny. If their paths crossed again, Bithiah would try to help Miriam if possible. The work she'd done today in aiding the injured had been valuable to all. It should be rewarded.

In the morning, Bithiah thought, she'd share the events with Mered and let things happen as they may. She wasn't about to make any ripples with Ramses or the pharaoh. Her station in the kingdom was still precarious. Until Moses secured his own position, Bithiah wasn't willing to create any conflict. Saving a single Hebrew girl from life in the harem and the attentions of the prince was not worth the price. The wind blew gently against her cloak as she closed her eyes and willed sleep to come. She hoped that in the morning she'd be able to think more clearly.

CHAPTER TWENTY-SEVEN

MIRIAM

THE WIND HISSED IN MIRIAM's ears as she ran. It tugged against her clothing and opened the cloak Bithiah had given her. Miriam pushed thoughts of the kind woman out of her head as she ran along the side of the ridge. Once she reached the top, she lay flat on the ground, catching her breath.

She dared a look back toward camp to see if she was being followed. It was too dark to see any movement below, but surely Bithiah and Ramses were wondering where she'd gone. Were they looking for her? Was Ramses rounding up a group of men right then to find her?

The darkness concealed both her and the soldiers and left her feeling like she was running blind. She rose again and crossed the ridge, then peered down the other side to where the smaller group of Hebrew soldiers was camping.

One of the fires was still glowing, but the others were out. She didn't dare seek refuge among those men because she might possibly put their lives in danger. She didn't know what the retribution would be if she was caught.

She half ran, half slid down the ridge and gave the camp a wide berth so she wouldn't alert anyone. By the time she was in the open desert, her skin was soaked with perspiration, but she didn't dare remove her cloak. It blended with the night sky and would give her protection from the sun in the heat of the day.

After a time, Miriam slowed, walking to catch her breath. She continued to trudge through the sand and rocks, heading in the direction of the palace. Once she neared it, she'd avoid the main roads. For now, the dark was her friend.

The sky was turning gray and violet, and the desert was coming to life. Insects skittered out of their holes, and the temperature rose degree by degree. Miriam knew the sun would be well toward its zenith before she reached Mennefer.

Her lips moved, whispering the words of a prayer. The sun started to rise, and the violet of the sky shifted into blue. Miriam couldn't remember when she'd last had water, but her throat felt as if she'd swallowed sand. Her breathing was shallow, and her lips had grown dry and painful. She licked them, but that only made them hurt more.

Her steps slowed. The air warmed, and Miriam shed her cloak. She looped it over her arm, but even that felt too heavy to carry, slowing her down even more.

The sun's heat intensified as it rose mercilessly in the sky, and there were no clouds in sight to give a measure of relief. The sand undulated endlessly before her, and if Miriam hadn't been taught to read the patterns of the traveling sun, she would have thought she was going in the wrong direction. How could Mennefer be so far?

Without water during her journey, she didn't know how much longer she could continue. She saw a group of palms up ahead, and she moved toward them, hoping it wasn't a mirage. When the warm sand beneath her feet turned cool, she knew the shade was real.

She lay down and curled up with the cloak to support her head. The night sounds of the desert had faded and been replaced by mosquitos and flies, which had found the same shade as Miriam. Gone were the voices of men. Gone was the prince of Egypt and his whispered words and unwelcome caresses. As she let her eyes close, Miriam figured she was about halfway between the military camp and the palace, and it had taken her several hours to get here. She couldn't go near the river because it was too close to Mennefer.

Anyone could find her at any time. It wouldn't be hard to spot her. She wondered if more of Pharaoh's army would be passing by. Or perhaps another group of newly recruited Hebrew soldiers. If she didn't find water soon, she might be lying here until Prince Ramses returned to Mennefer with Caleb and Aaron. What would her brother think when they discovered her cold, still body beneath the palms?

Miriam squeezed her eyes shut. They burned with tears although no moisture came. Her body couldn't even spare that much. "I'm sorry, Mother. I'm sorry, Father," she whispered. "I'm sorry, Aaron. I'm so sorry, Caleb."

Her body felt as if it was becoming part of the sand, heavy against the earth beneath her. She wondered if she'd ever see her loved ones again. She wondered what Caleb would do when he found out she'd fled from Prince Ramses.

Her eyes closed against the blue sky, and all she saw were Caleb's light brown eyes, the way his lashes framed his eyes, and his thick dark curls. The image made her want to smile, but she didn't have the strength to do even that.

* * *

Something was touching Miriam's face, yet no matter what she did, she couldn't get it to stop. She tried to raise her hand to push it away, but she had no strength. Then it touched her mouth, and she realized it was water.

Miriam forced her eyes open. Where she expected the blue sky and the brilliant golden sun, there was only darkness. Her breath left her body. Was she blind? Had she entered the next life?

And then someone touched her again, and she tried to pull away. Had Ramses found her at last, and now he was about to carry her off to his harem? Was he taking pity on her blind state? The harem women would point at her, laugh at her, and call her blind.

"Drink," someone said.

Miriam blinked and tried to see who had spoken. It wasn't Ramses's voice. One of his soldiers, then?

Water dribbled onto her mouth, then slid inside. When the water touched her throat, her muscles contracted, and she nearly gagged on it.

"Slowly." The man wasn't speaking Hebrew or Egyptian, but somehow Miriam understood his words.

More water, and this time Miriam swallowed. The pain jolted through her, and her head jerked forward.

"Take it slowly," the voice said.

Who was speaking to her? Who was giving her water? Miriam tried to focus, tried to see, but there was only darkness. All-consuming darkness.

And then something flashed—the man's eyes. She could see the whites of his eyes.

Miriam let her head fall back, and she realized the man's hand supported it so her head rested on the ground carefully. She could see the outline of his head now, and he wore a scarf that covered all of his face except for his eyes.

"Who are you?" Miriam rasped. "Am I in the afterlife?"

His response was a laugh, low and hoarse. He gave a cough, then said in passable Hebrew, "I am Katu. I am part of the desert, and I travel in the dark and sleep in the light."

A nomad, then. Miriam had heard of nomads who roamed the desert and lived off the land, but she had never seen one.

"Where do you come from?" she asked.

"Everywhere yet nowhere," he said.

She strained to see him in the darkness. "How do you know my language?"

"My mother taught me. She was a Hebrew, and my father a Hittite."

Miriam let the information turn in her mind. His Hebrew mother must have been captured during a Hittite invasion. "Where is your family now?"

"Dead."

The word was so final and spoken without feeling that Miriam shivered. She didn't know if she wanted to hear more than that. It was then she noticed the rocky ledge above them blocking part of the starry sky beyond. She was no longer at the group of palms where she'd collapsed. How had she gotten here? "Where are we?"

"I brought you to a place that will protect you from the heat," Katu said. "You slept a long time."

Miriam tried to sit up, but her body simply didn't have the strength.

"Rest," he said. "In the morning, you'll have to be moved again. Gain your strength while you can."

"This place isn't safe?"

"No place is safe for more than a night or two," he said, his voice low. "I've lived here most of my life, yet no one ever sees a trace." He brought the goatskin to her mouth again. "Drink."

She obeyed and relished the water sliding down her throat. Her head hurt, her feet hurt, her legs, her torso . . . but she was alive, and she had water. She would survive this too. Closing her eyes, she tried to let her mind and body relax, to heal and recover from her mad flight from Prince Ramses. If an entire day had passed, then Caleb and Aaron would know she was gone. What did they think or suspect?

Had the Libyans attacked again? Had the battle commenced, fiercer this time? Had the Egyptians finally defeated the tribesmen? Her mind tumbled with questions as her body dulled to the pain throbbing through it.

"What are you running from?" the man spoke again, startling her.

Miriam realized she must have been in the in-between place of sleep and wakefulness. What could she tell this nomad? For some reason, she didn't fear him, but she didn't know what information she could trust him with either. Could she tell him she was running from life in a harem, that she'd been singled out by the prince of Egypt?

"Ah, you don't have to say. I understand," he said in a gentle voice.

Miriam swallowed against her scratchy throat. Maybe she would tell him at some point.

"The more important question is where are you running to?" he asked.

Miriam let a smile touch her face. That was a good question. She wanted to go back to the village, back home to her parents, but she was afraid. And she didn't know if returning to her village would make things worse, and she didn't know if anything was wrong or if she was in trouble.

What kind of effort would Ramses make for one errant Hebrew?

"I live in the village north of Mennefer," Miriam said in a whisper. "I don't know if I should return though . . . if it will be safe for me or for my family."

"Ah," Katu said. "I understand completely. I too have reasons for living alone in the desert and never stopping for long at any place."

Katu was leaning against a rock, his knees pulled up and ankles crossed in front of him. She didn't know if she'd ever seen a man so thin, and she wondered about his age. In the dimness, he looked about her age, but his voice sounded much older and wiser.

"How long have you been living out here?" she asked.

He brought his hand up to rub his face. "More than ten harvest seasons." He must have expected her next question because he said, "I'm in my twentieth year."

The age didn't surprise her, but it meant he'd been living as a nomad since he was a ten-year-old child. "You were young when you left your home." She was guessing that he'd left after his family had died. What had his life been like with a Hittite father and a Hebrew mother?

"I never knew my father," Katu said. "He was killed in battle . . . after my mother conceived." He fell silent, then said, "My mother didn't know him either."

So his mother had been assaulted, then left with the results, which would have been devastating for any unmarried Hebrew girl.

"Did you live in a Hebrew village here in Egypt?"

"No," he said. "My mother could never return home with such shame. The other Hittite soldiers treated her cruelly, as their pleasure thing. She told me she escaped one night and fled to a desert community that had compassion on a woman with a large belly. Or so she thought at first."

Miriam watched him in the darkness as he spoke. He'd pulled off the scarf covering his head, and she could see his long scraggly beard on his angular face. His words were matter-of-fact, but he couldn't hide the hint of tremor in his voice.

"She might have been better off returning to her Hebrew village, even if she was ostracized by her own people and treated as a beggar. At least she wouldn't have been beaten."

Miriam sucked in her breath. Life could be so cruel. Whenever she thought her life was challenging, she learned that others were worse off. She and Katu went quiet, both lost in their own thoughts. Katu had been dealt a harsh blow, and right from the inception of his life, he'd struggled. "What happened to your mother?" Miriam asked after a moment.

He shook his head, and Miriam waited for him to speak. After a long silence, he said, "A man beat her to death for not giving him what he wanted." His head dropped, and he stared at his hands, then he said the next words in almost a whisper, "I killed him. That's why I had to leave."

The pain in his voice was unmistakable. Miriam looked away from him, her eyes burning with tears. Katu was a fugitive from an unjust life. He was a nomad because he couldn't find a safe place to live.

"You should come live in my village," Miriam said. "You can start your life over. You can live in honor of your mother's name."

But Katu was shaking his head. "I killed a man. It was murder, and for that I can never be trusted by another."

Miriam thought hard on what he'd said. Here she was next to a man who had killed another, but she wasn't afraid. He'd defended his mother's life.

"It wasn't your fault," Miriam said. "You did what any good son would do."

Katu nodded and remained quiet. He seemed relieved, as if sharing his burden had helped him relax. He scooted away from her and lay down, closing his eyes.

Miriam finally allowed herself to drift off to sleep, wondering what the dawn would bring. Her final thoughts before falling asleep were in thanks to Adonai for bringing her a man who had saved her life.

CHAPTER TWENTY-EIGHT

MOSES

Shouting awakened Moses for the second day in a row. They'd spent most of the previous day driving back the Libyans toward the western desert, and Moses raised his head with a groan. Were those foolish tribesmen back for a second beating?

There were bodies strewn about the battlefield as far as he could see. The Egyptians had been so exhausted the night before, they'd dropped off to sleep without bothering to move the dead.

The number of fallen Libyans far outnumbered the Egyptians. It had been a fierce fight, and now Moses stared in disbelief at the men who were preparing the royal chariots yet again.

He sat up, the motion making his throat pound and reminding him that he'd eaten little and drunk less. What he saw wasn't Libyans advancing on the border again but a group of men shouting in glee at two chariots racing up the ridge. The one in the lead suddenly slipped, pulling the horse backward down the ridge.

The men shouted their encouragement.

Moses rubbed the sleep from his face and climbed to his feet. Did these men never sleep? The sun had barely crested the horizon, and the Egyptian soldiers were acting like it was the middle of a festival day.

And then he saw the two carts that must have arrived during the night. They were filled with jugs of wine. The first soldiers to wake must have drunk their fill. And now the result was a boisterous chariot race.

The spokes of the wheels of the sliding chariot snapped, and the gathered crowd groaned collectively.

Moses shook his head and made his way past the men, stopping before the wine cart. He lifted a jug to his mouth, anticipating the taste of sweet wine, but the jug only dripped. It was empty. He tried the next, then the next. Finally he found one that was miraculously half full. He drank several swigs, making him feel like a new man. Now all he needed was a wash in a river or pool.

He leaned against the cart and watched the failing race a bit longer. He laughed with the men as the driver of the second chariot leapt out and frantically tried to stop his chariot from sliding. But the horse and chariot proved much too heavy, and soon the chariot driver was sliding down the ridge as well.

"Moses, there you are." Ramses's voice cut through the din.

Moses turned his head to see the prince approaching. He'd hardly seen the man since his arrival two nights before. Embroiled in battle or trying to snatch some much-needed rest, they hadn't had any time for conversation. And as far as Moses knew, Pentu was still resting and trying to recover. He'd been alert the day before.

"I'm looking for that Hebrew girl who came with Bithiah," Ramses said in a low voice. His gaze darted about as if he didn't want any of the other men to hear.

Moses froze, knowing he was speaking about Miriam, Caleb's betrothed, the same woman Moses had told his mother to keep watch over because of Ramses's interest in her.

"Isn't she helping my mother?" Moses said, keeping his eyes on the chariot race so he wouldn't have to look Ramses in the eye.

"She's been missing since yesterday," Ramses said, leaning against the cart next to Moses. "Or even the night before. I was speaking to her after everyone had gone to sleep, and then your mother showed up. When your mother left, the Hebrew girl was gone."

Moses didn't know how to answer. Ramses had been talking to Miriam in the middle of the night? He wondered what else Ramses had intended on doing before his mother had come upon the scene. A chill passed through him at the thought. Ramses was not a brutal man, but he'd been known to assign more than one Hebrew woman to the harem.

"Did you ask my mother?" Moses asked, his throat tight as he tried to make his voice sound at ease.

"She seemed surprised that the girl isn't anywhere to be found," Ramses said. He folded his arms. "I don't see how she could just vanish."

Moses didn't want to state the obvious and suggest that Ramses ask Miriam's brother or Caleb, but then Ramses said, "Bithiah said her brother is among the Hebrew soldiers. Go find him and discover what he knows." He straightened to move away, then stopped and turned back to face Moses. "Didn't you say she was betrothed?"

Moses met Ramses's gaze full on. The look in his eyes told Moses Ramses well knew Miriam was betrothed and to whom as well.

"She said she is," Moses said, because it wouldn't be wise to deny it. Ramses would find out soon enough.

Ramses's lips curled upward. "That's what I thought. Find the man she's betrothed to. Between him and the brother, one of those men knows something. If they are uncooperative, bring them to me."

Moses straightened himself. "Can't this wait until after we return to Mennefer? We still need to secure the valley."

Ramses's look was sharp, making Moses regret his words. "It can't wait, my friend." The words weren't friendly. "If she's been lost or injured, it will only grow worse with the passage of time."

Moses well understood the meaning behind Ramses's words. They were a threat and also a warning for Moses. For Miriam's sake, Moses hoped she'd found sanctuary someplace—wherever that might be.

"You're right," Moses said and stepped away from the cart. He picked up the jug of wine he'd drunk from earlier. "There's some left, but it is going fast."

Ramses chuckled and took the jug, drinking some of the wine.

Moses walked around the cart and crossed the camp in the still-early morning, heading toward the place where the Hebrews had banded together and camped. It wasn't that the Hebrew soldiers had purposely separated their sleeping quarters; it had happened naturally with the separation of culture and classes.

Before meeting with the Hebrew men who knew Miriam, Moses detoured to find his mother. He didn't have to search far. She was faithfully tending to the injured in the central camp that had been established as a refuge. Several other Egyptians were helping her, and they had plenty to do after yesterday's second battle.

When Bithiah saw him coming, she straightened quickly and walked over to meet him. "Moses," she said reaching for his hands.

He bent down and kissed her cheek, then kept his voice low. "What do you know about Miriam's disappearance?"

Bithiah said nothing for a moment. "Can you keep a confidence?" she said at last.

Moses was on full alert. Something had happened, and he wasn't sure if it was going to turn out well. "I can. And you need to know that Ramses is looking for her."

"Yes, I know," Bithiah said. "The first night we were here, Miriam and I set up camp together. Soon after, I went to help someone who was crying in pain. When I returned, Ramses was with her. He was . . . he was acting very interested, and the poor woman was frightened."

"Did he order her to the harem?" Moses breathed out.

"I am almost positive he did, although he hasn't said as much." Bithiah met his gaze fully. "She ran, Moses. She disappeared over the other side of the ridge, and I haven't seen her since."

"Where did she go? Back to the palace?"

"I don't think so," Bithiah said in a slow, quiet voice. "She's a smart girl and would know the consequences of disobeying the prince of Egypt."

Moses nodded. He tried to imagine Miriam fleeing in the middle of the night, crossing the desert alone . . . It was distressing. The possibilities of harm coming to her were endless. "Anything could have happened to her."

"I know," Bithiah said, clasping her hands in front of her. "We can only pray for a good outcome."

"If Ramses is involved and he doesn't get his way, I don't know if there *can* be a good outcome." He looked past his mother to the Hebrew camp. "Do you think her brother knows? Or the man she's betrothed to?"

"They haven't spoken to me at all if they do know anything," Bithiah said. "Perhaps they wouldn't dare call attention to it."

"You may be right," Moses said with a nod. "I'm going to speak with them now, if only to inform them she is missing."

Bithiah touched Moses's arm. "Be careful. I know you care for this woman in your own way. Ramses is watching all of us closely."

"He always has," Moses mused.

He left his mother and walked toward the cooking fire at the edge of the Hebrew camp, where the men were roasting desert pigeons. It smelled good, and Moses's stomach rumbled. He slowed his stride. The men had gathered around the fire. He recognized the palace scribe Mered and decided he'd know where Aaron and Caleb were.

"May I speak with you?" Moses asked Mered as he approached.

Mered was immediately on his feet and followed Moses several paces from the cooking fire.

The last time Moses had asked for a private conversation with this man was when Caleb was awaiting trial for theft. When Moses told Mered what his mother had said, the scribe went very still.

It was several seconds before he replied. "Miriam has been a fool. She'll get herself killed before anyone can ever catch up to her." He shook his head. "But perhaps she saw no other choice."

His response surprised Moses. "Even if she'd been sent to the harem," Moses said, "at least she would be alive. She'd be fed and taken care of."

Mered's dark gaze lifted and met Moses's. "*Alive* in what way? To a Hebrew woman like Miriam, living in the harem would be worse than death."

The two men looked at each other, each understanding without words. Finally, Moses said, "I need to speak with her brother and Caleb. Ramses wants to know if they have hidden her away somehow or know where she went."

Mered's jaw tightened, but he nodded. "I'll bring them to you," he said, then turned and hurried across the camp.

Moses watched him go and wondered again where Miriam could have gone. Maybe the Hebrews camping on the other side of the ridge had helped her. But the next morning, those same Hebrews had come over the ridge and joined the main army, and Miriam hadn't been with them.

By the time Mered brought Caleb and Aaron, the chariot race on the ridge had resulted in one severely damaged chariot.

Moses met the Hebrew men's eyes with steadiness, watching for their reactions when he asked them about Miriam. He hoped to be able to tell if they were speaking the truth. When he explained what he'd come to ask, Caleb threw a sharp look at Aaron.

Aaron raised his hands, his face pale as he looked from Caleb to Moses. "I haven't seen my sister since we arrived that first night and Prince Ramses brought his reinforcements. The last I knew, she was with the princess making rounds among the injured." He lowered his hands. "No one saw her yesterday?" He looked at Caleb again. "Not even you?"

"No," Caleb said in a quiet voice. He raked his hands through his hair. "Someone must have seen her leave. Which direction did she go?" He looked about as if he might happen to see her walking through the camp just now.

"My mother thought she saw her climb the ridge," Moses filled in, not giving them too much information yet, wanting to see their reaction and hear what they may or may not say. He cast a glance at Mered, signaling that the scribe needed to remain quiet.

Caleb's eyes immediately shot to the ridge, assessing its height.

"Did she join the soldiers on the other side?" Aaron asked.

"Nothing like that," Moses said.

Caleb's jaw was set hard, and his brows were furrowed as he studied the ridge. He looked back at Moses. "Something must have happened to make her flee. She didn't seek out her brother or me. She felt forced to leave without telling us anything." He gaze went to Mered. "What do you know about this?"

"Only what Moses has told me," Mered said, his eyes widening at the vehemence in Caleb's tone.

It was all Moses needed to see. He lowered his voice and said, "She fled the camp because of something that was said to her. Prince Ramses invited her into his harem."

Caleb's hands tightened into fists, and his face darkened. He stepped toward Moses, but Aaron's arm shot out, stopping Caleb from moving any closer.

Moses continued. "She has been gone a day and a half now. She might have made it back to your village safely." He knew his words weren't convincing any of the Hebrew men.

Caleb simply stared, and Moses sensed the man wasn't seeing him at all.

Moses looked over at Mered. "Ramses is very interested in knowing if any of you might be able to guess where she went or what happened to her. Any information would be appropriately rewarded."

Mered gave an imperceptible nod.

Relief coursed through Moses; Mered had understood him. Mered knew Moses was on their side, but his words and actions had to reflect that he was on Ramses's side and that Moses wanted to locate Miriam so she could fulfill Ramses's request. In truth, Ramses had more harlots than any young man in the land of Egypt. Why did he need this one Hebrew girl whom another man so obviously loved?

"We will report anything we discover," Mered said, speaking for all three Hebrew men. "If she does return to our village, we will bring the information to you."

Moses gave a brief nod, looked at all three men in turn, and said, "Thank you. I hope she is found safe." He'd said all he needed to say. He hoped they understood the meaning beneath his words.

He walked back across the camp, heading to report to Ramses. He wouldn't be telling the prince what he wanted to hear, but he hoped that with Caleb and Aaron now knowing, something could be done to ensure the woman's safety.

Moses didn't understand why he felt protective of this particular woman. Perhaps it was because her betrothed had been leading the Hebrews into battle on behalf of the Egyptians. And her brother was here now, and Miriam had risked her own life by joining Moses's mother on the battlefield to care for the injured—Egyptian and Hebrew alike.

It was easy to pick out Ramses among the other soldiers. He wasn't taller, but his presence was imposing. Everyone scrambled to do his bidding. Cleanup from the battle had started in full force.

When Ramses noticed Moses striding toward him, he motioned for Moses to join him by the cart, out of the main hive of activity.

"What did you learn?" Ramses asked, his eyes piercing.

Moses exhaled. "They know nothing. She might return to their village though, and if she does, they will inform us."

Ramses narrowed his gaze at Moses. "That is *all*?"

"I questioned them in multiple ways to determine whether or not they were hiding anything," Moses said. "You can be assured, on my honor, that they do not know where she went. They didn't even know she's been missing."

Ramses gave a short nod. "If she did head to her village, she might not arrive there alive."

"I know," Moses said. "The desert can be an unpredictable thing." He knew he was speaking two truths: one, that Miriam could come upon danger, whether it meant becoming lost or injured, and two, that Ramses could find her first.

CHAPTER TWENTY-NINE

MIRIAM

It had been five days since Miriam had fled the Egyptian camp. If Ramses could see her now, he might change his mind, Miriam thought as she studied her reflection at the river's edge. She and Katu had traveled downriver from Mennefer to wait out any possible search for her. The river here was clearer, and Miriam could see that her long dark hair had grown wild and matted.

Her face was smudged with dirt and sand, and her cloak was dusty. The only part of her that would be recognizable was her eyes. Miriam dipped her hands in the river and splashed her face with the water. She began scrubbing her face, and then, because Katu was farther down searching for fish, she pulled off her cloak and stepped into the lazy flow of water.

She'd been hiding beneath that cloak for five days, and this was the first time she'd taken it off. The water ebbed against her coarse linen tunic, soaking it immediately. The sand and wind and dirt had chaffed her skin and made her feel as if she was made of stone. She walked deeper into the river until it reached her knees, and then she sank down, reveling in the water drenching her skin.

Closing her eyes, she could almost believe she was bathing in the river next to her village and that it was late at night when all the others were asleep. She'd be alone, with no one to disturb her. She'd stay awhile, then walk back to the hut she lived in with her parents. Drying off, she'd spend the night on a mat and, in the morning, not have much else to worry about but getting her weaving orders fulfilled.

"Miriam," a voice hissed behind her, pulling her from her imaginings.

She opened her eyes to see that she was nowhere near her village and that she wouldn't be spending the night in her parents' hut.

Katu stood on the bank, his eyes wide as he stared at her. "I hear voices," he whispered and motioned with his hand for her to hurry out of the water.

She scrambled to her feet, but her soaked clothing weighed her down, making it difficult for her to get out of the water. As she stepped onto the bank, her heart filling with fear, Katu handed her the cloak.

Miriam pulled it on, ignoring the fact that she was soaking wet beneath. "Where are they coming from?" she whispered.

Katu put a finger to his lips, then grabbed her wrist and tugged her with him. Miriam hurried to keep up as Katu wound his way through the high reeds growing along this part of the River Nile, until he reached a dip in the earth.

He pulled her down with him, and they both sat on the ground, cross-legged, with the reeds reaching just higher than their heads.

They were concealed from a person who might be traveling along the river, but if that person decided to venture any farther into the reeds, they'd be easily discovered.

Miriam held as still as possible, waiting for her pounding heart to calm. After several minutes of not hearing anything, she looked over at Katu. "Have they passed by?" she said in a low voice.

He leaned forward and rose up just a little, peering through the reeds toward the river below.

Miriam leaned forward as well, and she almost didn't stop her gasp from escaping. Three Egyptian soldiers wound their way along the riverbank, walking slowly, too slowly. Their heads were down, eyes focused on the ground beneath them. It was plain they were looking for something or someone.

Me? Miriam wasn't sure, but it was a very real possibility.

Katu's eyes were as wide and full of questions as hers. His hand touched hers, and he drew her back to their original position.

The soldiers continued walking carefully as they examined everything, and Miriam could pick out the smallest of their sounds—the rustle of their tunics, the soft slap of their swords against their thighs as they walked, the crunch of a dried reed they stepped on, the clearing of a throat, a slight cough.

They weren't moving on, Miriam realized. She looked at Katu, knowing there was panic in her eyes.

He didn't look any better, and Miriam sensed that he might be regretting helping her now. If it was just him, he could easily flee from the soldiers and disappear back into the desert. But with both of them traveling together, there was more responsibility, more exposure, and more danger.

Miriam inhaled deeply, trying to calm herself enough that she could remain in her hiding place, as tempting as it was to jump up, scream, and dart away. She leaned forward again, peering through the reeds, unable to stand not knowing what the soldiers were doing now. Why weren't they moving on?

What were they looking at now?

They'd stopped at the exact place she'd come out of the water. Surely she'd left tracks, and they could see that they were wet and fresh. They might be able to detect Katu's tracks as well. Perhaps having two sets of tracks would throw them off. As far as any of the Egyptians knew, she was traveling alone.

One of the soldiers turned in her direction and seemed to stare right at her. Miriam clapped a hand over her mouth and then worried that the soldier had heard the action. She stared in horror and fascination at the soldier, waiting for him to alert the other men and point to where she and Katu were hiding.

But his eyes shifted, and he was no longer staring straight at her. Miriam's breathing started again. Had he not seen her? He turned his head to one side and then the other as if he was looking at the sky and checking the wind.

She exhaled and looked over at Katu. He pointed to the ground beneath them, then moved his hands and knees. He wanted them to crawl away from the soldiers. Miriam moved to her knees and crawled after Katu as he slowly moved through the reeds. When they reached a place where the reeds were shorter because they grew farther away from the river, Katu lay on the ground.

Miriam lay next to him. The sky above was an innocent blue, belying the way her pulse raced and perspiration stood out on her skin. The minutes passed too slowly before Katu rolled to his side and peered out through the reeds.

"What do you see?" Miriam whispered.

"They've left," Katu said, then added, "for now." He turned his dark eyes on Miriam. "We should start walking. Find a place to cross the river and travel on the other side."

Miriam expected to feel relief at the news that the Egyptian soldiers were gone, but unease continued to course through her, maybe because the soldiers had come so close and had examined the place where she had just come out of the river.

She climbed to her feet and followed Katu as he made his way back toward the water, taking a different route than the one they'd just taken. She watched Katu and marveled at how he could be so calm and decisive. Living as a nomad had made him into a man unlike anyone she'd ever known. He'd never chastised her for running from the prince or for trying to stay hidden. He'd just accepted it as what she had decided to do, and he had no thought for his own safety as he worked to protect her.

"Katu," Miriam whispered, and he stopped quickly, turning. That was another thing she liked about him—he took what she said seriously. "I can't swim."

He shrugged. "I'll swim for both of us, but we'll try to find a place that's shallow."

During the next while, Miriam and Katu picked their way through reeds, brush, and groupings of trees, trying to stay away from the main view of the river in case the soldiers returned, as the sun slid toward the western horizon. Miriam imitated the way Katu trod carefully, avoiding stepping on anything that might leave a trace that he'd passed through.

"There," Katu said, stopping and pointing. "I thought we were near."

Miriam looked in the direction he'd pointed. The river was faster here but much narrower. If it wasn't deep, it would be easy to cross with the help of a walking stick. "How deep is it?"

"Deep enough that you'll need to hold on to me," Katu explained. He crouched to the ground and scanned the river for several seconds.

"What are you looking for?" Miriam asked, crouching next to him. It fascinated her how much attention Katu paid to the land. He watched every movement, knew every rise or drop in temperature, and seemed to respect each plant and insect.

"There," Katu said, pointing again at the river.

Miriam turned her attention to the flowing water. At first she didn't notice anything unusual, but once she did, she couldn't help but notice. "Air bubbles," she said. "Crocodile?"

"Yes," Katu said.

A shudder passed through Miriam. "I guess we can't cross here."

"We'll have to change the location only slightly," Katu said with a slow nod. "But we will still be passing close by the crocodile."

Miriam stiffened. She'd done everything Katu had asked her to, but this—swimming past a crocodile when she couldn't even swim? "We can find another place. Even if we need to walk a little longer."

"There's no time," Katu said.

Miriam was about to ask him why when she saw it too.

Soldiers were coming along the path that wound by the river—the same three plus two more. They weren't taking their time now. They were walking with purpose, hardly looking left or right. They certainly weren't stopping to examine any muddy tracks.

"Where are they going?"

"They've discovered all they need to. Now they are traveling to the next village to deliver an edict. Look at what the lead soldier is carrying."

Miriam peered closer, noticing that he carried a papyrus scroll in his right hand. "What's the edict for?"

Katu looked over at her, his eyes somber. "I can't say exactly, but I'm assuming it's a reward statement for turning in a Hebrew woman who may or may not be traveling with another Hebrew."

"But how could they know?"

"Our tracks. My mother was Hebrew, and they can see it in the print of my foot."

Miriam shook her head—it was hard to believe—but Katu had a knowledge beyond what she could fathom. "Do you track people like that?"

"I avoid people and animals that way," Katu said. He looked directly into Miriam's eyes. "You have a choice to make. It's no longer safe to hide out in the outlying areas of Mennefer. Somewhere, somehow, you'll be recognized and turned in. If that edict offers a reward, you'll have reason to fear everyone you meet."

Miriam felt her breath grow shallow. What were her options? Cross the border? Take up residence among the Libyans or other foreigners? There didn't seem much hope in that, especially knowing how Katu's Hebrew mother was treated.

"What can I do?" Miriam asked, her chest growing tight. "Is it hopeless, then? Should I just return to Mennefer?"

Katu grasped her arm and lowered his voice. "I have a plan, but it's a wild plan. You'll have to put your faith in me."

Miriam focused on his dark eyes and sun-beaten face. She'd grown to trust this nomad, but she also knew she couldn't rely on him forever. "What is it?"

"You return to your village—"

"But my family would be in danger if they were discovered harboring me."

Katu didn't deny that fact or that danger. "Sometimes hiding in plain sight is the best way to hide."

Miriam shook her head. "I would put my whole village at risk if I was discovered." She looked away from Katu at the river that was moving, always moving. She wanted to return to her village, but it was too soon. Maybe in a year she could. As much as she ached from missing Caleb and her family, she could never live with herself if something happened to them because of her disobedience.

It was ironic to think of. She'd been taking many risks over the past few years, and all of them had the potential of endangering her family or herself and separating them all. But since she'd realized she loved Caleb and wanted to marry him, she had decided she needed to live a life less centered on her desires and wishes. Caleb was more important to Miriam than she was to herself. And with the realization, her family had become even more important.

Besides, a distasteful thought had entered her mind over the past couple of days. If she belonged to the royal harem, she might see Moses there. She couldn't bear to be a part of a harem her own brother might visit. She'd never seen the look in his eyes that she'd seen in Ramses's eyes, but Miriam wasn't about to take that risk.

"I could go and talk to your parents and let them know you are alive. We'll come up with a plan," Katu said.

"What's the plan?" Miriam pressed. "I can see something gleaming in your eyes."

"I have a couple of ideas. We could move into the village and pretend we are married."

Panic shot through her. The villagers would know who she was. How would they react to her pretended marriage to Katu? What would Caleb think? "No," Miriam said. "I'd rather become a nomad."

Katu's smile went wide. "I guess that answers my question as to whether there is any future between us."

Miriam let out a gasp. "Did you think—?"

He gave a small laugh, his face turning red, which completely mortified Miriam. "You can just say I am not surprised the prince of Egypt wants you to be in his harem," he said. "But also know that I am a lone man and not used to the company of another person, let alone a beautiful woman my age. You could say I dreamed a little." He held up two fingers spaced close together. "Just a little though."

Miriam could only stare at him; she had no idea how to respond.

"I care about you, Miriam, as you've probably guessed."

Her throat was thick, but she managed to say, "I care about you, Katu, as well. And I am ever so grateful for your kindness to me." Her eyes burned with emotion, and she had to look away. "I hope I didn't encourage any feelings of affection. You have become like a brother to me."

He cleared his throat. When Miriam looked back at him, she saw the moisture in his eyes.

"Thank you," he said. "No one has ever said as much to me. It's an honor."

She smiled, her heart hurting and soaring at the same time. "I could cut my hair, and we could travel as brothers."

He laughed, then sobered. "That might actually work."

Miriam tilted her head and studied him. "Let's go to my village, and you can consult with my parents. They will know more than we do and may have the right solution." It was risky, but Miriam knew that if she was to truly disappear, she wanted her parents to at least know she was alive. She wanted Caleb to know she was sorry. She wanted Aaron to know she was grateful.

Katu nodded. "We'll start traveling tonight. But we need to cross the river first." He was already scanning the area again.

The sun had nearly set, and Miriam's skin broke out into bumps. The crocodiles and hippos were much more active in the darkness than the daylight. If they crossed the river now, they could have an unpleasant encounter.

She grasped Katu's arm. "What are you thinking, Katu? You know I can't swim."

It still didn't seem to bother him. "We must cross now before those soldiers come back. If we wait until they pass by again, it will be too dark to cross."

Miriam looked down the river as if she was expecting the soldiers to appear. When they didn't, she took a deep breath. "All right."

CHAPTER THIRTY

MIRIAM

Miriam gasped as she surfaced above the water. The only thing that was keeping her moving across the river was Katu's firm grasp on her wrist.

"Kick," he said, his voice muffled in her waterlogged ears.

Miriam felt as if her whole body was filled with water. Her clothing weighed her down, and the current was swifter than she'd expected. Not to mention every foreign object in the water gave her a start as she wondered if some swimming creature was there to see to her demise.

"Hurry," Katu said, not for the first time in the past few minutes.

Miriam didn't question why he was in such a hurry. She didn't question what he was seeing that she didn't. Her eyes stung from being submerged in the river, and she blinked rapidly, trying to focus on the bank at the other side. She exhaled and kicked, propelling her more forward than downward. Forward was definitely better than downward.

"We're almost there," Katu said, his voice coming in pants.

It spurred Miriam on, knowing they were almost there and she could soon escape the murky water.

Something hard brushed against her foot, and she kicked frantically, propelling herself forward and running into Katu.

He must have felt it too because he practically shot out of the water, pulling her the rest of the way to the edge with him and scrambling up onto the bank. He tugged her through the reeds and up a hill until he finally came to a stop.

Miriam turned around to see the spot where they'd made their hasty exit from the river. A crocodile was just coming up on the bank. Miriam let out a small yelp. "He was there. Did you feel him? He almost got me."

Katu only nodded, his eyes wide. "Come," he said, pulling her farther up the hill. "We don't want to go anywhere near him now that he's shown interest in us."

Miriam was only too happy to hurry up the rest of the hill. And then Katu grabbed her arm and yanked her to the ground. She was about to protest when a whoosh sounded above her.

Her heart nearly stopped. Someone had shot an arrow in their direction.

"The soldiers spotted us from across the river," Katu said. "Pray that the darkness will be our friend right now."

Miriam felt cold and hot at the same time, and her body thrummed with nerves. Someone splashed into the water.

"They're coming across," Katu hissed in her ear. "We need to run."

Miriam nodded. She was sweating even though her soaking-wet clothes should have cooled her skin.

"The water will slow them down, and they won't be able to shoot arrows when swimming." He lifted his head slightly, then lowered it with a groan.

"What is it?" Miriam asked.

"Two of the soldiers have remained on the bank, which means they can still shoot at us," Katu said.

"What should we do?"

He turned his head and peered at her. "What do you want to do? You can run, and I can stay behind and distract them."

"No," she said. "We'll both run."

Katu's grin flashed in the almost darkness. He reached for her hand, and before Miriam had a chance to look back at the river, she was on her feet, running with Katu.

They moved down the other side of the hill, then turned north, heading back to Mennefer. They really only had two choices: run toward Mennefer or away from it. Either direction gave them about as good a chance as the other to outrun the soldiers and find a good hiding place.

Miriam knew Katu could run much faster than she could, but he was keeping it slower for her. If they separated, there was no doubt Katu would get away completely from the soldiers. Miriam was more grateful for her rescuer than ever.

If Ramses was sending soldiers to search for her in the first place, and if he was sending out an edict with a reward listed, his intentions of finding her were quite serious. She ran faster, and Katu picked up his pace as well. Miriam hoped it would be enough.

Katu wasn't spending any time or effort looking behind them to see if the soldiers were following. He led her through a grassy area, and then they arrived at an old quarry, which amounted to a collection of stones. As they reached the stones, Miriam realized it wasn't a quarry but the ruins of a former building or temple. "There's an old tomb here I found awhile back," Katu said, his voice a panted whisper.

He led her past several large stones and tumbled statues, then he reached a group of bushes. "Inside there," he said, pointing. "Hurry."

Miriam crouched low and pushed through the bushes.

Katu was behind her. "Keep going."

Miriam flinched as the branches tangled in her clothing and hair. She continued, ignoring the scratches against her skin until she was in a cave-like area. Darkness met her, and she couldn't see anything as she continued to crawl. Katu's words of encouragement kept her placing one hand in front of the other; she expected to run into something at any moment. She could smell the stale air and sense the confined space.

"That's good," Katu said, his voice sounding eerie. "You can stop now."

She moved to a sitting position. The only sound she heard was their breathing, which she decided was a good thing.

Katu's hand found hers. "You can move back a little more and rest your back on the wall."

Miriam did so, finding the stone wall pleasantly cool. She closed her eyes, trying to help them adjust to the darkness. When she opened them again, she still couldn't see well, but she could make out Katu's form next to her.

"You've had to hide here before?" she asked Katu.

"Once or twice," he whispered back. "I haven't been discovered yet."

Miriam exhaled and realized she was shivering. Whether it was from fear while running from the soldiers or from her still-wet clothing or from narrowly escaping the jaws of a crocodile, she didn't know. It was probably all three. But she was alive and safe. And Katu was alive and safe as well. She hoped she could say the same for her family and Caleb.

"Sleep if you can," Katu said, scooting next to her. "We'll wait out the night, and possibly the next day, before we continue north to your village."

Miriam's stomach grumbled with lack of food. Katu had been resourceful, but even her slave's diet was more plentiful than a nomad's. She ignored the emptiness and leaned her head against Katu's shoulder.

Somehow, some way, she slept. When she awakened, there was a faint light coming from the front of the burial chamber. She lifted her head, immediately regretting the action as sharp pain shot through her neck.

Katu was snoring softly next to her, his head tilted back, resting against the stone wall, his eyes closed.

She marveled that they'd slept at all sitting up. She supposed she was becoming accustomed to living as a nomad, and the small comforts she'd enjoyed in her village home were no longer necessary for survival.

She felt as if it had been weeks since she'd seen the sun. She crept to the entrance, careful not to disturb Katu, and made her way back through the bushes. She paused and listened every few seconds as she moved. If she heard any footstep, voice, or movement of a weapon, she'd hurry back inside.

But when she peered out at the gray sky, she saw no sign of another person. The clouds were low today, surprising Miriam. Would it rain? It was a rare event in the Nile Valley. But when it did rain, the land came to life. Flowers bloomed where there had been only sand before. Rivers formed where there had been only dry wadis. And grass grew in every crevice imaginable.

In the daylight, she could see the ruins more clearly. The area was not large, and Miriam decided it had been a smaller temple site. She wondered if there had been a battle here between two nations, being so close to Mennefer. Perhaps it was the last holdout of the Egyptian army during another era.

Something shuffled behind her, and Miriam turned with a start, though she knew it could only be Katu. She thought if they'd been sharing their hiding place with snakes or scorpions, the creatures would have already made themselves known.

"Katu," she breathed. "You scared me."

He came crawling up to her, his eyes blinking against the brighter light. Miriam smiled at seeing him look so disoriented. He scanned their surroundings, staying hidden behind the brush.

"What do you think?" Miriam said in a low voice.

He was silent for a moment, then said, "It's quiet, but I want to be absolutely sure. We'll start traveling at dusk."

Miriam's stomach protested in response.

Katu chuckled. "All right, I'll find us something to eat." He reached behind him and snatched the goatskin.

Miriam grabbed his arm. "Don't go if it's not safe."

"They're looking for a woman or for two people, not just a single man."

"Are you sure?"

"If you hear me scream, stay here until dark."

"Scream?" Miriam gaped. "That wouldn't be something I could ignore."

"It would be my signal for you to stay hidden," Katu said, giving her a half smile. "Don't worry about me. I have plenty of ways to evade the soldiers. A scream will just be a warning to you."

Miriam shook her head. "Stay here. We'll find something tonight."

But Katu was already crawling through the front bushes. "If they're here, they're here. If not, then they aren't. I'm hungry too."

Miriam watched helplessly as Katu stood and walked across the open space, scanning the area again and pausing every so often. She stayed watching for as long as he was within sight. When he disappeared in the direction of the river, all Miriam could do was wait.

It felt like hours had passed by the time he returned in a hurry. He ran across the ruins toward her, and she moved aside just as he plunged into the bushes.

"Inside," he rasped, and Miriam scurried after him.

A couple of paces into the dark opening, he stopped, breathing hard, catching his breath.

"Were there soldiers? Did they see you?'

He shook his head, still breathing hard. "I don't know; at least I don't think so. There were tracks everywhere."

Miriam went still. "Do you think they are waiting for us somewhere?"

"Possibly. I don't think they've given up yet." Katu handed her the goatskin.

Miriam took a drink of the cold water. It tasted fresh, and she had to stop herself from guzzling too much of it and making herself sick. "Where did you get the water?"

"I went south and found a well," Katu said, taking the goatskin back and drinking some of the water himself. "I had to wait awhile for the goat herders to move on."

"Were they Egyptian?"

"Yes. They were hardened men, and they lingered at the well much too long for working herdsmen. Either they were lazy, or they were waiting for someone."

"Like one of us?" Miriam whispered.

Katu nodded. "Or for the soldiers to return. They might even make up information to give the soldiers so they can profit." Katu opened the satchel that hung around his waist and removed several small fish.

Miriam wrinkled her nose; she preferred her fish cooked, but they didn't have the luxury of building a fire and eating a cooked meal.

Katu made quick work of cleaning out the fish with a dagger he kept in his satchel, then he removed the bones and handed her some meat.

It wasn't the first time Miriam had eaten uncooked fish, but she ate quickly, trying not to taste too much as she swallowed. When she was finished, she felt better. Katu had finished eating too and was stretched out on the ground, his eyes closed.

But Miriam's thoughts were tumbling too much to relax enough to sleep. She leaned against the stone wall and kept her eyes on the changing light outside, watching it go from gray to deep charcoal. She could smell the moisture in the air, foreign and heavy. And then the drops fell. Drops of rain from the sky, large and slow, impacting the earth and creating small circles of moisture.

Miriam crawled to the entrance to get a better view of the sky through the bushes. It was hard to tell the time of day, but she knew the sun must be setting. The clouds were low and dark. She reached out her hand and let the drops fall onto it. She flinched a little with each one.

Katu joined her, holding out his hand as well, a smile on his face.

"Do you think it will be a big rain?" Miriam asked.

Katu lifted a shoulder. "I think it's too early in the season for that, but we need to take advantage of this."

"What do you mean?" She leaned out farther and let the drops splash onto her face.

"We will leave now and head north to your village. The rain will be the perfect cover for our tracks." He was already reaching for the goatskin and his satchel.

Miriam picked up her cloak and pulled it around her shoulders. It had dried from swimming in the river, but it would just get wet again.

"Are you ready?" he asked, stifling a yawn.

Miriam felt the same weariness and wondered if she'd ever get a full night's sleep in a hut on a mat ever again. "I'm ready."

CHAPTER THIRTY-ONE

MOSES

MOSES GAZED DOWN AT THE temple construction site, Ramses and the newly recovered Pentu at his side. The site was amazing to behold, even beneath the threatening rain clouds. Hundreds of laborers worked to move the cut stones, heaving to pull the ropes secured around the rocks. If the slaves were allowed to attend Egyptian festivals, Moses sensed they would be contenders in any competition, especially after seeing their battle prowess against the Libyans.

The lower base of the temple was completed, and several granite columns had been erected. Moses could imagine the gleam of the granite when the clouds cleared.

"By the time the temple is finished," Ramses said, "I'll be surrounding it with my statues."

Pentu laughed. "You better not let your father hear you."

Ramses grinned. "He likes me to plan ahead."

"Ahead to his *death*?" Pentu asked, a smirk on his face.

"We can't ignore the cycle of life." Ramses pointed to a large hole being dug out several dozen paces from the temple site. "They're putting in a pool just as I requested."

"The pharaoh let you alter the building plans?" Moses cut in, surprised. Pharaoh Seti I was known for keeping everyone out of the architect room. But then again, Ramses was officially declared the crown prince now.

"My duties have doubled," Ramses said, pride in his voice. "Pretty soon you two will be bowing down when you greet me."

"I'll wait for the crown on your head," Pentu said.

Ramses slugged Pentu in the shoulder, and Moses smiled. But then he sobered as other thoughts crowded his mind. When Ramses did become pharaoh, their friendships would change. They wouldn't be spending time like this together. They wouldn't be having these kinds of conversations. Life had become more and more complicated lately, with his betrothal to Cena broken and the battle against the Libyans, but it seemed as if the whole kingdom was in a celebratory mood after defeating their foe earlier that week.

Pentu had mostly recovered, although he was happy to complain about his battle ailments, and fortunately Ramses had been diverted today from his quest in finding the Hebrew slave woman who'd helped Bithiah with the injured soldiers. Moses was keeping his eyes open and ears alert for any news of her. He knew Ramses had soldiers looking for her, but Moses hoped that as the days passed, Ramses would find new distractions and the Hebrew girl would be forgotten.

The stifling heat had yet to dissipate despite the threatening rain. Moses and his friends had spent most of the day inside with the viziers going over Egyptian law. As usual, Ramses had impressed everyone with his thorough knowledge as he'd argued that the Hebrew soldiers should be returned to their villages and their previous tasks. And those who'd died should be forgotten and counted as a sacrifice to the war gods.

But Moses had argued that the families of those who'd died should be compensated in some way since their soldier work hadn't been commissioned. None of the viziers had agreed with Moses, so he'd let the debate drop, remembering his mother's advice to avoid appearing as a Hebrew lover.

Then a debate had arisen between Ramses and Pentu about the laws that surrounded the Hebrew slaves—whether or not the taskmasters dictated the work hours each day. Ramses had told Pentu he'd show him the law in action and that each taskmaster was to work the slaves until sundown. Coming to the temple site had made Moses nervous at first. What if Caleb or Aaron were at this site? It would remind Ramses of Miriam, and there might be a confrontation.

"Watch, Pentu," Ramses was saying. "Any moment now the slaves will be called off the worksite."

Pentu grumbled, but it was clear he knew he was in the wrong. He'd argued that the slaves had to work until their tasks were done for the day, but Ramses had said that because the Egyptian taskmasters wanted their supper too, work ended at sunset.

As if the taskmasters had heard Ramses's words, a shout went up at the temple site below, and the slaves formed into lines. The workday was complete, and tools and ropes were left lying where they had last been used. The lines formed surprisingly fast, and Moses was impressed with the organization.

When one of the slaves moved slower than the others and didn't get into the moving line, a taskmaster stepped forward and whipped him. One such slave looked to be several years younger than Moses. Of course, there weren't any slaves close to Moses's age, since Pharaoh had ordered the deaths of all Hebrew male infants around the same time Moses had been born. He winced as the taskmaster drew blood. The young man scrambled to find his place in line.

Finally, he blended in with the rest, except for the red marks of the whip lines. Dirt and sweat clung to the young man's thin but strong body. Moses sensed the exhaustion the slave must feel. He wondered when the man had last had refreshment. He scanned the worksite, not seeing any jugs of water or baskets of food. Today had been extremely hot before the clouds had come in. Even with the cloud coverage now, the heat was sweltering.

"When do they return to the site?" Moses asked, following Ramses and Pentu as they made their way along the top of the ridge overlooking the temple site.

"Sunrise," Ramses said.

Near the horizon, the clouds broke apart briefly; the orange of the sky changed to purple and red. Moses glanced at the slaves again, seeing the glisten of perspiration on their backs as they walked along the path leading home. Several taskmasters followed, cracking their whips or shoving at the slaves to keep them in line. Moses furrowed his brow, pausing to watch again. The slaves were staying in their formation quite well; it seemed the taskmasters were being more aggressive than necessary.

"Come on," Pentu called, and Moses realized his friends were a dozen paces away now. "We're going to be late to the banquet. And it's starting to rain."

Moses couldn't recall which banquet Pentu was referring to. He was too caught up in watching the departing slaves. Then he remembered. Ramses's betrothed and her family were visiting again. The wedding was only a few months away. But Moses's attention stayed riveted on the slaves leaving the temple site. Raindrops started to fall from the sky, slowly at first, then a little faster. A female slave had fallen behind, and a particularly large taskmaster was shouting at the older woman. She looked too thin, and her nearly gray hair was pulled back and braided. It was obvious she was crying and very weak, but she hurried forward.

"You can stay all you want, Moses," Ramses said. "But I have a princess to see."

"Anxious, are we?" Pentu said with a laugh.

Moses was about to reply, but more shouting caught his attention. Ramses and Pentu slowed their pace and barked out a laugh. "Stupid Hebrew," Pentu said, but Moses didn't respond. He was riveted upon the scene below.

The old woman fell to the ground, and the taskmaster shouted something. She was shaking and trying to rise to her feet.

Pentu said something again, dozens of paces away now as he continued along the path, but Moses barely registered that the two men had left him to watch the scene alone.

He walked toward the temple site, his heart pounding as the taskmaster grabbed his whip and brought it down on the woman's frail shoulders. She was so thin and weak. And what had she done? Walked too slowly? Women her age should be home living out their twilight years without fear of abuse.

Suddenly another slave appeared, stationing himself in front of the woman. The taskmaster only paused a moment before he lashed out at the man. With the reprieve, the woman climbed to her feet, still crying, and it was clear her rescuer was telling her to get away.

Indignation burned hot in Moses's chest. The slaves seemed harmless, and the woman only struggled against her exhaustion. Surely that couldn't count as being defiant, not from an elderly woman. The young man was a different story. He stood erect, and his body was thick and strong. He'd seen many hours of hard labor, but instead of making him weak, they had made him strong. Moses thought he recognized the young man and wondered if he'd been one of the ones fighting the Libyans.

From Moses's vantage point, it was clear the slave could overpower the taskmaster if he chose. This wasn't even a fight he'd started out in, but he was defending the woman who had now disappeared to safety.

The taskmaster continued shouting and brought down the whip on the young man. He flinched at the beating but didn't fall to his knees or react in any other way. In fact, the Hebrew kept his stoic gaze forward, eyes unblinking.

Moses still moved down the ridge as the taskmaster continued to whip the slave. Eventually the slave, as strong as he was, couldn't stand anymore. No man could have. His knees buckled, and he fell to the earth.

Moses exhaled. Surely the taskmaster would leave now. The slave would have to nurse his wounds for many days as it was.

But it wasn't over. The taskmaster started to kick the man in the stomach as he ranted about dirty, lazy Hebrews.

Moses froze, staring. This was going too far. Wasn't it? Granted, he hadn't been around the building sites as much as Ramses and Pentu, but he had heard about slave deaths and executions. He had always assumed they were for crimes, though, not instances of defending a female slave who'd walked too slowly.

The rain came faster now, and the taskmaster started kicking the man's head. The slave wasn't moving anymore. The sound of the beating reverberated through Moses, filling his entire soul with despair and disgust. Was there no order or justice, even for a slave? The man had not even spoken for himself or defended himself. He had rendered himself completely helpless, and now he was unconscious.

Moses stopped next to a large stone, out of the taskmaster's sight. Moses's pulse raced, and his mouth went dry. He wanted to take the whip and show the taskmaster what it felt like to be brutally beaten. These people had fought by Moses's side against the Libyans only to return and be beaten by the very Egyptians they'd risked their lives to defend.

Moses exhaled, trying to remain calm. He was being foolish. It was only a slave. One of thousands.

One for whom it was too late now.

The taskmaster walked away, heading in the opposite direction from the slaves, leaving the young man broken and bleeding on the dirt that was quickly turning to mud. The taskmaster wiped the rain and perspiration from his face with the back of his hand, dragging the bloody whip. It trailed behind him in the dirt like a snake.

Moses looked again at the still body. Was the slave really dead? Before Moses could think better about his involvement, he stepped from behind the stone and crossed to the still form. His breath halted at the sight of the man's torn skin and crumpled body. He nudged the slave's shoulder with his foot. Nothing. The man would never open his eyes again.

What had this slave died for? His meager life was now over, his sacrifice perhaps in vain over an elderly woman who'd surely see many more harsh and violent days. Yet the brutal taskmaster walked away free— free to kill again and again.

The longer Moses gazed at the lifeless body, the more his rage multiplied at the injustice of a wasted life. Even though the man lived as a slave, subject to another's rule, he'd been *living* only moments before. And the one thing he had possessed was now taken away. Moses had never seen a man stand up for another human the way this young Hebrew had—without any thought for the consequences to his own life. The slave had merely stepped in to take the beating meant for another weaker person.

A voice cut through Moses's thoughts, and he realized the taskmaster had turned and walked back. The rain dotted the man's head and massive shoulders. "We don't need to bury him," the taskmaster said. "He'll be a good reminder when the other slaves return in the morning."

Moses peered at the taskmaster. The man had the slave's blood on his skin, and soon the rain would wash it away as if the man hadn't just killed someone. But the rain didn't cover the smell of death rising from the ground, invading Moses's senses. He found it strange that he noticed small details about the taskmaster. The man had a mole on the right side of his mouth, and he had a couple scars on his left shoulder. His face was long, his forehead broad. His kilt probably cost more than everything the dead slave owned.

Surely the taskmaster would be wearing a fresh one tomorrow, one that didn't have a slave's blood staining it. Moses wondered how long the new kilt would remain blood free. A day? A week?

"I can get you your own slave if you wish," the taskmaster said with a laugh, as if Moses's nonresponse didn't bother him. "Some of your royal friends give me a bit of payment to bring them a fresh young virgin. Just tell me where to bring her. Or him." The taskmaster chuckled, and the sound choked Moses like a plume of dark smoke.

He focused on the taskmaster's hands—the same hands that had just murdered an innocent man. The taskmaster was slowly winding the stained whip to put it away.

"I think I've seen you before," the taskmaster said. "Aren't you Moses? Son of Bithiah?"

Finally Moses spoke. "I am." He stepped forward, closing the distance between them. He brought his fist back and then slammed it forward, cracking the smiling man on the side of the head.

CHAPTER THIRTY-TWO

MIRIAM

THE RAIN WAS DRENCHING, MORE powerful than any storm Miriam could remember. She and Katu had spent the past few hours traveling as fast as possible, staying within sight of the river for the most part but taking detours when needed, trying to avoid making consistent tracks.

The rain helped cover their tracks, as Katu had said, but it also slowed them down, balancing out the danger. People were outside their homes, collecting rain in jars and jugs and bowls. Children screeched and played games, their parents laughing at them. It seemed everyone was celebrating the moisture falling from the sky.

Miriam knew that if the rain didn't stop, the River Nile would flood, and since rain was such a rarity, the people weren't prepared. But for tonight, the rain was a gift to Egypt.

Miriam and Katu slowed as they approached her home village. They'd skirted around the palace, and being so close had made Miriam feel shaky, but she focused on following Katu and said nothing, although she was sure he noticed her silence.

The darkness completely enveloped them, with no hope of the moon brightening their way, as it was hidden behind the dark clouds that continued to release rain. But relief mixed with anticipation as Miriam realized they'd made it this far. Now it was her turn to lead the way. Katu had done a fine job protecting them and navigating the desert for the past several days, but Miriam knew the roads, paths, rocks, and palm trees that surrounded her village. She motioned for Katu to follow her, and they crept through the darkness.

The first hut Miriam saw brought mixed emotions of apprehension and eagerness. She had arrived at her village, but what had changed? Had her family suffered because of her disappearance? Keeping off the main road, Miriam led Katu along the twisting paths, deeper into the village.

And then, suddenly, she was facing her home's courtyard. Everything was dark beneath the rain-filled sky. It looked lonely and isolated. Something didn't feel right.

"Wait here," she told Katu and then walked slowly to the front door. She tried the latch and was surprised to find it open.

Katu joined her at the door. "I'm not letting you go inside alone. What if the soldiers are waiting for you?"

But Miriam was already shaking her head. She felt the emptiness before she took a single step into the hut. She didn't sense that anyone was living inside, but she had to see for herself.

Leaving the door open, she walked into the damp interior. There was a musty smell as if the place had been closed up and hadn't had any fresh air passing through it for a while. Leaving Katu to make his own investigation, Miriam hurried to the small bedchambers. Her parents' chamber was empty and stripped of their personal things. Her own chamber hadn't been touched.

What did that mean? Had her parents been captured? Questioned? Punished?

Her eyes burned with tears. What if they'd been killed? She shook her head; she couldn't think like that now, or she wouldn't be able to make it one step farther.

"They're gone," Katu said, stating the obvious, but it was a question as well.

Miriam didn't have any answers. Her mind couldn't focus on the possibilities that might make sense. All she knew was that her parents were no longer living in their hut, and they'd taken their belongings with them.

"They had notice to leave," Katu said in a quiet voice, breaking the stillness of the hut as Miriam stepped back into the main room. "If they took their things, it stands to reason they left before anything could happen to them."

It made sense, and Miriam hoped it was true. But where had they gone?

"Where does your brother live?" Katu asked, moving to the door to look outside at the darkness.

It seemed Katu was the only one who could think straight. Miriam had been too caught up in wondering where her parents were. "He's not far," she said, her voice breaking. What if he was gone too?

She walked slowly out of the hut, passing by Katu, and stopped, gazing out at the rain and the rivulets of dirty water running through the courtyard. She moved around the hut and saw that her weaving looms were still in place. Her parents hadn't taken a cart; they'd just taken what they could carry with them.

She stared at the loom, then turned away. Katu still waited near the front door. They would go to Aaron's and hopefully find better news.

"Miri?" a voice whispered.

She gasped and whirled back around. A dark form was standing at the back corner of the hut. Only one person called her Miri. "Caleb?"

The man stepped forward, but it was still too dark to see him.

"Is that really you?" he said, his voice unmistakable.

Miriam stared at him as he walked toward her. Was this real? Was he real? She couldn't move, couldn't think. When Caleb stopped in front of her, her body was finally able to move, and she threw her arms about his neck.

His arms wrapped around her, pulling her tightly against him. "Is it really you, Miri?" he said against her neck.

Miriam couldn't speak; she just clung to him, feeling his solid body pressed against hers, his arms holding her up, his breath on her skin. She closed her eyes and simply breathed him in. All of her questions could wait. What mattered in this moment was that she was once again in Caleb's arms.

"Miriam?" Katu said.

She blinked open her eyes and released Caleb enough to turn toward Katu. "It's Caleb," she said in a low voice. She looked up at Caleb and into his hooded eyes as if to verify his presence. She didn't want to let him go, couldn't let him go.

But he released her waist and raised his hands to her face, cradling it gently. "Are you all right?" he said. "Where have you been?" His looked from her over to Katu, then back to her.

"Katu saved my life and brought me here."

Caleb turned toward Katu. Their eyes held, and Caleb reached out his hand. Katu grasped it.

"Thank you for taking care of her," Caleb said, his voice thick with emotion.

Miriam blinked back her own tears and laid her head against Caleb's chest, wrapping her arms around him. She didn't care that she was wet and he was damp and that if it were light, she'd scare away even a scorpion.

"Where are her parents?" Katu asked.

Miriam stiffened. Was this news she could bear? She was grateful that Katu had spoken the words, but now she didn't know if she could listen to Caleb's answer.

His arms came around her again, and he squeezed her gently. "They're safe."

The words settled over Miriam, warming every part of her soul. She looked up at Caleb. "Where are they?"

"As soon as we could get word to them . . . about your disappearance, Aaron took them to the northern village," Caleb said, trailing a hand along her cheek as if he couldn't believe she was really in his arms.

Miriam lowered her head and closed her eyes. "So Aaron is safe too?"

"He and his wife moved with your parents," Caleb said. "We all did." He looked over at Katu. "Since the Libyan invasion, there has been a lot of turmoil. Hebrew soldiers died in battle, and Pharaoh is recruiting more now. Families have been torn apart." His gaze went back to Miriam. "We are hoping that the relocation of your family won't create any undue notice with all of the other changes in the villages."

Miriam nodded, hoping Caleb was right. "Have the soldiers been here searching?"

"Twice," Caleb said, his voice strained. "I kept praying that if you came back here, I could find you before the soldiers did." He rubbed her arms. "I come here each night to watch. Tonight I almost didn't come because of the rain."

Miriam wanted to melt into his touch and forget about everything else. But it wasn't safe here at her parents' former hut. "I'm glad you came," she said, looking up at him. She felt honored just knowing this man.

"Where can we find shelter for the night?" Katu asked.

"Not in this village," Caleb said. "Are you up for more traveling?"

"We'll do what's necessary," Miriam insisted. She looked over at Katu. "Did you see anything inside the hut that might be useful?"

He shook his head. "I'm afraid we're completely dependent on your friend."

"All right," Miriam said in a quiet voice. "Let's go, then." She was all too happy to keep her hand in Caleb's as he led them down paths away from the village. As they traveled, she told him of her flight from the military camp and how she'd ended up at an oasis, where Katu had discovered her and forced her to drink water.

More than once Caleb turned to Katu and thanked him. The rain started to let up, but the clouds were still low, creating the darkest of nights. Caleb stayed off any main roads, and they wound their way along paths near new streams of water created by the rain.

Miriam was exhausted, but she tried to keep her trembling to a minimum so Caleb wouldn't notice. More than anything, she wanted to be reunited with her family. She pressed on, not complaining and not letting her step falter.

"We're almost there," Caleb said in a quiet voice, squeezing her hand.

Miriam didn't recognize the village in the darkness. She had passed by it before but hadn't personally known anyone who lived there.

When they reached the small hut, Miriam could hardly believe four adults lived inside. She hesitated when they walked up to the door, but Caleb knocked without a pause.

Heart hammering, Miriam waited, listening for any sign of movement. She was nearly ready to open the door herself when it finally cracked open.

"Aaron!" She threw her arms around him, and he almost stumbled.

"Miriam, is it really you?" He pulled back, examining her face in the dimness. "Are you all right?" His gaze went to Katu, then to Caleb.

"Miriam?" a woman said. Her mother.

Miriam fell into her mother's arms, and that was when the sobs came. Nothing needed to be said; it could all be communicated through their embrace. Miriam felt someone else patting her back, and she heard more voices. A lamp was lit, and the dimness fled.

She raised her head and saw her father, then embraced him, unable to speak. Her parents were alive and safe. Salome stepped toward her with a smile and embraced her as well. Relief pulsed through Miriam. Aaron and his wife were all right.

Through tears, Miriam introduced Katu and explained all he had done for her, and soon they were all embracing him and thanking him.

"You must stay with us," Jochebed said. "Come, eat." Always a mother, she busied herself with preparing food. Salome stepped in to help, building a cooking fire outside while Miriam's father led them to the cushions lining one wall.

"Rest, Miriam," he said, guiding her gently to a cushion. He took her wet cloak from her shoulders and went to fetch a dry rug.

She sank into the softness. It had been days since she'd touched anything so luxurious. Her father brought out the rugs and handed them out to her,

Caleb, and Katu. They all settled on the cushions, and not long after, her mother was offering them steamed barley, cooked fish, and a cup of warmed wine.

Miriam closed her eyes as she sipped the liquid. It moved down her throat, warming her whole body and bringing a feeling of contentment and blessing. "Tell me of your journey here," she said. Even though she was exhausted, she knew she wouldn't be able to sleep for a long time. Not when there was so much to catch up on.

Her parents settled next to her, one on each side. She reached for their hands and looked around the room at the others. Everyone she loved was here. Finally, everyone was safe.

CHAPTER THIRTY-THREE

MOSES

MOSES'S HAND THROBBED. HE'D HIT the taskmaster so hard the man had fallen back and stopped moving. Moses bent over him, the man's body lying in the dirt with his head twisted. He was utterly still. A shudder shot through Moses. The taskmaster was dead. Moses bent to pick him up and dragged him past the Hebrew's body.

His pulse beating wildly, Moses dropped the taskmaster into the dirt and began to dig a hole with his bare hands. It was dark now, but he worked to make a place to hide the dead man.

He'll never kill again. He'll never beat a helpless elderly woman or murder a young slave again. Moses focused on the words repeating in his head as perspiration broke out across his entire body. He rolled the large Egyptian into the shallow hole. The feel of the man's thick, lifeless body repulsed Moses, and the realization of what he'd done crashed around him. Moses tried to rise to his feet but sank back to his knees and vomited. He heaved until his strength was gone, then hung his head, his throat and mouth tasting of bitterness at the deed he'd done. Squeezing his eyes shut, he gasped for air, trying to calm himself.

When he caught his breath, he opened his eyes. He couldn't stay here. He had to leave, escape. With trembling hands, he moved the mud over his vomit, and then he started to pile the wet dirt over the dead Egyptian. Moses worked quickly, wishing he could erase what he'd done. He could be discovered at any moment. The punishment for murder was swift and fatal. Not even the best friend of the crown prince would receive mercy.

He relocated rocks to the burial site, spreading them so the animals wouldn't have access to the body too soon. He hoped the rain would conceal any other evidence of what had happened. Moses straightened. It seemed unreal.

Moses started walking out of the construction site, up the muddy ridge. The memory of the taskmaster's surprised expression wouldn't leave his mind. He could still hear the man's grunt and the sound he'd made as he'd fallen to the dirt. His burial spot was close to the slave's still body. Moses wished he could return the slave to one of the Hebrew villages, but he couldn't risk the Hebrews thinking he had killed the slave. He paused at the top of the ridge leading out of the site and looked down to where the slave's body was still exposed. Two lives had been wasted tonight.

Moses's shoulders sagged. He could not take back what had happened to the slave, but in a small measure, the slave's sacrifice for the elderly woman had been avenged.

Moses turned away from the place of death and headed back toward the palace, his mind in a daze. Perhaps he'd wake in the morning and this would all be a horrible dream. By the time he reached the palace, the rain had let up and torches blazed at every courtyard. In the light of the flames, he saw that the dirt and bruises on his hands were no dream.

He skirted the main palace building and entered a wading pool. Several guards saw him, though none of them asked any questions. Moses scrubbed off the remaining dirt and soaked away the blood and perspiration. Every part of his body ached, but he knew he had to go to his quarters and get dressed. His mother would be wondering what had happened to him, as well as Pentu and Ramses. He had to appear at the banquet so suspicions wouldn't arise if the Egyptian was found later and conclusions were made about when he died.

Moses entered the palace corridor, his kilt still damp. His skin prickled at the coolness of the interior. The shadowed corners appeared darker than usual, and the lit torches seemed to be watching him. His guilt and fear caused everything to feel strange and different. He slowed as he reached his chambers, not too far from his mother's.

Once inside, he lit an oil lamp and changed into a dry kilt, then surveyed his image in the copper length. He had a couple of scratches on his shoulder and definite bruises on his hands. Evidence. He didn't know how he could keep his actions concealed. Ramses and Pentu knew he'd stayed to watch the slave beating, so when the Egyptian taskmaster was discovered missing, what would the conclusion be? How long could Moses keep the truth hidden? He looked about his chamber. The platform bed, the jaguar rug on the floor, the tapestries . . . None of it meant anything—not now that he'd killed another Egyptian. Unease raised the hairs on the back of his neck. He wondered if this would be the last time he'd see the inside of his chamber.

He left and walked toward the banquet room. Music and laughter floated down the corridor, reaching him long before he turned the final corner. He stepped past the guards at the entrance and paused just inside the room.

The banquet was crowded with the royal family, court members, servants, and entertainers. A troupe of female dancers moved to the beating drums in the center of the room, entertaining the guests gathered at the surrounding tables laden with food. Ramses sat at the head table, reclining on cushions, his eyes on the girl he was betrothed to. Nefertari looked resplendent in a gold-trimmed tunic, a long Nubian wig, and enough kohl on her eyes to make her look the part of a temptress. But her smile was only for the future pharaoh.

Ramses didn't look over at Moses, which was just as well. He would be the next pharaoh, and Moses had just killed an employee of his father; he'd chosen to defend Egypt's lowest class.

A few people noticed Moses at the entrance, and he felt his face burn. Could they tell just by gazing at him what had happened? Had word already gone out? Moses turned his gaze to Pharaoh, who sat on his massive gold throne, eyes half open, with his hands clasped over his belly as he watched the dancers.

Pharaoh had a ruthless streak. Moses's own mother was far from his favorite child, and she had to live off the favors he sent her way. Moses felt diminished and guilty just being in the same room as the powerful man. Moses looked away, searching for his mother. His eyes connected with hers as she sat among the women. Her painted brows lifted, and he knew she was questioning why he hadn't appeared to escort her, why he had been delayed. Could he lie to his own mother?

Suddenly Pentu was at his side. "Come sit and drink some wine," Pentu said. "You look like you need to relax. Beset has a cousin here."

Moses didn't know what expression showed on his face, but he still tried to mellow it. He followed Pentu and settled on an empty cushion between two women. Both women smiled broadly, their scent of spice and flowers immediately invading Moses's senses. He didn't even ask which one was Beset's cousin.

"Hello, Moses," one of them said, her voice as deep as her dark eyes. He returned the greeting but had a hard time paying attention to her reply.

He pretended to be absorbed in the entertainment taking place in the center of the room, if only to avoid showing his increasing panic. The dancing troupe had been replaced by a snake charmer, and the audience went silent as they watched in awe.

The woman was whispering to Moses now, holding up a slice of melon. The fragrance was sweet, but Moses couldn't eat. He reached for his wine goblet and sipped, wishing it was stronger and more bitter. The woman next to him seemed to understand and put the melon back on the tray.

Another dance troupe started their performance, and the woman remained close, her arm and her thigh frequently brushing his as she talked with the other women. Moses swallowed against his parched throat. It seemed he couldn't drink enough wine to get rid of the dryness. When a messenger entered the room, Moses stared at the young man as he made his way to the pharaoh and gave his report.

The pharaoh's eyebrows drew together, but he made no move and didn't call a halt to the entertainment to make any announcements. Moses watched the messenger as the man left the room. Had the taskmaster's body already been uncovered?

Pentu leaned across the woman between them and tapped him. "Why the long face, my friend?" He gave Moses a slow wink and whispered loudly, "Moira will be pleased to escort you back to your chamber. That will cheer you up."

Next to Moses, the woman giggled.

The woman to his left also laughed and nestled closer to Moses. "Perhaps both of us can escort him."

Pentu chuckled. "Don't forget about me."

The second woman flashed Pentu a welcoming smile, then turned her attention to Moses again. She ran a finger along his forearm. The brush of her soft skin against his made his pulse hammer. Even if he was interested in either woman, if they knew what he'd just done, they would feel the same disgust he did—disgust at himself for having just killed a man, of having just watched another Egyptian beat a helpless slave to death.

While the two women turned their attention to Pentu, Moses looked over to where his mother sat. He could not lie to her. He could not face Ramses tomorrow or the day after, living as a traitor to Pharaoh, which made him a traitor to Ramses. A fire dancer began his routine in the center of the banquet room, drawing everyone's attention. Moses took the opportunity to slip away from the two women and out of the room. He hurried to his chamber, walking along the corridors, empty save for torches and guards. Somewhere, in someone's house, a wife and possibly children were wondering where their Egyptian husband and father was. In another much more modest household, a mother was grieving the loss of her son.

The thoughts and imaginings crowded Moses's head, making him want to scream until the thoughts fled. There was no way to make recompense. His punishment would be severe and would dishonor his mother. He had no other choice. He changed into his simplest kilt and put together a bundle that included a robe and a dagger. Then he paused at the entrance of his chamber before leaving. Despite everything, he had to say good-bye to his mother. He entered her chamber and found a sheaf of papyrus to write on. Words failed him. How did one say good-bye? How did one thank a woman who'd lived her life for him? But before he could write a single thing, footsteps sounded outside the chamber.

His mother came into the room. "Moses, what are you doing here?" Her eyes trailed to the papyrus in his hand. "I was worried about you but didn't find you in your chamber."

"I—" Tears stung his eyes.

"Moses?" She crossed the room and grasped his arm. "What's wrong, son?"

He exhaled, and suddenly it was all too much. How could he think his mother would be satisfied with a note? He sank to his knees. "Forgive me, Mother. I must leave Egypt. I have committed a horrible crime."

His mother knelt next to him, drawing him into her arms. "Tell me what's happened. Can it be that serious?"

"It is," he whispered. He held on to his mother for several minutes, and when he could speak again, he drew away and told her about the temple site and how he had watched the slaves being beaten. He couldn't meet her gaze as he told her how he'd killed the taskmaster and buried him beneath a mound of dirt.

"Oh, Moses," his mother said. She trembled in his arms, and Moses knew there was nothing she could do, save plead for his life.

After the humiliation of confessing his crime, Moses might receive mercy in the form of imprisonment or becoming a slave himself. He couldn't do that to his mother though. If he left, no one would have to know. His mother wouldn't be shamed in front of her family.

"I must leave right away," Moses said, his voice thick. "I do not know if I will ever see you again."

"Stay, Moses," his mother pled. "We will speak to Pharaoh together. He will listen and understand."

"No," Moses said, pulling away. "I have already made my decision."

The two of them stared at each other for a long time. His mother finally exhaled. Then, surprising Moses, she reached for his hands again. "I knew this day would come," she said. "Not in this manner, of course. There is something I must show you. It will help you decide how to live the rest of your life."

Moses stared at her as she released his hands and rose to her feet. In the far corner of her room, she unlocked a trunk. From within its depths, she lifted out a dark basket and brought it over to him, setting it on the floor between them.

"You've asked many times about your father, and I've never been able to give you an answer," she said in a soft voice. "Even my parents doubted when I first told them about you—and so it was assumed that I'd conceived you outside of marriage. After time passed, it was easiest to let everyone believe that as well."

Her gaze fell to the basket, and she continued. "The truth would have been too difficult for some people to accept—especially my father." She stretched out a hand toward the basket. "Moses, I did not know a man and conceive and bear you . . . I found you floating in the river." She looked up, and tears brimmed in her eyes.

It was all Moses could do to keep quiet and hear what she said next.

"No one knows the entire story. Not even my parents, as much as they had a hard time letting me keep you in the first place. Seeing their reaction when I wanted to keep and raise you as my own son made me realize I could never tell anyone."

Questions tumbled through Moses's mind, but he couldn't grasp even one to ask.

"Moses," his mother said, "you were born in an era when the pharaoh commanded that all Hebrew male infants be put to death."

It was true. But what did commands from long ago have to do with him? If he'd been sent down the river in a basket, it meant that his Egyptian mother was too poor and destitute to feed another mouth. She'd taken a chance that another woman would take compassion on her infant and didn't want the gods to bring a curse to her house for giving up a child she'd conceived.

Unless . . .

He stared at his mother, then shook his head. "No."

Tears fell from her eyes and dripped onto her cheeks. "Yes, Moses. You are Hebrew. I knew it the moment I opened the basket and saw you swaddled in a Hebrew cloth. I stared at you for a long time, trying to decide what to do. I was terrified. When I heard my handmaiden call out to me, asking me what I'd found, there was only one decision to make." She exhaled a shaky breath. "I removed the small blanket and hid it among the reeds. By the time my handmaiden joined me, you were naked and crying."

Moses couldn't move, couldn't comprehend.

"But you reached for me, my son," his mother whispered, "and that's when I picked you up and you nestled against my neck. You stopped crying right away, and I knew then that I would love and protect you. I would save your life. I would be your mother and raise you as my own, no matter the cost. An innocent child should not have to pay for the wickedness of a greedy man."

The breath left Moses as he let his mother's words sink into his heart. He was Hebrew. He had a father. A Hebrew mother. Possibly siblings. And they were slaves.

His gaze found his mother's—his *Egyptian* mother's—and then he wept.

CHAPTER THIRTY-FOUR

MIRIAM

A WEEK HAD PASSED SINCE Miriam arrived in the northern village. She'd slowly regained her strength and had started working in the granary with the other women, grinding barley and wheat into flour. She didn't dare start weaving again. It was too close to who she used to be, and she didn't want to be recognized by any royalty. No soldiers had come to the village, but Caleb had told her to be on guard. And Aaron reminded her of it every day.

Today she walked slowly to her parents' small hut. She knew the village layout well now and determined to stick to the less traveled paths. She found herself increasingly wary of large crowds, and she avoided them as much as possible. Katu was staying at her parents' hut as well. He seemed to enjoy sleeping in a regular shelter and not having to hunt or forage for every scrap of food. Her mother was spoiling him.

She saw Caleb nearly every evening, and she felt that she would never grow tired of being in his arms. As she neared her hut, taking a barely used path to reach the back, she heard someone coming toward her. Miriam moved into a group of trees and kept an eye on the approaching person.

It was a tall, thin man with a long gait. "Katu!" Miriam said, stepping out onto the path.

"There you are," he said with a smile, one that didn't quite reach his eyes.

"Is everything all right?" Miriam hadn't known Katu long, but since they'd lived as nomads together for several days, she recognized the sign of distress in his eyes.

"I need to leave, but I wanted to say good-bye to you first."

Miriam stared at him, not quite comprehending. "I thought you loved it here. I thought you'd stay and—"

He put a hand on her shoulder. "No. I never intended to stay." He dropped his hand and looked away.

She stepped closer, but he moved back. "What is it, Katu?"

Finally he looked at her again. "All of this is wonderful." He motioned with his hand to include the whole village. "Your parents have been so welcoming. And you . . ." He looked down and blew out a breath. "I hope you will have all the happiness in the world."

"Stay," Miriam said. "I will be happier if you stay."

He let out a half laugh, then leaned down and gave her a kiss on the cheek.

Miriam touched where he'd kissed her, unsure of what to say.

"Farewell," he said, taking a couple steps backward, his hand lifted in a wave. Then he turned and moved off the trail, walking away quickly. "Katu, wait!" Miriam said. But he didn't stop, didn't look back. "Where are you going? What are you going to do?"

He disappeared behind the trees, not pausing to answer.

Miriam couldn't believe he was truly leaving. She hurried after him, but by the time she reached the last place he'd been visible, there was no trace, no sound. She crouched to the ground looking at the plants and rocks at eye level, trying to see signs through a nomad's viewpoint.

"Katu!" she called out, standing. She looked at the trees, then at her parents' hut not far away, and then toward the River Nile. Which direction would he go? Toward Libya through the desert after crossing the river, then to the sea?

She exhaled and wrapped her arms about her torso. Katu had been her friend. They hadn't known each other for long, but she'd bonded with him like he was a brother.

She missed him already and felt the tears slipping onto her cheeks before she could stop them.

"Miri?"

She turned at the sound of Caleb's voice. Relief flooded through her. "Katu's gone. I don't know where he went; he just left."

Caleb reached her and wiped the tears from her face. "I know. He told me."

Miriam gazed up at him. "You knew? I don't understand," she said. "Why would he leave?"

Caleb linked his hands through hers. "He cared for you, Miri, more than a man cares for a sister."

The information deflated her. She remembered the conversation they'd had while hiding in the tomb, but it had been lighthearted, and she'd believed Katu would get past those feelings and want to live in a village community. She thought perhaps he'd meet someone else he wanted to marry. "He said something, but I didn't take him seriously."

Caleb gave a small nod, watching her closely. "You care for him too."

"Of course," Miriam said, and when she saw Caleb's eyebrows furrow, she rushed to say, "But not the way he wants me to." She fell quiet, looking down at the ground and wondering if there was anything she could have done or said that would have made Katu stay in the village and feel more comfortable.

Caleb's fingers touched her chin and lifted her face so she was looking at him again. "Do you love me, Miri?"

His voice was so earnest that Miriam wondered how he couldn't know. "Yes, Caleb, I love you. More than anything."

His fingers moved along her jaw, then down her neck, finally resting on her shoulder. "Then marry me. Tomorrow."

She wanted to say yes, but *tomorrow*?

"I know it sounds crazy," he said, "but men are going to continue to fall in love with you if you don't marry me and let them know you're mine." He grinned.

"Men aren't falling in love with me." And then she closed her mouth, her mind flashing back to Ramses—who was certainly not in love with her and wouldn't have cared if she was married or not—and Katu . . . who'd been hurt enough that he couldn't even live in the same village.

"See, you know I'm right," he said, sliding his arms around her waist and kissing her forehead.

He lingered, and she let him. What was stopping her? Soldiers could come and drag her away, Caleb could be called to fight in another battle, she could get injured in the granary . . . But if she married Caleb tomorrow, they'd at least have tomorrow together and hopefully the next day.

"All right, Caleb, I'll marry you tomorrow," she said, smiling up at him.

His eyes widened, then he whooped and picked her up, swirling her around.

She laughed. "Put me down. Someone will hear you and come running."

"Or stay hidden in their huts."

"Or that." She was still laughing when Caleb bent to kiss her on the mouth. She sighed against his lips and let her heart soar.

* * *

It was a small wedding. Only Miriam's parents, Aaron and his wife, and the village elder were in attendance in the courtyard behind the humble hut. For a few seconds, Miriam wished that Katu could have been there, but she understood now why he hadn't stayed. If Katu felt for Miriam even a small measure of what she felt for Caleb, she wouldn't wish that on him.

"You look beautiful," Caleb said as he reached for her hand. They stood facing each other in the courtyard, beneath a linen canopy her mother had borrowed. The sun was setting, casting its warm glow into the courtyard and making the sand golden and the rough stone wall shimmer like silver.

Caleb wore a shawl over his shoulders, and he was more handsome than Miriam could remember. She looked at him through her embroidered veil, which had been her mother's wedding veil too. She felt a blush rise to her cheeks at the way Caleb's gaze pierced the fabric.

The elder began to recite the *kiddushin* while Miriam looked into Caleb's eyes, her pulse racing. Then the elder spoke the ceremonial marriage words, and Miriam promised to take Caleb as her husband, and he promised to take her as his wife. Miriam's thoughts spun as Caleb's words of promise wrapped around her. She was really doing this; she was truly getting married.

When Jochebed handed over the ceremonial cup of wine, Caleb took a sip, then held it out to Miriam. She lifted her veil and took a sip, then gave the cup to her mother to hold again. Her father stepped forward and gave the ceremonial ring to Caleb.

Caleb took the ring, then turned to look at Miriam again. Sliding it onto her finger, he said, "You are now consecrated unto me with this ring according to the law."

The warmth of Caleb's fingers and the weight of the ceremonial ring brought tears to Miriam's eyes. She not only saw the love in his gaze but felt the love from his touch. She had doubted so many times that she'd ever experience marriage to a man she loved, first because she hadn't wanted to marry and then because she didn't know if she'd ever make it back home safely.

"From the beginning," the elder continued, "the Lord created male and female."

While he spoke, Miriam walked around Caleb seven times. When she stopped and faced Caleb again, he reached out and lifted the corner of her veil, then placed it on his shoulder. Miriam smiled as he then removed his prayer shawl and wrapped it around her shoulders.

"What the Lord has joined, let no man put asunder," the elder said.

Salome stepped forward and placed woven garlands made from palm leaves on Miriam's and Caleb's heads. Then Jochebed held out a bowl of blessed water, and both the bride and groom dipped their hands in it.

Miriam's father cleared his throat as the elder stepped back, and then he read their signed marriage contract. He bowed his head and offered a prayer to the Lord, blessing them. When he finished, with tears in his eyes, he smiled at Miriam and Caleb. "The words of our forefathers, Jacob and Joseph, have been fulfilled today," he said in a reverent voice. "'And let your name be named on them, and the name of your fathers Abraham and Isaac, and let them grow into a multitude in the midst of the earth.'"

Everyone said amen, and then her father embraced Miriam. "Praise the Lord," he whispered in her ear.

Miriam held on to her father for a long time. And then she was swept into her mother's arms, then Aaron's, followed by Salome's. Afterward, it was time to embrace her new husband.

He stepped toward her and lifted her veil. Miriam gave a nervous laugh, but then her nerves turned into full twisting when he bent down and kissed her in front of everyone.

The small gathering cheered, and Salome began to play a timbrel. Miriam's parents started clapping, and Caleb held out his hand to Miriam. "Would you like to dance?"

She laughed and was soon caught up in a dance with her new husband.

They danced until the sun disappeared and the evening grew dark. The oil lamps in the courtyard were lit, and Jochebed and Salome brought out the wedding feast of pigeon meat, cooked squash with lentils, and figs soaked in honey. Miriam sat in her place of honor to be served and cast frequent glances at Caleb.

The later it grew, the more anticipation coursed through her. And then suddenly the meal was over, the music had faded, and her parents and brother and sister-in-law had bidden them farewell. Her parents would stay in Aaron's new hut for the night, leaving Caleb and Miriam alone.

Caleb turned to Miriam, a smile on his face, his hand extended. He didn't say anything, just looked at her with his hand held out to her.

Miriam's throat tightened, and nervousness flushed through her. But looking into Caleb's warm brown eyes made her feel safe. She knew he would take care of her, protect her, and not let anything or anyone within his power hurt her. She trusted him. Completely. And that was perhaps the best gift she could give to any person.

She placed her hand in his, and he pulled her close. His other hand came up and cupped her chin, and he lifted her face to his.

"I love you, Miri," he said in a low voice.

His words rippled through her, settling into her soul. She tightened her fingers around his. "I love you too, Caleb."

He closed his eyes and leaned down, then brushed his mouth against hers in a soft kiss. She found herself kissing him back, urging him on, demanding. He chuckled quietly and scooped her up into his arms.

She wrapped her arms around his neck, holding on but also taking the opportunity to get closer to him. She nestled her face against his warm neck. She didn't care where he was taking her as long as they were together.

Caleb carried her into the hut they'd be sharing alone tonight, and Miriam's heart thumped as she felt a fullness of joy she could have never dreamed of. No matter what happened after today, she'd have this moment and this memory with the man she loved more than anything.

CHAPTER THIRTY-FIVE

MOSES

MOSES RAN HIS FINGERS OVER the gold pieces his mother had given him as if to assure himself that he still had wealth. He'd brought little with him on his flight—a bit of food, his dagger, a robe, and the gold pieces. He'd settled into a grove of palms just outside one of the Hebrew villages to watch the comings and goings of the people—*his* people. As each slave passed by, he wondered if he had any family connection to them. Of course, it was impossible to tell. There were thousands of slaves, dozens of villages spread up and down the Nile Valley and Delta, and he was only one person. One man who'd been missing for eighteen years.

His true parents could be dead. He may or may not have any siblings living or otherwise. He grieved over leaving his Egyptian mother . . . Was it only the night before? He'd slept little, but it seemed a lifetime ago that he'd fled the palace. As the sun set, he was reminded of that same time the day before, right before the beatings had started.

Surely the Egyptian taskmaster had been missed by now and the family of the slave knew about the young Hebrew's demise. Another day had passed, one filled with work and activity. For all Moses saw, life had continued. Both Egyptian and Hebrew life.

What was happening at the palace now? What were Ramses and Pentu thinking about his disappearance? Had his mother told them his true identity? Were they searching for him?

He wondered what his life would have been like if he had been raised in one of the Hebrew villages, if his parents had hidden him from the pharaoh, and if he'd become a slave worker. Would he now be returning home to a simple meal?

The shadows lengthened, and the air finally began to cool, bringing needed relief to Moses. He pulled out a flat piece of bread that was quite hard now and bit off one end. After an entire day away from the palace, he was hungrier than he'd ever been in his life, especially when he realized he had no idea when he'd eat next. He imagined this was how the Hebrews felt every day.

A group of slaves approached, passing by on their way to the village. Their ages were mixed, from boys to older men; it seemed there was no specified age one had to be to work as a slave. He listened to the conversation in Hebrew and was able to pick out many of their words.

It was hard to look away from the passing men. Could one of them be his father? His brother? Behind the men, a group of women walked. Moses looked hard to see if he could spot the elderly woman from the day before. But she wasn't in the crowd. The women were the last of the slaves to return to the village. The road beyond was deserted. Soon, Moses realized, they'd have a chance to eat and rest. He let himself find comfort in that.

Some of the men started to sing a song of simple, repetitious phrases crooned over and over, but the tone was hopeful. Moses didn't understand the words, but he marveled that the slaves could find the desire to sing after a grueling day of work and abuse. Despite their hardships, they were a community, one in which they loved and supported each other.

Moses was so entranced by the singing that it took him awhile to notice that three young women had tarried behind. They walked slowly, their arms linked as they whispered and giggled together. For a brief moment, Moses was reminded of the women from the banquet the night before. The Egyptian courtiers had been more sophisticated and worldly, while these young women wore heavily repaired clothing and had bare feet, but they seemed equally delighted to be sharing secrets with friends.

"Hello there." A man's voice sounded from across the road, speaking in Egyptian.

Moses snapped his head to look at the man who had come out of the trees opposite him. Paser. Moses's stomach clenched. Anything or anyone who surrounded Paser was not good news. As if knowing his thoughts, three more men emerged from the trees, one whom Moses recognized as being a constant follower of Paser.

Moses had never liked Paser. The man was the son of one of the prominent viziers and was often thrown in with the royal children, much to everyone's resentment. He was proud of the fact and saw no class difference between him and someone with an actual royal title. But a Hebrew slave would hardly know the difference by the way Paser acted.

"Returning home so soon?" Paser said.

The young women stopped to stare at him. They huddled together, their eyes wide. If they'd had encounters with Paser before, they were right to fear him. Moses hadn't believed half the stories Paser told, but now he was wondering if they were all true.

Paser's friends' gazes fastened on the young women, their expressions greedy.

Moses rose to his feet and removed his dagger from his satchel. No one could see him yet, but every part of him recoiled at the thought of using a dagger after just seeing what his bare hands could do.

"The night's too young to be returning home," Paser continued. "There is much enjoyment to be had right here with us."

Moses didn't know if the girls understood Egyptian, but by the fear in their eyes, he guessed they understood enough. Paser took a step forward, and his friends quickly surrounded the women.

One of them screamed, but Paser stopped her with a hand over her mouth. "For that, you will be first." He dragged her to the ground, and his friends laughed.

The other two women started crying, only making the men laugh harder.

Moses moved out of the trees, his dagger ready. "Let the women go," he said. He wasn't about to humor Paser and bargain. It was either they set the women free, or they'd have to fight him.

Paser twisted from his position where he held the first woman on the ground. "Moses?" He grinned. "You can have a turn after me."

Moses advanced, keeping his dagger in front of him. "Let the women go, Paser."

Paser barked out a laugh. "If you're not here for entertainment, then you best leave. Pharaoh has been looking for you."

Dread pumped through Moses at the words. So his crime had been discovered. It was just as well that he knew before leaving. Now there would be no doubt in his motivations. He lunged at the nearest man, his dagger slicing into the man's arm.

The man screamed, and the two women were able to scramble away. But they didn't go far, obviously waiting for their friend.

Moses didn't waste any time; he fought the next man and the next, although they brought out their daggers. It wasn't hard to best them; they didn't have the training and skill he did, nor the rage.

Someone grabbed his shoulder and yanked him back, causing him to lose his footing.

"You fool!" Paser shouted.

Moses twisted against Paser's grasp, pain shooting through his head as he fought to get loose and face Paser straight on. "You are like an insect beneath my feet," Moses said, slamming his shoulder against Paser.

Paser fell to the ground, and Moses was on top of him in an instant, holding the blade at his throat. "I will use this," he growled.

Paser's body trembled, giving Moses an odd sense of satisfaction.

"I have no use fighting against you," Paser croaked out. "Pharaoh is after you anyway." He cleared his throat and spat into Moses's face.

Moses didn't move a muscle as he glared down at his foe. "Call your friends off and never come to this village again."

Paser's eyes narrowed, but he shouted, "Send the women away. We have more important things to do tonight."

As the women scurried away, Moses climbed off of Paser. He watched the men slink into the darkness and head toward the palace. Moses knew he had only a short time to disappear completely. Paser would tell the pharaoh immediately, and then guards would be seeking him.

It was nearly dark by the time he picked up his satchel. Blood ran down his arms, but he didn't have time to bind his wounds. The sooner he left the Nile Valley, the better. As he walked away from the village, he turned a final time. Cooking fires had been lit, evidenced by the curling smoke rising from several locations. He hoped the young women would find safety and peace tonight in their homes.

Moses shuddered to think what the next day might bring for the slaves, and the next day after that. He couldn't very well stay here and defend them all, not when the next sighting would bring about his capture.

He slung his satchel over his shoulder, wincing at the movement, and with his dagger still clutched in his hand, he climbed the nearest rise. He turned and scanned the land of his birth. In the distance, Mennefer glowed like a piece of gold in a dark pool, and the nearby Hebrew villages appeared tranquil in the deepening twilight. The wind picked up, tugging at his kilt, reminding him of the passage of time and the few moments he had to escape.

"Farewell, Mother," he said. A farewell to the woman who had raised him.

He looked toward the Hebrew villages. "Shalom, Mother," he said to a second woman, the one who had given him life. This farewell was in her language, only a whisper on his lips as he turned out of the wind and took his first steps into the wilderness.

End of Book 1

ACKNOWLEDGMENTS

WHILE READING THE BOOK OF Exodus in 2014, I wondered if the story of Miriam had been fictionalized. Of course everyone is familiar with the film adaptations of Moses and the Exodus, but I was interested in what had been done in literature form. Finding very little, I started to draft a few chapters from Miriam's point of view. Knowing the scope of the book of Exodus, I decided that any story told during this era couldn't be contained in just one volume; it was an epic story and deserved epic treatment. My initial idea was to write a three-book series, starting with a book on Miriam, followed by one on Moses, then concluding with Aaron. I quickly realized Moses wasn't going to be quiet in Miriam's story, so he became a main character as well.

As with all my historical work, I relied heavily upon others' expertise. My father, S. Kent Brown, has been my prime resource in scripture analysis. And both he and my mother, Gayle, were willing to read this manuscript under a strict deadline. I'm a lucky daughter to have such great parents who are not only willing to read my work but who are also foremost experts in the subject matter.

Many thanks, as well, go to Susan Aylworth, who read the early version of this story and helped me with characterization and asked me a million questions for clarification. Continued thanks go to my critique group for their years of putting up with me and always being there: Lu Ann Staheli, Michele Holmes, Jeff Savage, Annette Lyon, Sarah Eden, and Rob Wells.

I'm also immensely grateful to my publisher, Covenant Communications, and the great people who work there: Samantha Millburn, as my primary editor, is the best cheerleader. Managing editor Kathy Gordon has been very supportive and enthusiastic, giving me much-needed confidence. Many thanks to managing director Robby Nichols, who has been supportive from my very first book with Covenant in 2004. I also appreciate the efforts of the sales, marketing, and design teams, namely Tammy Kolkman, Margaret Weber-Longoria, and Stephanie Lacy, who all come together to create a stellar product.

Final thanks to my husband and children, whose support means the world to me.

ABOUT THE AUTHOR

HEATHER B. MOORE IS A *USA Today* best-selling author of more than a dozen historical novels and thrillers written under the pen name H.B. Moore. She writes women's fiction, romance, and inspirational nonfiction under Heather B. Moore. This can all be confusing, so her kids just call her Mom. Heather attended Cairo American College in Egypt, the Anglican School of Jerusalem in Israel, and earned a bachelor of science degree from Brigham Young University in Utah. Visit Heather's website here: www.hbmoore.com